BACK CHANNEL

A FRANK YAKABUSKI MYSTERY

BACK CHANNEL

RON CORBETT

 roncorbettbooks.com

ottawapressandpublishing.com

Copyright © Ron Corbett 2025

Printed and bound in Canada.

Cover: Joanna D'Angelo
Interior: Magdalene Carson RGD
Author photo: Julie Oliver

Library and Archives Canada Cataloguing in Publication

Title: Back channel / Ron Corbett.
Names: Corbett, Ron, 1959- author.
Series: Corbett, Ron, 1959- Frank Yakabuski mystery ; 2.
Description: Series statement: A Yakabuski mystery ; 5
Identifiers: Canadiana 20250292076 | ISBN 9781990896385 (softcover)
Subjects: LCGFT: Detective and mystery fiction. | LCGFT: Novels.
Classification: LCC PS8605.O7155 B33 2025 | DDC C813/.6—dc23

AUTHOR'S NOTE
This is a work of fiction. All places and characters are imagined. While the story takes place somewhere on the Northern Divide, there are no literal depictions of any city or town on the Divide.

For Pat and Terry McGregor

BACK
CHANNEL

1

BACK CHANNEL

FIRST CLUE

Springfield, 1865

The agent arrived as the sun was falling behind the Northern Divide, casting dark-purple shadows upon the river. The air cooled at the same time and the agent's breath was showing when he beached his canoe. He pulled the boat through fifty feet of spring mud. Hid it behind a hackberry bush.

With the canoe hidden the agent rested on his haunches and took a last look at the Divide. He could see it clearly from this stretch of river — the Tectonic plate that had ruptured the earth millennia ago, creating the high ridge of land he had travelled in the shadow of for fifteen days. It was a journey that had left him with a fatigue so complete and self-erasing that much of what was about to happen would later seem a dream to him.

He stood and began to walk. The agent was tall and lean, with taut muscles running from collar to heel, although they were hidden this day beneath loose-fitting leather britches, a thick wool tunic, a caribou jacket. He walked until he cleared the darkening pine forest and stood upon a cliff overlooking a giant bend in the river.

A town had been built along the bend. The agent looked down upon sawmills and matchstick factories, pulp kilns and shake houses, a hissing, clanging, kerosene-lit stretch of river that was never quiet and never still.

He made his way down into the valley and was soon on a dirt road crowded with other men. Mill workers and shantymen fresh from the winter camps, their long beards matted with pine needles. Government notaries and forward-steerage clerks, stumbling out of taverns after lengthy visits on their way home, suspenders hanging beneath their waists, frockcoats unbuttoned.

Each man turned his head when the agent approached, to avoid looking upon his face. Then watched the agent's back until losing it in the crowd. Protruding from the pockets of the caribou jacket were the heads of beaver clubs and dressing knives.

When the agent had nearly walked the length of the bend he turned inland and went down a dirt road with a forward-steerage company at the corner, a dry-goods store after that, then wood-frame homes that grew larger the farther he came from the river.

He stopped at the last house. This house was built not of wood but quarried limestone, with turrets and buttresses and too many windows to count. There was a fenced courtyard, and behind that, a six-stall livery. The agent opened the gate, approached the back door and rapped a brass knocker three times.

When the door swung open a woman stood before him.

"You're late," she hissed.

"Where is he?"

"His study. He's in a right foul mood, too — you should have been here on time."

The agent pushed the woman aside and entered the house. On time. He thought that was funny.

1

MEAGHAN MCKENNA arrived at the Springfield police station early one morning. Although it was mid-May, she wore a winter parka with soot stains around the collar, heavy denim pants, and hiking boots. Her long blonde hair was straight as an ironing board. She told the receptionist she needed to see a detective.

"What seems to be the problem, Miss? Maybe I can help."

McKenna, who would turn eighteen that summer, gave the receptionist a confused look before asking, "Are you a detective?"

"No."

"Then, how can you help me?"

The receptionist told her the detectives were busy, but she could wait until one was free. The girl sat in the wooden chair the receptionist pointed toward and in a few minutes was asleep.

When she was shaken awake an hour later, a man stood over her. He was a big man, his bulk blocking the overhead lights and in the darkness the girl briefly forgot where she was. Then she heard — "Miss, I'm told you're looking for a detective" — and she remembered.

"Yeah . . . yeah, I am."

"I'm Detective Frank Yakabuski. How can I help?"

McKenna looked up at the man. He was still blocking the overhead lights. "I need to talk to you about my mother."

"Has something happened to your mother?"

"Yeah . . . I can't find her."

Yakabuski stood back and took a closer look at the girl. She spoke with an accent that wasn't French, or Polish or Cree, an accent that hinted at a second language, but he couldn't place it. "What do you mean, you can't find your mother?"

"She hasn't been home in more'n a week now. There's a doctor says she's dead, but that ain't true." The girl looked at her boots, then back up at Yakabuski. "If you're a detective, you gotta figure out what's goin' on here."

The girl sat in a chair in Yakabuski's office, her boots barely touching the floor. She had turned down an offer of something to drink and still wore her parka.

"Sure you don't want to take off your coat?" Yakabuski asked her again. "It can get warm in here."

The girl shook her head. "I'm good."

"Nothing to drink?"

"No, thank you."

"All right, what's your name, Miss?"

"Meaghan McKenna."

"How old are you, Meaghan?"

"Seventeen."

"Shouldn't you be in school today?"

"Don't go to school. Haven't in a while." The girl gave him a puzzled look. "I'm here 'bout my momma. Shouldn't you be askin' questions 'bout her?"

Yakabuski took a steno pad from the drawer of his desk. Turned to a blank page. "What's your mother's name, Meaghan?"

"Agnes. Agnes McKenna."

"And when did you see her last?"

"Saturday."

"This past Saturday?"

"Yes, sir."

"Where?"

"On our farm . . . we live near Port Henry, just upriver from there a bit."

Port Henry. That was it. The accent Yakabuski couldn't place. It was the flat vowels and hard consonants of someone from the Back Channel of the Springfield River. Not quite a second language. But close.

"What was your mother doing when you saw her last?"

"Goin' collectin'. It was market day the next day. She never come back."

"What was she collecting?"

"Fiddleheads this time of year."

"You searched the woods around your farm?"

"For the first couple days, yes, sir"

"Why did you stop?"

"'Cause of that doctor you got up there, the one I was tellin' ya 'bout."

"The doctor *I've* got up there?"

"Yeah, he's a government doctor . . . you work for the government, right? Maybe you know him. Doctor Atkinson?"

Yakabuski put a hand over his mouth, so the girl wouldn't see his smile. "I'm afraid I don't. What do you mean, he made you stop searching?"

"He called me . . . well, not me, we don't have a phone, but he called Mrs. Dorchester, my neighbour, and he told her I needed to come to Port Henry and ID my momma. He told Mrs. Dorchester she'd drowned in the river, and he had her body. I told Mrs. Dorchester she should call that doctor back and tell him he shouldn't have bothered her none, 'cause that woman ain't my momma."

Yakabuski looked at the girl. People grieving. It had been happening forever, yet to his amazement, people were still finding new ways to do it

"You've refused to ID the body?"

"No, sir."

"Didn't you just say . . . "

"What I *refused* to do was waste everyone's time by goin' down to Port Henry to look at some dead woman I don't even know."

Yakabuski stared at the girl for a few seconds. "Sure you

don't want something to drink?"

"I'm sure."

"Not too warm in that jacket?"

"I'm good."

"Meaghan, is there anyone who can do the identification for you? Your father, maybe?"

"He's dead."

"Any aunts or uncles?"

"I got an aunt that's crazier than a jay, and a little brother who's crazier than her. Will one of 'em work for ya?"

"I guess not. Meaghan, I'm sorry for what's happened to you, I truly am. If you need help, for the challenges you're about to face, I can put you in touch with the right people. But refusing to ID your mother won't bring her back."

"Do ya think I'm stupid?"

"No, not at all. You appear to be a smart young woman, you're obviously independent, and resourceful, heck, you got yourself here this morning — no one is judging you, I just think — "

"My momma has nightmares 'bout the Springfield River," she interrupted. "I don't know why she has 'em. She ain't never told me, but she's had 'em her whole life. Never seen her once go near that river. Washin' clothes, cleanin' fish, those ain't ever been Momma's chores. So, you tell me . . . how did she *drown in that river*?"

Yakabuski returned the girl's imploring look until it became too painful for him, and he had to look away. People grieving. When he was a soldier in Bosnia, he'd marched into a badly destroyed village on the outskirts of which an old man sat in the vestibule of a church that had been shelled until it was nothing more than a facade.

The old man wore a three-piece suit with a rose pinned to the lapel. He told Yakabuski he was waiting for his wedding to begin. Had he seen his fiancée? She was late.

What's real and what's not, when you're grieving, that can

get mixed up better than a finger painting. "Meaghan, if what you're saying is true, why not go to Port Henry and prove it? Wouldn't that solve . . . "

The girl looked shocked. "What did ya just say?"

Yakabuski sat straighter in his chair, cleared this throat, but before he could answer the girl continued, "If I was from the Mission Road Estates, 'stead of from the Back Channel, would you be sittin' there askin' me to prove anythin' to ya? I come here this mornin' to report my momma missin' and it looks like that's all I'm goin' to be doin.'"

With that, Meaghan McKenna stood and left. Not bothering to say goodbye. Not bothering to hear what the detective she had travelled nearly two hundred miles to see might say next.

Yakabuski watched her through the open door of his office, surprised to see she knew the way to the stairs, although there were a few turns and she had walked the route only once. She was just tall enough that her head was showing above the cubicle partitions in the detective squadron.

She walked without hesitation. With ease. Although she carried a chip on her shoulders that Yakabuski figured must be as wide and heavy as the Back Channel itself.

CONSTABLE DONNA GRIFFIN sat in the chair Meaghan McKenna had been sitting in ten minutes earlier, listening to Yakabuski explain the reason for the girl's visit.

When he was finished, Griffin said, "Port Henry? Is that even in our jurisdiction?"

"It is."

"I thought it was all Mounties up there."

"They have Smoke Island, which has the Black Duck Reserve, right across the channel from Port Henry, but they're not on the mainland. We have the river all the way to Ferguson Falls."

"That means Port Henry is the last town in our jurisdiction, is that right?"

"Last town you can drive to, if you're heading up the Divide, that's right."

Donna Griffin had been living in Springfield for six years, right after graduating from college in Toronto. No one thought she would stay, assumed she would add some patrol experience to her police foundation courses and be back South as quick as she had a decent job offer.

Yakabuski thought the same thing at first. Until the day he learned Griffin came from money, old money even. Her great-grandfather once held the patent on automobile headlights. Griffin's parents had never worked a day in their lives, and they were not happy with their daughter's decision to become a police officer on the Northern Divide.

When he heard that story, Yakabuski figured the odds of Donna Griffin sticking around might be better than most people thought.

"Port Henry is at the end of an old colony road that never

got finished and probably never should have been started," said Yakabuski. "There was no reason to go up there. Not much reason to go there today. The town was a mistake. The government gave out land grants before the road was finished, and people got stuck."

"Got *stuck*?"

"Maybe marooned is a better word. When you're on the Back Channel it can feel that way, like you've been left behind, abandoned.

"Get up there much?"

"Not anymore."

Griffin crossed her legs, then uncrossed them. Unless she was sitting in front of a computer screen, she had trouble staying still. "But you did once? You're about to tell me the fishing is good, aren't you?"

"It *is* good, but no, that's not why I went. There's a market in Port Henry. When I was a kid, my dad took me."

Griffin had begun tapping her feet, and twirling her hair, which she had just cut and maybe she missed it, thought Yakabuski, because she was often twirling strands of her now-shortened, blonde hair. She had also begun jogging in the morning, and Yakabuski knew that was to lose weight, although he didn't think she was overweight. Not much, anyway. "A farmer's market?" she asked.

"I guess you can call it that. Although no one on the Back Channel is a farmer. You can't grow anything up there. The land is all marsh, and rock, the Port Henry Market sold what people could forage, or scavenge, or steal, I suppose. My dad went for the chaga mushrooms."

"Chaga mushrooms? Never heard of them."

"They grow on birch trees, high up, so you need to climb the tree to get them. Dad thought they cured ulcers. Not sure if that's true. His ulcer turned out to be a kidney stone."

While Griffin was laughing, Yakabuski thought back to those Saturday morning drives with his father to the Port Henry

Market, travelling along the Springfield River for most of the trip, the river getting wider the farther north they went, not able to see the far shore after a while, like they were driving beside a Great Lake. Then they reached the southern tip of Smoke Island, and everything changed. The sun disappeared behind the cliffs on the island. The river split into two channels, one wide and navigable, the other narrow and dark, with shoals and reefs that made it impassable for anything but a flat-bottomed barge.

Fifteen miles up this channel was Port Henry.

"How did the girl get here?" Griffin asked. "She didn't look old enough to drive."

"She's small for her age. Said she was seventeen. Not sure how she got here. Never had a chance to ask her." Yakabuski kept thinking about Port Henry. How many years had it been since he was last there? Thirty? No, must be closer to forty.

"That's a long drive. What would it be, four hours?"

"Closer to three."

"Long way for your dad to go for some mushrooms."

"We were coming from High River. It was about ninety minutes."

"Right, I forgot . . . but that reminds me, your dad phoned while you were interviewing the girl. He wants you to bring the fish when you go see him. That's what he said — 'bring the fish.' Make any sense to you?"

"It does."

Griffin flashed him a mischievous smile. "Yak, I'm making no comment on the state of the Yakabuski family when I ask you this, but — doesn't your dad have your cell number?"

"He likes phoning the detachment. I think he has a crush on Sandra."

"The receptionist? Oh, that is too funny."

"Or maybe it's you."

"You're joking, right?

"He likes you, Griff. And I haven't missed a call on my desk phone this morning. Sandra must have patched him through to you, not me."

Griffin looked momentarily alarmed. But then she smiled and said, "Sandra knew you were interviewing that girl. She wouldn't have put a call through to your phone."

"Ummm, that must be it." Yakabuski stretched his arms above his head. At six-foot-four, he could almost touch the ceiling. "Then again, he *does* like you, Griff. Maybe more than he likes Sandra."

"Very funny. Let's get back to the girl — if her mother was a suspicious death, the doctor in Port Henry, the one who has the body, he would have notified us, right?"

"That's right."

"But he hasn't."

"Right again."

"Which means — there's nothing for us to do."

Yakabuski stood and took a windbreaker from the back of his chair. "Right — if there's no suspicious death report, there's nothing we need to do."

He slipped his arms through the windbreaker and reached for the zipper.

Griffin said, "So . . . why do I think that's *not* what you're doing?"

"I don't feel good about the way I treated that girl, Griff," he said. "She told me her mother never went near the river. Why would she lie about a thing like that?"

"She probably wouldn't."

"That's right — she probably wouldn't. Maybe someone needs to go up to Port Henry and talk to that doctor."

3

BEFORE LEAVING SPRINGFIELD, Yakabuski stopped by his father's apartment and dropped off a cooler of fish. Opening day for char had been two weeks ago, and the fishing at Entrance Bay, where Yakabuski kept an ice-fishing hut during the winter, had been spectacular.

When his father opened the cooler, he broke into a wide smile. "You caught those last night? Are they frozen?"

"Nope. They've been lying on ice, but they're fresh. If you cook them today, it'll be like having a shore lunch."

"That's what I'll do, then. Can you stay?"

"Afraid not, Dad. Busy day."

"Why don't you come back? Tell me what time you can be here, and I'll have a plate ready for you."

"I'm out of town today. Heading up to Port Henry."

"Port Henry? What in the world are you doing up there?"

"Need to talk to a doctor. He has a body that got pulled out of the river."

"Suspicious death?"

"He doesn't think so."

His father gave him a curious look, and Yakabuski told him about Meaghan McKenna's visit. As he talked, his father rolled his wheelchair to the built-in wall pantry and began pulling out spices. Rosemary. Coriander. Sea salt. Coarse ground pepper.

Going next to the fridge, he opened the door, looked inside, and groaned. Yakabuski knew what that meant.

"No lemon, Dad? I don't have time to pick one up for you today."

"Don't worry, I can do it. I need groceries, anyway. Guess

I'll be doing that before lunch."

"Why not have them delivered?"

"You want someone else to pick out my vegetables?"

His father gave him an uncomprehending look. Then he reminded Yak that he had a new Dodge campervan in front of his apartment building, sitting in, what he had begun to boast was, "the best parking spot on the south shore." Almost worth a bullet.

Six years ago, Yakabuski's father had walked into a Stedman's department store in High River, looking to buy some mosquito netting for his hunt camp. He was followed five minutes later by a stick-up crew from Montreal. His father saw one of the robbers pull a balaclava over his face and stay by the front doors, while the other two headed toward the offices. They covered their faces with balaclavas as they made their way to the back.

George Yakabuski approached the first robber and yelled at him to put his hands in the air — that he was under arrest. George was an old-school cop — more than thirty-one years on the High River police department the day he walked into that Stedman's store — and he believed if a cop told you to put your hands in the air, that's what you did.

His father didn't have his service revolver. Didn't have back-up. Didn't even have his badge. The robber looked around to see if he was missing something, then pulled a sawed-off shotgun out of his parka and fired.

Doctors later said only Geroge Yakabuski's tremendous height and girth saved him; that for most men the shotgun blast would have hit them square in the chest, shredding their internal organs. On Yakabuski's father, who was the same size as his son, the metal fragments hit lower, striking his hips and lower back, saving his life, but rendering him a paraplegic.

"I keep forgetting you have that van," said Yakabuski. "Got any speeding tickets yet?"

"How could I get a speeding ticket? I know just about every

cop in town."

"Just about — those are the important words. What if you fly by a cop you don't know?"

"Then I'll drop your name. Every cop knows about the last man standing at the Ragged Lake shootout. It's in a book somewhere."

"I wish you'd stop teasing me about that book."

"Sorry, I keep forgetting."

His dad chuckled and rolled his wheelchair to the window of his kitchen. His apartment was on the twelfth floor and looked out on the Springfield River. He had to fight to get the apartment, the superintendent of the building telling him when he moved in that the "accessible units" were on the ground floor, and that's where he needed to go. Yakabuski's father told the superintendent all the accessibility he needed was an elevator. He would take an apartment with a river view.

"You going to your nephew's party next week?" his dad asked.

"Wouldn't miss it."

"How about bringing your girlfriend. Don't you think it's time we met her?"

Yakabuski let out a sigh. "That's another thing you keep forgetting, Dad. I don't have a girlfriend."

"What do you call her, then?"

"You going to tease me after I just brought you fish? Who do you torment when I'm not here? Had any fights with the neighbours, yet?"

"Neighbours, *smeighbors*, who cares about neighbours? You're not answering my question."

"That's right, I'm not. Can't fool you, can I?"

"Bring her to Justin's party. I want to meet her."

Yakabuski gave his father a quick hug. "I better be heading out."

"I think you're crazy to be leaving this time of the day. It's a long drive."

"Do you think I'm crazy to be going at all?"

"You mean because there's no suspicious death report?"

"Yeah."

"No, you're doing the right thing. Girl says her mother never went near the river. Why would she lie about something like that?"

4

WHEN YAKABUSKI ARRIVED in Port Henry, Dr. Peter Atkinson was waiting for him in front of the Food Town grocery. Yakabuski was surprised to see that the doctor had baby-fat cheeks, greasy hair, and acne scars on his forehead. He looked like a teenager.

He spoke like one as well, sounding petulant and aggrieved when he said, after shaking Yakabuski's hand, "I am *sooo* glad you called, detective. Hopefully you can talk some sense into that girl. She's making everyone's life difficult."

Atkinson was a recent medical school graduate, hired by Northern Head Start, a government agency that recruited medical graduates to work in places like Port Henry. If they agreed to work for the government for five years, their student loans were repaid in full. The key qualities you needed to be recruited by Northern Head Start were crushing student debt and no residency offers.

"How is she making everyone's life difficult?"

"The body can't be moved until it's been formally identified. It can't stay in the Food Town cooler forever. Honestly, I've never had a situation like this before."

Yakabuski looked at the doctor and wondered how many situations he'd had before. "Girl doesn't believe her mother drowned."

"Girl can believe anything she wants — *after* she's ID'd the body."

The doctor stomped his feet a few times. Blew air into his hands, although it wasn't that cold. "You said you needed to see her?"

"I do."

"Follow me."

The two men entered the Food Town and made their way to the walk-in cooler at the rear of the grocery. They walked down an aisle of just arrived summer clothes, Yakabuski looking at a display of golf shorts and wondering how brave you needed to be to wear such garments in the woods around Port Henry. At the end of the aisle the doctor unclasped a thick metal door, and they walked through a commercial curtain of floor-to-ceiling rubber slats that made a slapping sound as they passed through.

The body lay on a metal shelf near the entrance to the cooler, hemmed in by bags of frozen peas and hamburger patties. It was zipped inside a dark-green sleeping bag with a hood, though not all the way; a few pale blonde hairs poked through the teeth of the zipper.

The doctor eased the zipper down. "How far do you want me to go?"

"All the way."

He tugged it open, then stepped aside as Yakabuski moved forward. A woman lay before him, her age difficult to pin down — although no longer young. That was safe to say. Her eyes were deeply recessed, as though they'd begun to burrow backwards in their sockets, as if they had seen too much of the world and begun to retreat. Her blonde hair was grey at the roots, and it looked like it hadn't been dyed in a long time. Her skin was deeply wrinkled, although you didn't notice the wrinkles right away because of the bruising and contusions on her face. Her jaw was clearly broken. Her nose was broken as well, splayed back and showing bone.

"She's in bad shape," said Yakabuski.

"The river did that. She was out there a couple days."

"She drowned?"

"Absolutely. You can tell by the blueish discolouring of the skin. That's called cyanosis, and it means she was alive when she started swallowing water. Rigor mortis is consistent with a drowning victim. There's blood in the middle ear as well.

She drowned."

"The blood has pooled in front of her body; that's consistent with a drowning victim as well, correct?"

The doctor gave Yakabuski a surprised look. "If the body was facing down, yes, that would be another sign of drowning."

"A lot of damage to her face."

"Which would be consistent with a downward-facing body. She was dragged along the bottom of the river."

"Why aren't the same abrasions on her knees? And her feet?" Yakabuski asked.

The doctor looked to where Yakabuski was pointing. "Hard to say. But this woman died by drowning. There's no doubt about that."

"How much do you know about the Springfield River, Doctor Atkinson?"

The doctor gave Yakabuski a suspicious look. "Why do you ask?"

"Well, you're saying it's the river that killed her — that's what you're saying, right?"

The doctor took so long to answer it seemed as though he were a contestant on a game show. Eventually, he said, "There's no doubt the river killed her. That is correct."

"Then I think you should know something about your killer. Know something about how the current works, how it flows on the Back Channel of this river, where you say this woman drowned. Those would be good things to know, wouldn't you agree?"

The doctor didn't answer. Yakabuski continued.

"On a river, the current bounces off the rocks and anything else in its path. It doesn't *pull you* toward an obstacle. It's the reason white-water kayakers don't get smashed to pieces each time they go out. The contusions and abrasions on her face — there are too many of them. Drowning victims don't have faces that look like this. It doesn't matter how long they've been in the water."

The doctor took a step backward, as though trying to put some distance between him and Yakabuski, or between him and some bad-news truth that had suddenly trapped him in the stand-up cooler of the Food Town grocery.

"The cyanosis, the skin maceration, the blood in the ears — I'm telling you; this woman drowned."

"I know she drowned," replied Yakabuski. "What I don't know is who attacked her before they tossed her in the river."

5

MEAGHAN MCKENNA lived ten miles upriver from Port Henry, in an original settler cabin made of pine logs and chinked mortar that had turned yellow with age. The cabin had four small windows — one for each wall — and a front door that Yakabuski knew would be exactly six feet tall, because that's what they all were.

He leaned over the steering wheel of his Jeep Rubicon and looked around. The trees surrounding the cabin were spruce and white pine. No cedar. No hardwood. There would never be much sun around this cabin, no matter the time of day, no matter the season. A Ford Escort with bad rust around the tire wells was parked in front. Out back, clothes were hanging from a wash line.

As he sat in his Jeep, a boy walked out of the cabin and stared at him. He looked to be seven or eight, with long blond hair and a blue hoodie with the logo of the University of Florida. He wiped his nose on the sleeve of the hoodie and kept staring as Yakabuski got out of the Jeep.

"I'm looking for Meaghan McKenna," he said, as he approached the boy. "Is she here?"

"Out back," answered the boy, pointing his thumb over his shoulder.

"She your sister?"

"Yeah."

"Is she busy?"

"Busy?" said the boy, and he gave Yakabuski a questioning look, as though he didn't understand the word. He wiped his nose again.

"Out back?" asked Yakabuski.

"Out back," answered the boy.

Yakabuski walked behind the cabin, where he found Meaghan McKenna standing beside a picnic table, folding clothes. An old woman sat at the end of the table, smoking a cigarette.

"Meaghan, I hope I'm not disturbing you."

The girl gave him an unfriendly look and kept folding clothes. "Just doin' the wash. Don't know if you can rightly disturb a chore like that . . . why you here?"

"I've just come from seeing the doctor."

"Didn't think you were going to do anythin' 'bout my momma."

"I don't recall saying that. You may have a better memory of our last meeting than I do. I do remember that it ended rather abruptly."

The girl's hands clenched the edge of the plastic laundry basket. She raised her shoulders and leaned forward. It looked like a football stance. If Yakabuski was expecting an apology from the girl for walking out on him, he was about to be disappointed.

"May we go inside and talk?" he asked.

"You want to go inside?"

Yakabuski heard panic in the girl's voice, and he suspected the reason. Meaghan McKenna could probably count on the fingers of one hand how many times a stranger had been inside her home. And none of those would have been good times.

After a funeral. After a bad storm. After a cop drove down the laneway and said they needed to talk.

The way poor people lived was usually a family secret. Something not shared with others. "If you prefer, we can talk on the porch," said Yakabuski. "Would that be easier?"

He could see the relief spread across her face. As noticeable as wind moving through a wheat field. "Yeah, that'd be easier. Let me put these clothes away, first."

The girl nodded toward the woman at the end of the table. "Aunt Lizzie can bring you out front."

The old woman stared at Yakabuski but didn't move. After a while, she reached into the pocket of her cardigan and pulled out a pack of Camels.

"You a cop?"

"Yes ma'am. Detective Frank Yakabuski."

"From Springfield?"

"Yes ma'am. I'm here about Agnes. She'd be your . . . sister?"

"Ya askin' me or tellin' me?"

"I'm sorry?"

"If you're askin' me, you gotta let me know that's what you're doin'. So, I know I gotta talk to you. It's not polite, makin' me guess."

"I'm asking you."

"Ain't my sister. My niece. I'm older than I look. Thought you were a detective."

Yakabuski waited for the woman to stop laughing, then he asked, "This is an original settler's cabin, isn't it? When did your family come to the Back Channel?"

"McKennas were some of the first," she said. "Not many've been here longer than us. Why are you here? Is Agnes in trouble"

"No ma'am, not at all."

She gave Yakabuski a suspicious look and finally lit her cigarette. From inside the cabin, Meaghan yelled — "If she ain't comin', just leave her there. I'll see ya out front."

The chairs on the porch were made from poplar branches twisted into shape. The cushions were woolen blankets, folded to fit. They were comfortable chairs with a clear view of a fast-moving creek that ran through a stand of white pine, and beyond that, in the far distance, the Northern Divide. Purple and cobalt shadows were inching down its southern flank as the sun began to drop.

They sat in silence until the girl asked. "You've seen the doctor?"

"I have."

"And?"

"I believe you're right. Your mother didn't go near that river."

"But you're here now. You must believe the woman the doctor has in Port Henry is . . . "

"It's your mother."

"Thought the doctor said she drowned."

"He did."

"I don't understand."

"I believe your mother was assaulted and then put in the river. She drowned, but it wasn't an accident."

"She was murdered, is that what you're telling me?"

"I'm sorry, Meaghan, there still needs to be an autopsy, but yes, it looks that way to me."

It seemed to Yakabuski he heard a clock ticking somewhere inside the cabin. He felt certain it was a grandfather clock. Had that sort of sound. "Did your mother have any enemies? Is there anyone you can think of who might have wanted to harm her?"

The girl looked away and it seemed to Yakabuski that her body sagged, as though something inside had gone flat. Although it was such a fleeting movement, he couldn't say with certainty that's what he'd seen.

"Can't think of anyone," the girl said.

"Your father is dead, is that right?"

"That's right."

"Do you have any other family?"

"Other than Lizzie and my brother? No, they're all I got."

Yakabuski closed his steno pad and looked out at the shadows moving down the Divide. He had more questions but decided they could wait a day. He had one question left that he couldn't avoid.

"Meaghan, the doctor still needs someone to make a formal identification. Can your aunt look after your brother for a couple hours?"

6

MCKENNA FOLLOWED Yakabuski to the Food Town. The heater on the Escort was broken, and she spent the first few minutes of the drive wishing she had brought a sweater. By the time she reached the main road, though, the heater had started half-working, and it didn't seem so cold. Nothing to complain about, anyway.

She hoped the identification wouldn't take long. She wanted to start looking for her mother's killer. That night. Before the cops got in her way. Before the killer got spooked and ran.

Although she doubted that was going to happen. Whoever killed her mother probably lived on the Back Channel and anyone from the Back Channel would know running from trouble made you look like an idiot when it caught you. Always better to stand your ground and fight.

Yes, she had gone to Springfield to report her mother missing, but she didn't need the cops anymore. She thought they could be useful in finding her mother, when she thought her mother was alive, but now that her mother was dead, she didn't need the cops.

Don't trust cops. Don't trust anyone. Take care of yourself, first.

Her father taught her those "golden rules." That's what he called them. His golden rules. As if to show his family how they worked, he walked out on them as soon as a doctor confirmed Robbie was a wet-brain baby.

Her dad lived downriver for a few years after that, with a girl not much older than she was, but then he got cancer and died within two months of being told about it. Her mother said that was her dad getting his "just desserts." That's what

she called his death. Just desserts. Maybe. Meaghan wasn't
sure about that.

Before heading out to Port Henry the detective asked again if
she could think of anyone who would want to hurt her mother,
and again she said no one came to mind.

"What happens now?" she asked him.

"After your identification, your mother will be moved to
Springfield so the regional coroner can examine her. That will
likely happen tomorrow."

"Examine her . . . you mean an autopsy?"

"That's right."

"Don't I need to say yes to that?"

"Not if it's a homicide. I'll be back tomorrow as well. I'll
bring another police officer with me and that will be the start
of our investigation. Where it goes from there . . . we'll know
more tomorrow."

"What will ya be doing tomorrow?"

"Interviewing people. Who do you think we should talk to?"

The question confused her. "Isn't that the same question
you already asked me — who would want to hurt my momma
— just using different words?"

The cop had laughed and then asked, "How old are you
again, Meaghan?"

"Seventeen," she'd answered.

"And you're not in school?"

"No, sir."

"You should be."

The girl nodded. She should be doing a lot of things.

And as soon as this cop was gone, she could start doing them.

McKenna stood in the parking lot of the Food Town and
watched Yakabuski's Jeep go over the berm surrounding Port
Henry, the one the government had built years ago to keep out
the spring floods. She watched the Jeep's taillights rise and then
vanish into the marshland the other side of the berm. When

she was certain the cop had gone, she started her car.

The identification had been brutal. Her mother lying on a metal shelf in the cooler of the Food Town, her face busted up, her eyes staring off into . . . *what*? Heaven's Gate? The Promise Land?

Don't make me laugh.

Those eyes had looked scared and old and sad — her mother's eyes — and she would carry that image in her head the rest of her life.

Weren't you supposed to close a dead person's eyes? She thought that's what you were supposed to do, and she hated the doctor for not having done that. And for making her come down to Port Henry.

Her mother was dead, the doctor hadn't help her none, and it seemed right and proper to hate him. She drove over a wooden causeway that cut through a marsh, then down a meandering road that brought her to a trailer park on the north shore of the bay, where the permanent population of Port Henry lived.

Most of it, anyway. Some people still lived in settler cabins along the Springfield River, like she did, or somewhere along the Racine River, the tributary that emptied into the Springfield just upriver from Port Henry; but most people living along the Back Channel — permanent, not seasonal — lived in the Port Henry trailer park.

Which was ringed by abandoned cars and busted ice-fishing huts, rusted RVs and twisted wooden boats — a protective ring road of junk, a non-governmental berm that kept out nothing. The girl parked her car and began looking for a trailer.

A dark red trailer in the shadows and gloom of early dusk was hard to find. She walked up and down the rows of trailers, past men sitting on the steps of doublewides, or on fold-up camp chairs with tall-boys in their hands. A barred owl hooted over the water. Cookfires were being lit.

And then she found it. Perched on a knoll. A trailer that was separate from the others. A place of honour? A place of banishment? The girl knew either answer was possible, given the man who lived there.

She knocked on the trailer's door and waited, gazing down at the shadows growing in size and number upon the bay. When the door finally opened a man wearing a coffee-stained undershirt and green factory pants stood before her.

"What do you want?" he asked.

"Want to talk to ya 'bout my momma."

"Why?"

"Want to find out if you killed her."

The trailer smelled of work socks and mold and old man sweat. They sat at opposite ends of a small kitchen table. The man's hair was white and long. He pushed a handful of it off his eyes and said, "Agnes was killed? I heard she drowned."

Meaghan gave him a nervous look. The man was old enough that she shouldn't need to worry about him — what he might do to her — but he was big enough that she couldn't do that. He had the girth of a boat frame.

"Someone beat her up and threw her into the river. She couldn't swim."

"Says who?"

"Says the cops. They've been up here already. They'll be back tomorrow. *Investigating.*"

The man stroked his chin. "What's that got to do with me?"

"When I was in town last month, I seen you arguin' with her."

"Don't remember that. You sure it was me?"

"I know what you look like good enough."

"What was we arguing about?"

"Didn't hear all of it . . . somethin' 'bout money."

"You fuckin' pup — every argument is 'bout money. Sooner or later, that's what you're fightin' 'bout." He took another bunch of hair, pushed it to the back of his head. "I never had words with your mother."

"You're lying."

"Be careful what you say to me, Meaghie."

The man licked his lips, a languid, sweeping motion that showed the backside of his nicotine-stained tongue. The girl shuddered at the sight of it. Like a black snake moving in a pool of still water.

"Just like a fuckin' McKenna," the man said. "Come into a man's house and insult him. You better be *real* careful what you say to any cops, Meaghie."

"Are ya not goin' to tell me what you were fightin' 'bout? Gonna let me draw my own conclusions?"

The man suddenly jumped from his chair, knocking over the table. He took two giant strides and grabbed her by the throat. She raised her knee to kick him, but he swatted it away and pushed her against the wall.

"*Men* draw conclusions, Meaghie, not a child bitch like you."

"Stop it, you're hurting me."

"'Cause I *want to hurt you*. I can do that anytime I want, Meaghie. You need to *understand* that."

"Big man . . . choking a girl."

"I'll do more than fuckin'—"

He didn't finish the sentence. Just then a woman and a teenage boy walked into the trailer. The woman gasped and the hand around the girl's throat went slack.

"What's going on here?" the woman asked, not raising her voice, and not seeming as surprised as you might have expected.

"Can't ya see? Grandpa is just having some fun with a McKenna. Ain't ya Poppa?" said the boy.

The man ignored the question. He looked at the girl, then did an off-balance spin and returned to the overturned table. He sat it upright, found the bottle of Crown Royal that had fallen to the floor, found the rocks glass that had landed beside the bottle, and poured himself a drink.

He emptied the glass in two gulps, then grabbed Meaghan by the arm. "She was just leaving," he said, and then he shoved her outside.

7

THE HIGHWAY WAS ALREADY in shadows when Yakabuski left Meaghan at the Food Town and began the drive back to Springfield. Already dark, although sunset in Springfield was at least two hours away.

The sun always disappeared early on the Back Channel, a natural phenomenon that happened because of the cliffs on Smoke Island, which rose more than eighty metres at their highest point and were never less than sixty. When the sun fell below those cliffs it was nighttime along the Back Channel, even though it was afternoon everywhere else along the Divide.

As though the Back Channel had its own time zone. To go along with everything else it uniquely possessed. Like health care that was neither healthy, nor caring. Poor people didn't get health care, thought Yakabuski, they got indentured help from medical school graduates who possessed the experience and expertise of June bugs.

And promises. The poor always got promises, too, let's not forget about that. It's what grows best in places like the Back Channel. Promises of a better day, a better tomorrow, a better whatever, because today sure wasn't offering you much.

Yakabuski had often wondered why people stayed in places like the Back Channel. Live on bad land long enough and misery gets passed down through the generations — tough days, bleak horizons, the scorn of strangers who don't even know your name — that's the family inheritance. So why stay?

Yakabuski was still pondering the question when he cleared Smoke Island and the sun returned. It was always a strange sensation when that happened, as though you had been sailing beside a supertanker for a long time and finally got ahead of it.

Not that the sun improved his mood any. Yakabuski thought of Agnes McKenna lying on the metal shelf of the Food Town cooler, her face weathered and scarred long before it was brutalized, her hair sponged together like clumps of seaweed, clouded eyes staring up at a corrugated tin roof, where a light bulb swung from a yellow extension cord.

The indignities done to the murdered — they seemed infinite to him right then.

Yakabuski drove until he found himself pulling in front of Rachel Dumont's townhome. *You shouldn't be doing this*, he told himself. *You should drive straight home; you should do it now.*

But he was telling himself this even as he was knocking on her front door.

Rachel Dumont put a teacup in front of Yakabuski and sat beside him on her living room couch. She was still dressed in the clothes she must have worn to her government job that morning: a dark blue skirt that covered her knees, a white blouse that was buttoned to her neck. She brushed out a wrinkle on the skirt and said, "Can you believe I've never been to the Back Channel?"

"That's easy to believe. The north-shore highway dead-ends at Port Henry. Unless that's where you're going, there's no reason to ever be on that road."

"What's it like?"

"It's wild country. Wild and poor, only one town of any size, and Port Henry's not much more than a wharf and a lumber yard these days."

"Sounds like the townships."

"The townships are suburbia compared to the Back Channel."

"That can't be true."

"It is."

Dumont scrunched her face into a little pout and Yakabuski took another sip of his tea. He wasn't doing a good job of describing the Back Channel. Maybe the task was beyond him. Or maybe he just became clumsy around Rachel Dumont.

His money was on the latter option. Their friendship had been slow developing, a thing more implicit than stated. But the facts were becoming hard to dispute. Yakabuski was at Dumont's apartment three or four times a week. She contacted Yakabuski whenever she wanted advice, legal advice at first, now everything up to possible prom dates for her daughter, Grace, and should she be worried about the options?

There were reasons for the slow pace. The seventeen years difference in their age was one. Another was her last name. Rachel was the only child of Gabriel Dumont, the last great chief of the Travellers, a near mythic group of criminals from the Far North, or so the folk songs were being written even as they sipped their tea that night.

Gabriel Dumont's reputation had only grown since his death. For many along the Divide, he had become a folk hero. Grace even had a poster of her grandfather in her bedroom. It showed him in full buckskin and beard, a photo taken outside his home in Cape Diamond, with what looked like herb bags hanging from leather straps around his belt.

Although they could have been scalps.

You couldn't tell with certainty what they were, not even if you held a magnifying glass right up to the picture. That poster had caused a month-long rift between Rachel and her daughter, and Yakabuski still wasn't sure if she had made the right decision by allowing the poster to stay.

"When I was a child, I thought the Back Channel was the most exotic place on the planet," he said.

"What?"

Yakabuski put down his teacup. "You asked me to describe the Back Channel. That's my description. I used to think it was the most exotic place on the planet."

"Really?"

"Absolutely. I went up there with my father quite often when I was a boy. We went to the market in Port Henry. My sister used to go too, until Trish tried to free a blue heron from its cage and then she couldn't go with us anymore."

"What was a heron doing in a cage?"

"Oh, there used to be all sorts of birds at that market. Maybe there still are. I could have bought a hawk once, but I couldn't talk my dad into it."

"Why in the world would you want a hawk?"

Yakabuski looked puzzled. "Why in the world *wouldn't you*?"

Dumont laughed so quickly she nearly spit out her tea. She swallowed just in time, although a small trickle dripped onto her chin. She dabbed at it with a napkin. "If you ever have a hawk as a pet, don't bring it here."

"How about a red? They're not big. And it's just a hawk. I wouldn't bring over a wolf."

"You can't have a wolf as a pet."

"Sure, you can."

"You know people who have wolves as pets?"

"What — you don't?"

She wasn't quick enough this time. Tea shot from Dumont's mouth in a stream that hit a butter dish and then splashed into the air like a mini geyser. Yakabuski laughed so quickly, he nearly did the same.

He enjoyed teasing Dumont. Enjoyed seeing her laugh. Even though he wondered sometimes if he were putting up barriers, behaving like a smitten schoolboy who pulled pigtails and chased girls during recess, because he didn't know how else to behave. It was possible. He often felt young and foolish around Rachel Dumont.

Still, her laugh was a wonderful thing to hear, and he didn't mind making it happen. "Is your mouth empty?" he asked. "I need to make sure before I tell you that I knew a guy who had two of them."

"Two wolves as pets. You are *so* making that up."

"Scout's honour. The guy lived in High River, and he found the wolves as cubs. That's the only way you can have a wolf as a pet, can't do it when they're older, not even if you get them when they're injured. Although they all take off on you eventually, cub or no cub. Hawks are different. A hawk will stay with you."

"How do you train a hawk?"

"I knew a guy who did it by putting food near a nest. Food was in a tray tied to a rope, and he waited until one of the fledglings started eating the food, then he spent two weeks bringing that tray closer, and closer, until one day the bird hopped onto his hand and that was it. Ready to train. The guy told me that's how Mongolians caught golden eagles."

Dumont had a far-away look in her eyes when Yakabuski finished his explanation. He suspected she was thinking about something other than red hawks and Mongolian eagles. Grace had a steady boyfriend, her first, and although the boy would not confirm it, he was almost certainly a pledged member of the Travellers.

Rachel had fought to keep her daughter shielded from the Travellers, protected from a family legacy she found shameful and dangerous, but often these days it seemed like she was losing that fight. That her daughter was slipping away from her. Inch by inch. Temptation by small temptation.

"Why didn't the mother protect the fledgling?" she asked.

"Maybe because it was never in any danger. It hopped onto the hunter's hand and left. It was free will," answered Yakabuski.

"The fledgling was deceived and put into service of the hunter. It didn't know what was about to happen to it. Where is the free will in that?"

Yakabuski was now certain that Dumont was thinking about more than birds. He felt just as certain that staying on this topic would end badly for him. Especially if he said another kind word about Mongolian eagle hunters.

"My nephew is having a birthday party next week," he said. "My sister is organizing it. I saw my dad earlier today. He'd like to meet you. He'll be at the party, of course, and I was wondering, if you were free that night, if it doesn't seem like too strange an idea to you, maybe you could . . .

"Are you asking me to a party, Frank?"

"My dad would really like to meet you. So would my sister. Is that strange?"

"Not strange at all. The daughter of Gabriel Dumont; They'll need to take a number."

"It's not like that at all, Rachel. My dad and Trish could care less about your last name. They'd just like you to be there. I know they would."

"What about you, Frank? Would you like me to be there?"

"Of course."

"You should have led with that."

She gave Yakabuski an annoyed look, but he was wise enough, this time, not to talk. Before long, she was laughing. "I enjoy teasing you," she said. "What does that say about me? Nothing good, I'm sure."

Dumont told him she'd love to go to the party, and they finished their tea while watching a show on television about people working on a boat. Not a fishing boat. Or a naval ship. A yacht in the Caribbean. A show where nothing of consequence ever happened. It was one of Rachel's favourite television shows.

When Yakabuski left that night she walked him to his Jeep. It was the first time she'd done that. As though she wanted a few more minutes with him.

"It didn't always work," said Yakabuski, when they were standing beside his Jeep. "I should have told you that earlier, so you can quit blaming the mother."

"What are you talking about?"

"The eagle fledglings that willingly went off with the hunter. It wasn't always that way. Sometimes the fledgling needed to be snatched.

"The Mongolians preferred if the bird came willingly, they believed it made them better hunters, but if the fledgling didn't come, they would just snatch it. You shouldn't be so hard on the mother. Maybe she just knew the options."

THE SPRINGFIELD RIVER was beginning to appear out of the darkness, a blue line slowly getting embossed onto a black background. Yakabuski and Griffin stood beneath the *Welcome to Port Henry* sign on County Road 44, drinking coffee from metal travel mugs. The sign had been erected on a knoll overlooking the river and the cops looked down at the reappearing waterway and the buildings starting to take shape along the shoreline.

There wasn't that much to Port Henry. A public wharf. A post office. The Dickinson Hotel and Tavern. Coogan's lumber yard. A four-room school. A six-room medical centre. The Food Town. The residential buildings consisted of some original settler cabins, a score of new builds, and as many as a hundred trailers on the north shore of the bay. Most of the trailers were still hidden in the fading darkness, although a few were beginning to be visible in the early light.

It was Griffin who spoke first. "Regular holiday spot, isn't it? Get any better when the mist burns off?"

"Not really."

"What I thought. So — where do we start?"

"Treat it like a regular homicide. We've lost a couple days, but let's imagine we just found Agnes McKenna's body. What would we do?"

Griffin didn't hesitate. "Canvass the neighbourhood."

Yakabuski took a sip of coffee and pointed at a white, clapboard building. "We'll start with the post office."

"You think it'd be open now?"

"Postmaster will be living there."

"Oh," said Griffin, sounding embarrassed. Yakabuski began walking to his Jeep. "This place takes some getting used to.

Wait until we reach those trailers."

Yakabuski knocked on the back door of the post office for nearly ten minutes before someone answered. When the door opened a man stood there, wearing a bathrobe many inches too short for him.

He had his head turned down, cinching the cord of the bathrobe, and muttering in a loud voice, "What's your dang hurry at this time of day? You know we're not open 'til . . . "

Then he looked up and saw the cops.

"Who in sweet blazes are you two?"

"Morning sir. Apologies for getting you up this early. We're with the Springfield Regional Police. I'm Detective Frank Yakabuski and this is Constable Donna Griffin."

The man looked at Griffin and cinched his robe a little tighter. "You're cops?"

"That's right."

"What are you doing here?"

"Investigating a homicide, I hate to say."

"In Port Henry?"

"Agnes McKenna. Did you know her?"

"*Of course* I knew her. I'm the postmaster."

"Of course . . . What's your name, sir?"

"Stinton Halliday."

"I need to ask you a few questions, Mr. Halliday. May we come in?"

The postmaster gave Yakabuski a suspicious look. "I don't mean to be rude, but I don't see how I can help you much. Agnes McKenna didn't live in town. I didn't know her too good. Lots of men you can interview who knew her better than me . . . *a lot* better."

The postmaster winked at Yakabuski and gave him a smile. It was an uncertain smile. The kind nervous people have when they think they have said something clever but are unsure.

Yakabuski said, "What you just told me Mr. Halliday, that's

why I need to speak to you. I think a postmaster knows what's going on in his community better than any mayor, better than any police officer. What do you think, Mr. Halliday — am I wrong about that?"

The postmaster's chest grew a few inches right before them. Puffed right out like the throat of some freak-of-nature bull frog. "I think you're a smart man," he said.

Yakabuski stepped into the post office. "I hope you can get a pot of coffee going for us, Mr. Halliday. I'm nearly out. What about you, Griff?"

The living quarters of the postmaster were as humble as a backwoods parson's. The main floor was one large room that had a kitchen sink and a small fridge at one end, a couch and television at the other end. In the middle of the room a large oak table was strewn with stamps, envelopes, tape guns, and unfolded boxes. There were stairs leading to a second floor, where Yakabuski suspected there would be a small bedroom and a bathroom. The building had a sloping roof and there wouldn't be room for much more than that.

Halliday put on a pot of coffee and went upstairs to get dressed. When he came back, he was wearing grey slacks, a white shirt buttoned to his Adam's Apple, and a blue cardigan that had a Canada Post crest where his heart would be.

Halliday looked at the freshly brewed pot of coffee and said, "I think I have three cups here somewhere."

But he didn't. It was almost sad, thought Yakabuski, a man having only two coffee cups. One to wash, and one to use, he supposed. Who needs a third? The postmaster rummaged around in his cupboard until Yakabuski said, "I'm fine using my travel mug."

"Me, too," said Griffin.

"Well, I guess that'll work," said Halliday.

He refilled the cops' travel mugs, then made a cup for himself and took a seat at the table. Halliday's cup also had a Canada

Post logo on it. "I thought Agnes drowned," he said.

"We believe she did drown," said Yakabuski. "But we don't believe it was accidental."

"Someone drowned her?"

"No, someone assaulted her, then threw her in the river. She couldn't swim. What can you tell us about Mrs. McKenna."

Halliday pursed his lips, as though he had just bitten into something distasteful. "Well, she's a McKenna. Those people are always trouble. She was married to Bobby McKenna till he up and left her one day and moved in with some teenage girl."

The postmaster stroked his chin. "Bobby's brother was killed trying to rob a bank in La Toque. That was about ten years back, I guess."

"What was his name?"

"Clifford . . . Cliff McKenna."

Yakabuski wrote the name in a steno pad. He motioned for the postmaster to continue talking.

"There were a bunch of brothers, and they were all like Clifford. Couldn't tell 'em apart, to be honest with you. And Bobby's daddy — he was one of the biggest moonshiners these parts have ever seen. There's a lot of McKennas up and down this channel and there's probably not a one of them that's ever done an honest day's work."

"What about Agnes?"

A confused look came to the postmaster's face. "That's what I've been telling you."

"No, you were telling us about her husband, her father-in-law. What about *her?*"

"Well, she's a McKenna."

The postmaster shrugged his shoulders. He seemed annoyed at needing to repeat obvious truths. Yakabuski took a sip of coffee and looked at Griffin. She put down her travel mug.

"What does that mean, Mr. Halliday?" she asked. "Was Agnes McKenna a bad person? Did she do bad things? We've found no criminal record for her."

The postmaster snorted. "How often do you think the law comes up here? You two are the first cops I've seen in . . . well, I don't rightly know when I last seen a police officer up here."

"I'm asking you if she was engaged in some sort of criminal activity. Is that what you're saying, Mr. Halliday?" Griffin continued. "If you know any details, you need to tell us."

Halliday snorted a few more times. Clumsy snorts that made his eyes bulge. "Do *I know* any details? How 'bout she used to hang out at the lumber yard on pay days, and she never worked there. Why do *you* think she'd do a thing like that? Or, how 'bout I seen her in this post office so high on meth-am-*phetamines* that she was jimmying open the mailboxes with me standing right behind her."

Griffin looked at Yakabuski and her lips twitched as she suppressed a smile. He had been right. While Halliday had been suspicious and tight-lipped when Yakabuski was asking the questions, with her he was boastful and verbose. Wanting to impress her. Wanting to show his superiority.

"Please, go on," she said.

"Well, I'm not surprised to learn she was murdered. Let's put it that way," he said.

"That's not a detail, Mr. Halliday."

"No, but McKennas get killed. That's a *fact.*"

"Who might have killed her, Mr. Halliday?"

"Take your pick."

"I'd rather you did that."

Halliday gave Griffin a surprised look. That had been too abrupt.

"Names, Mr. Halliday," said Yakabuski, stepping back in. "That's what Constable Griffin wants from you. Names of people who may have wanted to harm Agnes McKenna. If you know any, of course."

"Well . . . " Halliday leaned back in his chair, stroking his chin again. "The Murphys would be worth talking to. They hate the McKennas. And they've killed each other before. If you go way back, you find those stories. They had a feud of some sort."

"About what?"

"Who knows? Don't take much to have a feud 'round here."

"Are there any Murphys in particular who come to mind?"

"Walton Murphy is the head of the family. You'll want to speak to him. He lives over in the trailers. Most people call him Wally. His son, Donnie, you probably want to find him, too."

"Who else?"

"She had boyfriends. Maybe it was one of them."

"Names, Mr. Halliday."

"Like I'd know? If you don't have a postal box, I don't know you. And her boyfriends — they tended to be seasonal."

Yakabuski started flipping through the pages of his steno pad. "Body was found ten days ago, on May 10."

"I suppose. It was a Monday. I remember that. Body was found in the harbour by Bobby Laforest. He was running a barge, bringing in some slag from the mill on Smoke Island."

"They still dump slag in the bay?"

"Sure do. They need to dredge it now, to keep enough draft, but that's where most of it still goes. When the pulp mill is running. Not as busy as it used to be."

"You remember it being busy?"

"I'm born and raised, detective. My family was one of the first to come up here. Yes, I remember."

"People used to call this place Slag Bay."

"They've called it a lot worse than that," the postmaster said.

"Doctor figures she'd been dead three days by the time she was pulled out of the river."

"Lots of bodies pop up after three days."

"Which means she was likely assaulted the previous Friday. Anything unusual happen in Port Hope that day?"

"Nothing unusual ever happens in Port Hope," Halliday muttered.

"Is that right? Yet here I am in your kitchen, asking you questions about a murder."

Halliday's head snapped back so quickly it was like he'd been slapped in the face. It was the mildest of reproaches, but the postmaster reacted as though he'd been punched. Yakabuski wrote something in his steno pad.

Griffin picked up the questioning. "When was the last time you saw Agnes McKenna, Mr. Halliday?"

"Not that long ago. She came in for her mail."

"When would that have been?"

"Couple weeks back, I guess."

"How often did she come in for her mail?"

"Not that often. She lives upriver. Not that easy to get into town when you're upriver. It's all private roads, none of 'em in good shape. 'Specially in the spring."

"What about her daughter? How well do you know Meaghan McKenna?"

"Don't know her at all. She never comes into town. There's a brother too, isn't there? A kid with problems."

"Her brother is developmentally handicapped, that's correct."

"Don't even know what the boy looks like, that's how often those two come to Port Hope. Lot of people like that in the marshlands. Hell, I don't even know how you'd count 'em all up, the people out there. It's Crown land. Lots of people living off the grid. Even families that have been here right from the start, like the McKennas."

"Wouldn't you know how many people are living along the Back Channel? They'd come here to get their mail, wouldn't they?"

"I only have seventy-six boxes. Most of my mail is general delivery. Like the McKennas."

"Why would the McKennas be general delivery? They were one of the first families up here."

"That's right. They came the same year my family did."

"So — why no box?"

"Boxes cost twenty dollars a year."

9

WHEN THEY LEFT the post office, most of the mist had burned away and Griffin got her first clear look at Port Henry. There were men working in the lumber yard. Children playing on the rocks behind the school, which was two double-side trailers welded together, four rooms in total. Someone was having a cigarette on the stairs behind the Dickinson House tavern. A slag barge was in the harbour.

"Where to now?" asked Griffin.

"Postmaster says she spent time at Coogan's."

Yakabuski and Griffin started walking toward the lumber yard. There was no fencing around the main yard, the way there normally is, and they could see stacks of wood, some already cut into twelve-board lengths and bark stripped, waiting to be trucked to a Coogan mill downriver. There were several work trailers and mini-silos holding dirt and rock salt, a row of dented pickup-trucks, a repainted school bus with Coogan Lumber written on the side. And, sticking out like sore thumbs, a Rubicon Jeep and a Land Rover, parked just inside the front gate.

They headed toward one of the trailers when a forklift with some logs in its basket pulled up beside them. The driver kept the forklift moving in its lowest gear.

"Can I help you?"

"Looking for the yard manager," answered Yakabuski. "Is he in one of these trailers?"

"One on the left. You're a cop, ain't you?"

"Detective Frank Yakabuski."

"That's what I thought. Are you sure it's the yard manager you're looking for?"

Yakabuski stopped walking. "Why wouldn't it be?"

"Just thought there'd be a connection. Mister Coogan is here today."

Thomas Coogan III looked so much like photographs of the original Thomas Coogan it startled Yakabuski. The first Thomas Coogan had been rich enough to get his picture included in high school history books and Yakabuski instantly recognized the long patrician face, the receding hair line, the pouty mouth.

"A murder in Port Henry?" said Coogan, after Yakabuski told him about the death of Agnes McKenna. "Hard to believe. Has there ever been one?"

"Not one that went to court."

Coogan chuckled. "That's a cynical answer."

"Maybe, but a truthful one. Your company has been around long enough to know that."

Coogan Forestry was founded in the heyday of squared timber, when lumber barons were some of the richest men in the British Empire. They sold the wood that England needed to build war ships, which was white pine, such a prized commodity back then, bush camps along the Upper Divide were routinely attacked, timber cribs stolen, and men killed, just to obtain the wood. Stealing squared timber was how the Shiners street gang started, back in the 1840s.

The old-growth pine stands along the Back Channel had all the lumber barons salivating when the colony road to Port Henry was surveyed and the stands were first seen. They all bought timber rights, only to discover the water level on the Back Channel was too low to run logs down to Springfield.

But when everyone else left, Thomas Coogan stayed. Probably for the same reason a handful of settlers stayed after the colony road was cancelled. He was stubborn. He had invested heavily in land along the Back Channel. And he didn't want to admit what a fool he'd been.

Coogan also stayed because he found a way to make money

on his timber rights. There were several stands of black oak on those rights, and oak didn't need to be run down the river like pine. Oak cost ten times more, and you could load it onto barges and ship it to mills in Springfield and still make a profit. Not much — nothing like the riches a man could make from floating a forest of pine downriver – but it was enough to keep Thomas Coogan from running.

"Did you know Agnes McKenna?" asked Yakabuski.

"I know the last name. McKennas have been up here a long time. Not sure if I knew anyone named Agnes. Do you have a photo?"

"No."

Coogan shrugged his shoulders. "Then, I probably don't know her."

"The postmaster told us Mrs. McKenna used to come to your yard on pay day. He said she got thrown off the property a few times."

"Is that right? What was she doing?"

"Selling meth. That's what he thought, although he wasn't sure. He also thought she might have had a boyfriend working here. Maybe several, over the years."

"I'd take anything Halliday tells you with a grain of salt. He's a fussy old gossip, that one. Selling meth to my workers? I doubt that."

"You're saying it's not true?"

"I'm saying I doubt it. Although what my workers do on pay day . . . "

Coogan shrugged his shoulders and smiled, leaving the rest unsaid.

"What about Mrs. McKenna getting thrown off your property? Is the postmaster wrong about that as well?"

"How in hell would I know? Do you think that's part of my job — lumber-yard bouncer?" Coogan laughed. It was a good-natured, come-over-here-so-I-can-slap-you-on-the-back sort of laugh. "Is that what you think, detective?"

"No. Although I thought you might have been given an incident report about something like that. So, the name — Agnes McKenna — means nothing to you?"

"I'm afraid not. Maybe if you had a photograph."

Yakabuski looked over at Griffin, then back to Coogan. "What brings you up here today, Mr. Coogan?"

"The price of oak," he answered with a grin. "It's been on rather a roll these days. Don't know if you follow news like that, but I'm looking at some of our stands. I want to make sure the numbers I'm seeing on my desk in Springfield are the real numbers."

"Doing your due diligence."

"That's right."

"How many stands are you inspecting?"

"Four. Been here since yesterday. I have one more before I head back." Coogan looked around the trailer. "Don't mean to be rude, but I was hoping to be done by now, and on the road. Will this take much longer?"

"Shouldn't. If there's someone waiting to go out with you, you can tell them we'll be done in a couple of minutes."

"No, it's just me. I have the same vehicle you do, Mr. Yakabuski. A Rubicon. I saw yours parked in front of the Post Office. I won't have any trouble getting around."

"And the Land Rover?"

He looked surprised. "Land Rover? I didn't see a Land Rover when I arrived. Must belong to one of my workers."

It was Yakabuski's turn to look surprised. "Really? How much do you pay your workers?"

"Oh, a good wage, detective. And if they have any overtime, which isn't hard to get in the spring, they can make out like the proverbial bandit. With me the proverbial bank that's just been robbed." He let out another good-natured, frat-boy laugh.

Yakabuski thanked him for his time. As they were leaving

the yard, Griffin said, "Something's bothering you. What is it?"

"Trying to figure out why he just lied to us."

"About not knowing the victim?"

"Don't know if that's a lie. Maybe."

"What, then?"

"Him doing his due diligence. He's inspecting his timber stands, but he's doing it without a tree-marker."

"That's wrong?"

"About as wrong as it gets. If you don't have a tree marker, you're wasting your time. How much wood you have, the board feet, the quality of it — you'll never be more than guessing. Coogan would know that."

"So, he's lying about why he's in Port Henry."

"Seems that way."

They had made their way back to the post office. Yakabuski leaned over the hood of his Jeep and stared at the lumber yard. He watched Thomas Coogan exit the trailer, look around, then get into his Rubicon and drive away. Yakabuski watched until the vehicle disappeared through a back gate in the yard. He looked back at the trailer and frowned.

Griffin said, "There's something else, isn't there?"

"Yeah — I'd also like to know who's driving that Land Rover."

10

YAKABUSKI TOLD GRIFFIN to wait in the Jeep while he went to the trailer park and continued the canvass.

"Anyone walks out of that trailer, take a photo," he said. "Anyone goes near that Land Rover, take a photo. Your phone any good?"

"Please."

"That's what I figured. Wait here 'till I get back."

It was hard to tell how many trailers were on the north shore of the harbour. Many of them had ice fishing shacks in their yards, or garden sheds, or discarded truck cabs. Where the trailers started, and the junk ended was a guessing game. There could have been scores of trailers. There could have been hundreds. It was that big a ramshackle.

Turning left from the lumber yard, Yakabuski walked past a line of well-maintained, A-frame houses, then some log cabins, a farmhouse with a wrap-around porch, a three-story Victorian with ornate bargeboard that looked as out of place as a spaceship would have. He kept walking until he reached a stand of tall spruce, the ground wet and spongy beneath his feet.

When he cleared the trees, he arrived at a wooden causeway that cut through a marsh. The slatted boards were old and rotten, didn't look strong enough to carry the weight of a pickup truck, and yet, this was how everyone living in the trailer park got in and out of Port Henry.

He was surprised at the sorry state of the causeway, until he remembered the general rule of maintenance and repair among most people living along the Upper Divide. Maintenance was to be avoided during fishing and hunting season.

And repairs were only to be done once the object in question had stopped working.

The homes he had just passed on the south shore were different. Well maintained. A few even sported fresh coats of paint, gleaming in the morning light. These would be the homes of the managers at Coogan, the owner of the Food Town. The young doctor was renting one, Yakabuski knew. This was the good part of town.

A ridiculous concept, but also a universal one. Didn't matter how small a town was — how insignificant or remote — people would find a way to have a good part of town and a bad part.

Yakabuski remembered clearing a squatter's camp near La Toque once, one that was in danger of being swept away in the spring floods, and the men who ruled that camp, the leaders, all owned shopping carts and slept against a rock fence that blocked the wind.

That was the good part of town.

People always found a way to pick winners and losers. You couldn't stop them from doing it even if you tried. So much a part of human nature, it was done with everything, not just houses — clothing, bank accounts, spouses, children, teeth . . . Who was a winner? Who was a loser?

The bad part of town — in a place like Port Henry, the concept was absurd. It was also, for all practical purposes, the trailers on the north shore of a weedy bay.

Yakabuski cleared the causeway and was making his way toward the trailers when he heard what sounded like a fight.

"Whatsa matter? Can't take it boy?" a man yelled.

"Screw you!" someone yelled back.

"Think you can talk to me like that? Stop your gawdamn runnin' 'round."

"Why? So, you can hit me again?"

"Why you little—"

The rest of the sentence was interrupted by a roar of laughter. "That's tellin' him, Garland," someone yelled.

Yakabuski broke into a run. He came around a trailer and saw a knot of men standing and stomping their feet. Inside the knot were two other men, although Yakabuski couldn't see them clearly.

No one noticed him approach. When he was ten feet away, he yelled, "Morning, gentlemen!"

The men turned to look at him and the circle broke. Yakabuski had his first good look at the two men who were fighting. One looked to be in his late fifties, with shaggy hair, and a barrel chest, blood dripping from thick tufts of hair on the back of his hands.

The other man wasn't a man. Not yet. He was a teenage boy, with a torn shirt, sunken chest, bloodied face, and a left eye he was having trouble keeping open.

No one said anything until the man with the bloodied hands said, "Yak — what the fuck are ya doin' here'?"

"Donnie Murphy — are you trying to kill this boy?" Yakabuski replied.

"Shit, boy's all right. Just a little blood."

"Looks to me like he may need medical attention."

"Nah, just a few stiches 'round the eye, that's all. His mother knows how to do that."

"Is he your son?"

"He is. And he deserved what he was gettin' Yak. He surely did. Go ahead, Garland, tell him what you were doing."

The boy gave his father an angry look and spat on the ground.

"All right, I'll tell him. I caught the boy stealing lumber. And copper line. And yeast. Boy was doin' it when I weren't around, when I had my back turned to him."

"Thought you'd be proud of initiative like that," Yakabuski said.

"Proud? The boy was stealing *from me*. He was planning on

setting up his own fuckin' still. *To compete with me!"*

The men roared with laughter. One stepped forward and patted the boy on the back. The boy smiled back at him through chipped teeth.

"A commercial squabble?" said Yakabuski. "That's what I just witnessed?"

The man looked at Yakabuski, ran a hand through his hair, not noticing the blood on his fingers. Or, not caring. "Well, yeah, I guess so — the squabble part, anyway."

The men roared one last time, then began to disperse and head back to their trailers, the entertainment finished for the morning.

11

GARLAND MURPHY sat in a wooden chair by a kitchen window; his mother stooped over him with needle and string. From time to time the boy would scream and his mother would slap him on the head and tell him to be quiet.

The boy's father had washed his hands and changed his shirt and was now sitting with Yakabuski at a linoleum kitchen table. The trailer was filled with wooden carvings: birds, bears, sailing ships, a large one with a castle and two men walking a cobbled path.

"You still carving, Donnie?" asked Yakabuski.

"When I have the time."

"Still sell at the market?"

The man nodded.

"Agnes McKenna was getting ready for the market when she was killed. Reason I'm up here today."

"She was killed? I heard she drowned."

"After she was assaulted and tossed into the Springfield River."

"Didn't know that — what does that have to do with me?"

"I'm canvassing the area. You drew a bit of attention to yourself this morning. Always been good at doing that, haven't you, Donnie?"

"Don't know what you're talking about."

"Yes, you do."

Murphy laughed and scratched his belly. Yakabuski remembered Donnie Murphy selling carvings at the Port Henry Market. Out the front of his stall, that's what he sold. Out back, he sold moonshine. And magic mushrooms. And ran boxing matches after the sun went down.

They used to be a regular market attraction, Donnie Murphy's

Saturday night maulings. He'd rope a ring around a cluster of pine trees and men would go at it. Murphy set odds and took bets. Yakabuski's dad raided the fights a few times and maybe that's why Murphy tried to recruit him one summer. Thinking the cop would stay away if his son was one of the fighters.

A plan that backfired when Yakabuski said no, and his dad raided the fights one more time. Murphy was charged with racketeering and human trafficking after that raid, charges that were dropped as soon as the crown attorney had a close look at the file and said, "The offense is moonshining, isn't it?" But it kept Murphy at the regional detention centre for three months.

"Are you still running fights at the market?" asked Yakabuski.

"Are you still a cop?"

"Can't be much of a secret if you are."

"Then it shouldn't be much work for you to find out."

"How old was I when you tried to talk me into fighting for you, Donnie. You remember? Would I have turned sixteen yet?"

"How the hell would I know how old you were?"

"That's right. Didn't matter. Anyone ever die in one of your rings, Donnie?"

"No one who knew what he was doing."

After saying this, Murphy stuck out his lantern jaw and clenched his teeth. Prepared to have an old argument one more time; prepared to defend a belief, a world view, that was intrinsic to Donnie Murphy.

Wasn't my fault.

"I'm told your family didn't get along with the McKennas. Is that true?"

"Who told you that?"

"Is it true?"

"Thought you were just canvassing. A question like that makes me think you were always going to come here. Which is it, Yak?"

"You're living less than a mile from where our homicide

victim was found. Yes, I'm canvassing the area, and yes, I was always going to knock on your door, Donnie."

"Lying to me before you even start asking your cop questions. Hear that, Garland — in your own kitchen a cop will sit there and lie right to your face."

"I'm not lying Donnie. I may just have more questions for you than I do for regular people."

Murphy snorted, looked at his son, snorted again. "Regular people. You're funny."

"Is it true? Did your family not get along with the McKennas?"

"I don't know. Ask my dad."

"You wouldn't know about something like that?"

He gave Yakabuski a quick sneer. "That's what I just said, ain't it?"

"Where does your dad live?"

"Red trailer on the hill," Murphy pointed out the kitchen window. "He won't be there, though. He's out in the boat, deadheading."

"When's he back?"

"He wants to have some logs for the next market. He could be out a few days."

"When did you last see Agnes McKenna?"

"Probably at the market."

"How did she get along with the other vendors?"

"I don't know. Probably not good. McKennas don't have a lot of friends."

"Not like the Murphys, right?"

"Don't believe me? Ask around. Go talk to a Hardwick."

"Why would I do that?"

"One of the Hardwick boys tried to court Meaghan last year and she hit him on the head with an ax. Butt end, but it put the boy in the hospital for a week. She told him if he come back to her farm she'd hit 'em with the other end. Hardwicks were none too pleased 'bout it. Boy drove fifty miles to see her. Some people are startin' to say the girl's just as crazy as her little brother."

"Tried to *court* her?"

"That's what he said."

"Maybe the boy deserved it," said Yakabuski. "The butt end, anyway."

Murphy laughed and spittle flew across the linoleum table. He wiped it away with the back of his hand and then wiped his hand on his pants. "Girl's turning into a looker, though, the boy weren't wrong 'bout that. She won't be on the Back Channel much longer."

"Where will she go?"

"I don't know. Someplace that ain't here."

"Did Agnes McKenna have any enemies that you know about?"

"She had ex-boyfriends. They're always enemies, ain't they? Works the same way as ex-wives?"

"I thought she was long-time married."

"That didn't stop her none. Didn't stop Bobby none, neither. Hell, they could both find their way into town on a Saturday night, if you catch my drift."

"Do you know any of the boyfriends' names?"

"I've got a bad memory these days, Yak. Sorry."

"You sure about that? I was thinking about buying a carving."

Murphy scratched his chin. "You were? Well . . . maybe I can remember a few . . . "

"Write them down for me." Yakabuski pushed his steno pad across the table.

As Murphy wrote, Yakabuski picked up a carving. It depicted a vagabond walking down a cobbled road, a pole over his shoulder, his worldly possessions in a bag tethered to the pole. Behind the vagabond walked another man wearing a jester's hat. The jester was pulling a cart.

The attention to detail was astonishing, the precision of the cuts so exact there seemed to be emotion in the eyes of the vagabond, and the eyes of the jester. Nothing was crude, everything was shaded and nuanced. The hands that had bloodied a boy's face earlier that morning had also carved this scene, something that didn't seem possible to Yakabuski. As though there were two people living inside the body of Donnie Murphy.

It took him a minute, turning the sculpture over in his hands, examining it, to notice there was a human skull protruding from the vagabond's sack. And that the cobbles on the path were not stones but the heads of people dead and stacked, waiting to be collected by the funeral carriage that was the jester's cart.

Donnie Murphy had carved a scene from the Great Plague. Maybe the two sides of the man weren't as irreconcilable as Yakabuski had briefly thought.

"Is that the one you want?" asked Murphy. "That one's not cheap. A lot of work went into it."

"You couldn't pay me to take this one, Donnie. How much for the cardinal?"

As Yakabuski neared his Jeep he saw Griffin smiling and waving at him from the front seat. He opened the door and threw the cardinal onto her lap. "Brought you a present. Why are you so happy?"

"What's this?"

"The price of a few leads," he answered and handed her the list Murphy had written. "These are some ex-boyfriends of Agnes McKenna."

Griffin was turning the wooden sculpture over in her hands. "This is beautiful. Who did it?"

"Donnie Murphy."

"One of the men the postmaster was telling us about?"

"That's right. Are you ever going to tell me why you're grinning like a banshee?

"Banshees are big grinners? I didn't know that. But you were right — there was someone still inside the trailer when Coogan left. The guy took off about a half hour later."

"In the Land Rover?"

"You got it. I took lots of shots of him, and the vehicle. If I had better cell reception, I would have run the plates already, but here's something strange . . . I think I know him."

Griffin was punching her cell phone screen as she talked. "Or I'm *pretty sure,* I know him; I recognized his face . . . I just can't remember the name."

She stopped hitting her phone and thrust it in front of Yakabuski. "Recognize him?"

Yakabuski stared at a middle-aged man with short hair and big glasses, wearing what looked like a camel hair trench coat.

"That's Walter Crawley."

"I know that name. Why do I know that name?"

"Because you live in a city with three rivers running through it. He's the water commissioner."

II

PEOPLE DROWN
ALL THE TIME

SECOND CLUE

Springfield, 1865

The man raised a crystal glass and gestured toward a nearby credenza. The agent shook his head.

"What, you don't drink?"

"Not tonight."

"What's wrong with tonight?"

"What's right with it?"

"What in the devil is that supposed to mean?"

"Just a question. I believe it's time I started asking some."

The agent rubbed his brow. His fatigue had deepened as he'd entered the house. Almost overwhelmed him as he trod down a long hallway lined with oil paintings of wigged men in red military uniforms. In the air was the smell of paraffin and lard, polished wood, and old port — the sweet, treacly odors of powdered wealth.

At the end of the hallway, he'd entered a room with oak-panelled walls and glass-enclosed bookcases, curtains thick enough to be throw rugs. On the walls hung more paintings of wigged men sitting astride sturdy horses. In one corner there was a stone fireplace with a fire burning.

The crystal decanters that sat on the credenza were filled with liquid that seemed to match the dark red in the oil paintings.

Beside the credenza, in front of a bay window, behind a large oak desk, sat Angus Arnprior, Colonial Governor of the Northern and Upper Divide.

Who stared at the agent and said, "I don't pay you to ask questions, Adams. I pay you to report on my land, something which you're late doing. Now, you won't even have a drink with me? You're a fuckin' cheeky bog, aren't you?"

If the agent was offended by the governor's remarks, he gave no sign. He unlaced his caribou jacket, and threw it open before sitting, the motion catching a glint of light off the brass dagger strapped to his thigh. Dropping into the chair before the desk, he let the jacket slide over the backrest and furl onto the floor.

"Why are you late?" Arnprior asked.

"Had trouble leaving."

"Why?"

"A dispute."

"What's that supposed to mean? You should have been here weeks ago."

The agent's fatigue was now so deep, so thick and enervating, the governor's voice sounded far away. Like an echo. "Have you seen it?" he asked

"Seen what?" Arnprior roared.

"Your land."

"Jesus, I'm not here to answer your questions, Adams. Give me your fuckin' report."

"I've come a long way, governor, in service of the king, as people like to say. Perhaps you can grant me the courtesy of an answer. Have you seen it?"

The governor stared at the agent but didn't answer. He drained his glass, stood and walked to the credenza, where he mixed himself another whisky soda, keeping his back turned to the agent.

"Why would I ever want to fuckin' see it?" he asked. "That's why I employ bogs like you."

He laughed and returned to his chair. Rolled the ice in his glass. In the quiet of the study the rolling ice sounded louder than it should have been. Like dogs barking late at night.

"That's what I thought," the agent said. "Well, let me tell you about your land, Governor. You have swamps that can't be surveyed. There's no end to them. What isn't swamp is stone, a rock ridge that cleaves the water, sending it either to the north or the south, and if you can find an inch of level ground anywhere on *your land you've found something precious. Swamp and rock. That's your land, Governor. What you've been giving to people as settlers' grants."*

The governor smiled and patted his belly.

The agent had known many governors. He had never known a thin one. "Have you met any of them?" he asked.

"Met whom?" the governor answered with a yawn.

"The people you've been sending to the back channel of this river."

"Now you're starting to annoy me, Adams — on what fucking occasion would I ever have met them?"

The agent shook his head. "Then allow me to tell you about them, governor. They build rock fences. That's how they spend their days; for there is little else for them to do along that channel. They can't grow anything on the land you've given them. They no longer possess money for steerage home. So, they spend their days building rock fences.

"On that back channel, rocks determine the worth of a man. If a fence has used many stones, then the man who built it is considered industrious. If a fence has used many different rocks — if it's elaborate or ornate in some way — then that man is considered rich. Strange way to see the world, wouldn't you say, Governor?"

Arnprior made a dismissive sound that was half-snort, half-chuckle, and when the agent knew no other answer was forthcoming he turned away. He looked at the barrister's bookcases, the crystal port glasses, the slow burning fire beyond the hearth.

"I've heard a rumour about the road."

Arnprior stopped patting his belly. "Rumours flow through this town more often than logs. Nowhere near as valuable, though."

"I thought this one was worth a penny or two. Do you plan on completing the road, Governor?"

Arnprior glared at the agent. He leaned forward, as if about to say something, but he seemed to think better of it, for he suddenly leaned back and said nothing.

The agent caught the portly man's reflection in the leaded glass of the bookcase, and a great sadness overcame him.

Had it always been wrong? he wondered. Or had it become wrong? There would be a difference, and the difference would matter. To him. To God. Maybe even to those living high upriver on the governor's land, although he doubted if there was much that still mattered to those people.

He turned back to face the governor. "I've decided those fences are improvements. I've brought the papers."

The governor's smile disappeared. "You've done what?"

"You heard me."

"That was a rather stupid thing to do, Adams."

There it was. Always wrong.

The agent stood. "You're a man of no curiosity, Governor. Every governor I've known has been the same, so I suppose there's no shame to it, merely the way you were raised. Knowing this, I know you won't care about what I'm going to say, but I'll say it anyway. I've worked on four continents, been land agent for railway companies, mining companies, even an Indian emperor, once, but I've never seen land like yours . . . it's unholy."

"Unholy?"

"I cannot think of a better word. The back channel of this river is the land God gave to Cain. Shame on you for not seeing that."

Arnprior's face turned scarlet red, and his knuckles whitened around his whiskey glass. "You're tired, Adams. It's understandable. You were upriver a long time. I'll forgive you for what you just said. I'll also put in a requisition with the quarter master for a bonus — meritorious service, that's what we'll call it — that'll get you fifty quid and a damn fine letter, on top of what I'm already paying you!"

The agent turned up the collar of his coat and said, "I want neither your forgiveness nor your letter, Governor; and I won't be taking your money. I want no more part of this scheme."

"Scheme? Is that what you just said? Have you lost your mind?"

"Good day to you"

"What . . . you're leaving? You think you can just get up and leave?"

"I'm a free man, Governor, not one of your indentured settlers, so yes, that's what I think. It is also what I'm doing."

"You can't just . . . What do you . . . ? Fine. Go ahead and leave. You can put your papers on my desk."

"I'll be taking the papers with me."

Surprise flickered across the governor's face. But it was fleeting. Without saying anything more, he reached for the handle of a desk drawer.

When the agent saw this, he pulled his dagger from its leg sheath and threw it.

To Governor Angus Arnprior, third colonial governor of the Northern and Upper Divide, it would have seemed a continuous motion; his land agent reaching inside a caribou jacket, removing his hand, extending it; looked like the beginning of a handshake; looked almost friendly.

The governor gasped when he felt the dagger enter his chest. His surprised look returned, although just as fleeting as before. His eyes began to close, and he slumped forward. When he hit the desk there was a knocking sound, an ordinary, rap-on-the-door sort of sound.

His left hand still reached for the desk drawer holding the Colt pocket pistol. His right still clutched a half-finished whiskey and soda.

The agent walked around the desk, hefted the governor's body back in the chair and removed the dagger. He wiped the blade clean on Arnprior's embroidered tunic, then let him fall forward once more. There was a louder, not quite as ordinary knock this time.

The agent left the study and walked down the hallway, past the blood-red paintings and the crystal bowls of cut chrysanthemums sitting upon the many side tables. As he opened the courtyard door he heard the maid scream.

12

CHIEF BERNARD O'TOOLE looked at his computer screen, then over the top of the screen to Yakabuski and Griffin.

"This was taken yesterday?"

"Shortly before noon," answered Yakabuski.

"Outside of Coogan's lumber yard in Port Henry?"

"Yes."

"And you think Commissioner Crawley being in Port Henry is significant, because . . . ?"

"I don't know if it's significant. I just know the timing is odd," Yakabuski said.

"You think he knew the victim? Agnes . . . "

" . . . McKenna. I don't know if he did. I haven't interviewed him."

"I find it unlikely that they knew each other. The victim, from what I've read, was born and raised on the Back Channel and rarely left the place."

"I doubt if it was rarely. More likely never."

"Exactly. So how could she have known Mr. Crawley?"

Yakabuski shrugged his shoulders. "I haven't interviewed him."

"What else did you get from canvassing? Constable?"

Griffin leaned forward. "We have the names of some ex-boy-friends. We ran the names. Each one has a criminal record."

"It doesn't seem like our victim kept good company."

"No, you can't say that she did. Two of the exes have convictions for assault, one of them a domestic battery charge. Elmer Tilson. He did two years plus-a-day for it. Federal time."

"He beat his wife."

"Yes."

O'Toole turned back to Yakabuski. "The ex-boyfriends seem like a more promising avenue of investigation than the water commissioner."

"I think it's too early in the investigation to know what's promising."

O'Toole snorted again. Louder this time.

"Did you get anything else?"

"I interviewed Donnie Murphy."

"Donnie Murphy? Why do I know that name?"

"He's been in the cells a few times."

"A bootlegger?"

"Among other things. A few people told us there's some sort of feud between the Murphys and the McKennas. Goes back generations. No one knows how it started. There's hatred between the two families; no doubt about that, we saw evidence of it."

"Some old family grudge? Why would that get someone killed today?"

Yakabuski shrugged. "At the moment, we don't know if there *is* a feud. We'll need to interview some more Murphys and some more McKennas to find out if that's true. Donnie Murphy has a father we haven't interviewed yet — Walton Murphy. The patriarch of the family. He was out on his boat yesterday looking for deadheads."

"When will you be able to interview him?"

"Donnie said he'd be at the next market." Yakabuski said.

"When is that?"

"A week from Saturday."

"How are you going to work the case until then?"

"The ex-boyfriends are in Springfield, sir," Griffin said. "The ones that aren't in prison, anyway."

"We'll finish those interviews, go to the market, and see where we are," added Yakabuski.

"The Back Channel Market; it's been a few years since I've been there," said O'Toole.

"Constable Griffin will go with me, so we'll be able to conduct multiple interviews," said Yakabuski. "Lots of people on the Back Channel are hard to track down, but everyone comes out for market day."

"Have you ever been to that market, constable?" O'Toole asked.

Griffin shook her head.

"Don't buy a bird," said the chief. "It'll just take off on you."

"Sorry — don't buy a *bird?*"

"You haven't told her anything about the Back Channel Market, have you, Yak?"

"Not that much."

"Well, constable, consider it a cultural exchange," O'Toole said with a smile. "Yak, when you're done interviewing the ex-boyfriends, I'd like an update."

"Will do," said Yakabuski, rising from his chair, Griffin following. "So, the water commissioner — he's a no go?"

"For the moment," answered O'Toole. "Seems to me, there's plenty of work we can do before we need to drag the water commissioner into an active homicide investigation. Find out more about our victim. Let's start there."

13

MEAGHAN MCKENNA sat on her porch, looking at the path running beside the creek, wondering when her uncle would get there.

It surprised her that he had yet to arrive. Liam Burke had always been protective of his little sister, always willing to help her, even if her uncle's idea of protection and help were different from most people's.

Hell, different from anyone who wasn't in a federal pen, she supposed.

He lived in Springfield now, although he had cabins and cookhouses up and down the Back Channel, places that you kept far away from if you valued your health. Her uncle sold methamphetamines, primarily to the Popeyes, a biker gang in Springfield. She had known these things since she was a child.

No one had ever tried to hide it from her. Not her uncle. Not her mother. Certainly not her father, who was often in debt to Liam Burke, and once had his arm broken by him, to speed up payment.

His left arm. Not his working arm. He was family, after all.

When her father left, her uncle even came and stayed with them a few days, sleeping on the porch, as it was early summer when her dad took off. No one from the Back Channel ever walked out on someone during winter. Why add to your problems? You want to ditch someone, wait until spring.

Uncle Liam had offered to kill her father. She'd heard him make the offer when he was out on the porch with her mother, middle of the night and the pair of them chatting away like a couple of grey jays.

"Bastard deserves it," she'd heard her uncle say. "Why let

him get away with it, Aggie?"

"He may come back."

"You can't want him back . . . Bobby McKenna is the laziest piece of shit I ever met. You never should have married him, but now you get a chance to wash your hands of him. Tell me where he's staying. I'll do it tonight."

"I don't want you getting into trouble. He's not worth it."

"I won't get into any trouble. Bobby will just disappear. Do you know how easy it is to disappear up here?"

"As easy as . . . Oh, damn . . . Just like . . . Damn, why can't I do this?" Her mother had been trying to snap her fingers but couldn't do it.

"'Cause you're higher than the rafters in an Amish barn," her uncle answered, and they started laughing, just killing themselves laughing at how easy it would be to make her father disappear.

If they could only snap their fingers.

She was still remembering her uncle's visit when she heard footsteps on the porch behind her. She turned, expecting to see her little brother, or Aunt Lizzie, but saw instead a man walking toward her. He wore a denim shirt with the sleeves cut off, denim pants with a cowboy buckle larger than a beer can, steel-toed cowboy boots. His black hair was slicked back and shining in the moonlight.

She smiled at him. "'Bout time you got here."

Liam Burke reached into the packsack that sat at his feet, took out a can of beer and handed it to her.

"Thanks."

"Want to smoke a spliff?"

"No, it's too late. It'll just keep me up."

"I've got some indica. That won't keep you up."

"It does with me."

Her uncle nodded and reached back into his packsack, took

out a baggie of marijuana and a pack of rolling papers. He sat on the steps of the porch, a can of beer beside him, and began rolling a spliff.

While he was doing that, his niece told him about her visit to the Food Town, and what that big cop from Springfield had told her. Burke lit the spliff and took a couple of drags. "So, that's how she ended up in the river," he said. "It didn't make any sense to me, when I heard that. Your mother was scared to death of that river."

"She was. I never knew why. Do you?"

"Not 'till now."

Meaghan gave him a puzzled look. "What do ya mean, 'not 'till now'?"

Burke took a deep inhale of the spliff, held the smoke for a few seconds, then let it out slowly, his head tilted back so he could watch the smoke drift up into the pine. When there was no more smoke, he said, "I knew a guy once who was scared to death of cars. He never learned how to drive, never owned a car. Didn't make any sense to me, someone being that scared about something that wasn't part of his life. Then one night the guy went out and got himself killed in a car crash. His girlfriend was driving. She made it, but he was dead 'fore the car wheels stopped spinning. You gotta figure he knew."

Meaghan thought about that. "You think momma knew she was gonna drown one day?"

"I think she did."

"How would that work?"

"I don't know. Maybe God gives some people a warning."

"Didn't do her any good."

"No, it didn't."

They didn't say anything for a while after that. Sat in silence as Burke finished his spliff, blowing the smoke up into the trees.

"I thought you would'a been here 'fore now," Meaghan said.

"I didn't think it was your mother at the Food Town. Thought that kid doctor fucked up. You know if the cops have any suspects?"

"Don't think so.

"Who do *you* think done it?"

"Walton Murphy."

"Fuckin' Murphy. I should have known. That family should'a been bug-sprayed years ago. Why him?"

"Seen him arguin' with Momma 'bout a week 'fore she went missing."

"He came here?"

"No, down in Port Henry. In front of the post office."

"What were they arguin' 'bout?"

"Money. I didn't hear all of it. I had Robbie with me and when they started up, I took him away. I went to see the old bastard the other night, and he denied it, but he done it all right. I seen it in his eyes."

Her uncle was still standing, rocking back and forth on his cowboy boots, heel to steel-tipped toe, heel to steel-tipped toe. The boots looked expensive. Tony Lama, she thought.

"You seen it in his eyes?" he asked.

"Yeah."

"Maybe you got the same gift your momma had. No doubts 'bout him?"

"None."

Her uncle stopped rocking. He put the baggie of marijuana in his packsack and rezipped the pocket.

"You not stayin'?" she asked.

"No, I've got work to do. You take care, Meaghie. I'll be back soon.

14

CARL PATTERSON WAS the second name on Donnie Murphy's list. It was a name that jumped out at Yakabuski. He'd arrested Patterson five years ago. He also knew where Patterson could be found on a Thursday morning.

The Raftsmen Café was starting to fill up with the early lunch crowd when Yakabuski arrived. The diner opened at 6 a.m. and closed at 6 p.m. sharp, even though it served breakfast, lunch, and dinner. The owners of the Raftsmen believed if you were eating your evening meal after the sun went down you were leading a profligate and sinful life.

"Carl Patterson here, today?" Yakabuski asked the woman behind the cash register. She pointed toward the rear of the restaurant. "Out back. His shift started an hour ago. You a cop?"

"I am."

"Is he in any trouble?" She was an elderly woman who wore brown, thick-framed glasses tethered to a metal chain, and she slid the glasses up the bridge of her nose so she could see Yakabuski better.

"I don't know — is he?" Yakabuski said.

"Clean as driven snow, far as I know." Then she smiled and added, as she patted Yakabuski's forearm, "but I'm an old woman — what do I know?"

"More than you'll ever tell," he answered with a wink. The woman was still laughing when Yakabuski reached the swinging doors at the rear of the restaurant and walked into the kitchen.

A Vietnamese cook was stirring a pot of what smelled like fish stock. Another was pulling a large bag of beef burgers from a stand-up freezer. Behind them, Carl Patterson was raising the door of a Hobart dishwasher. Steam came hissing out of the machine to swirl around his arms, his chest, his face.

"Carl," yelled Yakabuski. "I need to talk to you."

Patterson waved steam from his face and when he saw Yakabuski he groaned. "I don't need to talk to you, detective. Not unless you're here to arrest me."

"Why so unfriendly, Carl? What have I ever done to you?"

"Are you fuckin' kiddin'? You *arrested* me!"

"All right, that's one. What else have I done to you?"

Patterson gave him a confused look.

"See, there's nothing else. You have no call to be so anti-social."

"*Anti-social*? I did two years 'cause of you, two years *plus* a day, that's federal time, Detective Yakabuski, all 'cause of some bullshit charge that never should have gone to court."

"When you have seventeen stolen . . . "

"Fifteen."

"Carl, when you have *fifteen* stolen televisions in your living room, you get arrested."

"They weren't mine."

"That's right, they weren't. That's why you were arrested. Now, come out from behind that Hobart and talk to me."

The Vietnamese cooks had stopped working and were staring at the two men. Their bodies had shifted slightly, so they were angled toward the stairs leading to the basement. Steam still swirled around Patterson's head.

"We can talk in the alley, or we can go down to the detachment. Your call," said Yakabuski.

"What do we need to talk about?"

"Agnes McKenna."

"What about her?"

"She's been murdered."

The cooks headed toward the stairs. Carl Patterson swept the last of the steam from his face and stepped out from behind the Hobart.

"Alley works," he said.

The alley behind the Raftsmen was crowded with stacks of wooden crates and bulging garbage bags waiting for garbage day. The smell reminded Yakabuski of a commercial fishing pier.

Patterson lit a cigarette. "I didn't know Agnes was dead," he said. "When did it happen?"

"About ten days ago," Yakabuski said. "We don't know the exact day and time."

"In Port Henry?"

"That's right. Her body was found in the harbour. She'd been assaulted and thrown into the river."

Patterson thought about that for a few seconds. "I'm sorry to hear that. I liked Agnes. But I don't know why you're talking to me. I haven't seen her in years. Haven't been to Port Henry in years, either."

"How many years?"

"A few. Before you rousted me on that bullshit grand theft charge, so . . . a few."

"What were you doing in Port Henry?"

"Working for Coogan."

"The camps or the mill?"

"Both."

"How long?"

"Two years. Almost three."

"How did you meet Agnes McKenna?"

"At a party," he said with a shrug. "Agnes liked to party."

"What do you mean by that?"

"Means I met her at a party. There were always parties in the trailers up there."

"Whose trailer?"

"I don't know. There were a lot of trailers in Port Henry. A lot of parties."

"You can't remember whose trailer? You need to try harder, Carl."

Patterson scowled, slipping his hands into his jean's pockets. "You can't come here and strong-arm me just 'cause you feel like it, Detective Yakabuski. It ain't right."

"One more thing you can add to the list of injustices that have befallen you during your short and troubled time upon this planet."

"What?"

"Whose trailer, Carl?"

Yakabuski got another nasty look. "Might have been her brother's."

"I didn't think she had a brother."

"Who told you that."

"Her daughter."

Patterson shrugged his shoulders. "What can I say?"

Yakabuski rested his foot on a wooden crate and stretched out his back. He didn't say anything, choosing to wait out Patterson.

"I still don't know why you're here," Patterson grumbled. "There weren't nothin' serious between us. We'd hook up on paydays, party some, then I'd go back to work, and she went home. Guess she went home. Don't really know where she went. I never asked."

"Sounds like a sweet courtship."

"What?"

Yakabuski rolled his eyes. "Were you fucking her the whole time you were working for Coogan?"

"Yeah . . . I guess. Some weeks we didn't hook up."

"Were you paying her?"

"For sex?

"Yes."

"No fuckin' way. I've never had to do that. I never *will* have to do that."

"You're a regular romantic, Carl. It's touching."

Patterson gave him an uncomprehending stare.

"Let's see if I have this straight," continued Yakabuski. "You hooked up with Agnes McKenna on paydays, for sex you didn't pay for, because that is something you have never done, and never would do . . . why on paydays, Carl?"

"What?"

"Why only on paydays? Didn't you want to get laid any other day of the week?"

"'Course I did. Nothin' wrong with my equipment . . . "

"Then why only on paydays?"

Until then, Carl Patterson had only shown Yakabuski two facial expressions — anger and confusion. Now, he leaned against the Hobart, ran a hand through his sopping wet hair, and took his time about answering the question. He appeared thoughtful and reflective.

He's about to lie, thought Yakabuski.

"Weren't no special reason," Patterson finally said. "I felt like partying on payday. Most men do. Maybe you're different."

"You're lying to me, Carl."

"Ain't lying to you, detective, I'm telling you the — "

"Why only on paydays?" Yakabuski interrupted.

"Already told you, a man feels like . . . "

"Are you *trying* to spend the night in a holding cell?"

Carl Patterson's face cycled through his go-to expressions of confusion, then anger, but this time he ended with something different, a weary, what-can-you-do look of resignation. "Guess it don't matter much if she's dead," he said. "She sold meth."

"Agnes McKenna was a meth dealer?"

"Yeah."

"I find that hard to believe. I've been to her cabin, Carl, and there's no sign of a meth lab there. Or anywhere close. I can smell a meth lab a mile away."

"She got it from her brother."

"The one whose trailer you partied at on paydays?"

"That's right. At least, that's where people said she got it. I don't know if it's true. But she didn't cook it, you're right about that — Agnes was dumb-fuck ignorant about how her drugs got made."

"Why didn't her brother sell the drugs directly to you? You bought it at his trailer, right?"

"I always figured he was doing his sister a solid, letting her make some money."

"You never bought from him?"

"No. Tried once, went to his trailer and the motherfucker acted like he didn't even know me. I'm banging his sister, partying at his trailer every two weeks, and the dude's like, "Meth? Don't know what you're talking about, bro.""

"What's the brother's name?" Yakabuski asked.

Patterson gave him a puzzled look. "You really don't know?"

"I wouldn't be asking you if I did."

"You're not pulling my leg or anything? You talk funny to me sometimes. It's hard to tell."

"What's the brother's name, Carl?"

"Liam Burke . . . her brother is Liam Burke."

Yakabuski stood there, trying not to look surprised. Although he was almost certain he was failing miserably. Carl Patterson had just given him the name of the biggest meth dealer in Springfield.

15

THE BIRTHDAY PARTY for Yakabuski's nephew was held that weekend in the ballroom of the Mission Road Golf and Country Club. Justin had asked for pizza at a nearby bowling alley, but his mother, Yakabuski's younger sister, Trish, had not only shot down that idea — she'd seemed scandalized by it.

"A *bowling alley*?" she'd said. "You can't be serious, Justin. It's your eighteenth. You need a venue befitting the occasion."

Justin Lawson wasn't sure he needed a "venue" at all, but he knew arguing with his mother was pointless, especially when she was in party-planning mode, that periodically occurring state of mind that gave his mother more energy and determination than a time-share salesman short on his quota.

"This is for a teenager's birthday party?" Rachel Dumont whispered to Yakabuski when they entered the ballroom. Spread out before them were forty-four tables (his sister told him the number later) with linen coverings, linen napkins, and cutlery settings that included salad, dessert, and oyster forks — to accompany the one you used for dinner.

A birthday banner was stretched between two of the chandeliers in the room with the words: *Happy 18th Justin!* Another banner, with the same message, was stretched between two marble columns framing the stage. On the stage itself was a DJ who had brought more speakers, screens, and equipment than a NASA deep-space exploration capsule.

The ballroom was packed, every corner crowded with guests milling around tables piled high with canapés and appetizers: the classic tomato bruschetta, prosciutto-wrapped melon, salmon pâté on crostini, and more. Others clustered at one of the three open bars. With drinks in one hand and hors d'oeuvres in the other, guests drifted along the red carpet that rolled out the open French doors onto the flagstone terrace that resembled an Italian piazza. There they lingered at yet another open bar or settled into chairs beside a gurgling fountain.

"Yes," said Yakabuski, grabbing Rachel's hand and heading toward the terrace. "This is a teenager's birthday party."

"It's . . . amazing."

"Not that amazing. You should see what Trish does at Christmas."

They walked onto the terrace, took two glasses of wine offered to them by a waiter wearing white gloves, and sat beside the fountain.

"What does your sister do at Christmas?" asked Rachel. "Rent reindeers?"

"Rent? That's for amateurs. Trish has her own herd. They're quartered in the stables out back."

"You know — I almost believe you."

"Wait until you meet Trish. Then you *will* believe me."

And just then, as if scripted, as if she were entering from the wing, stage left, Trish Lawson appeared in front of them.

"Frankie, you made it!"

"Wouldn't miss it, Trish," he said. His sister had already spoken to him twice that day, to confirm his attendance. "Trish, I'd like you to meet Rachel Dumont."

"Why, Rachel Dumont, as I live and breathe, I have heard *so much* about you. What a pleasure to finally meet you."

Trish bent down and gave her a hug. Yakabuski was pleased to see it was a real hug, not the air kiss she often gave.

"It's a pleasure to meet you, too," said Rachel. "The ballroom looks wonderful."

"Do you really think so? I wasn't sure about the banners. It seems like cheating, to have them both with the same message. But what else do you say, right?"

Rachel nodded. "Right."

"And the appetizers were an absolute chore. Do you believe my son wanted *chicken wings*?"

"I believe it. I have a teenage daughter. She would have wanted poutine."

Trish's face scrunched up, and her body trembled when she heard the word poutine. "Honestly, I wonder some days why we even bother. And how is your daughter doing?"

"She's fine, thank you."

"You know, the entire town was praying for her. And when she was found, oh my, I still remember how relieved, and grateful everyone was. Grace is such a pretty name. It suits her."

"Thank you."

Trish turned to Yakabuski. "Have you seen Justin?"

"Nope."

"I'll send him over when I see him. He's anxious to see you, Frank. Have you promised him something for his birthday?"

"I may have a little something."

"Of course you would. Well, I should mingle. It was *so nice* meeting you, Rachel. We'll get a chance to chat more inside. You're sitting at the head table, with us."

With that, Trish Lawson was off, headed toward the ballroom, air-kissing and arm-stroking her way through the crowd as quickly and effectively as though she were wielding a machete.

"There's a *head table*?" Rachel asked. "Frank, this is all a bit much. I thought I was attending your nephew's birthday party, not some . . . *gala*. I shouldn't be sitting at a head table. I don't even *know* anyone here."

"I don't know half the people myself, Rachel. Trish always goes over the top. Didn't I warn you?"

"You did. But this is *way* over the top. This is . . . sub-orbital."

"That's good. Sub-orbital. I'll have to remember that. Trish does tend to boldly go where few have gone before."

"I'm not even dressed right for something like this. Why

didn't you warn me?"

Yakabuski leaned back in his chair and gave her an appraising look. Rachel was wearing a bright, floral summer dress and white shoes with heels so low they resembled ballet slippers. Her long, black hair was pulled back and she wore little make-up, just a touch of rouge and a thin line of pale-red lipstick, no mascara as her lashes were long and full and there was no need. Her eyes were bright blue, one of the distinguishing features of many Metis from Cape Diamond: vivid blue eyes shining beneath onyx-black hair.

"You look perfect," said Yakabuski. He cleared his throat and leaned forward to say more, when his nephew appeared.

"Uncle Frank!"

Yakabuski turned and grinned. "Justin!" He stood and shook hands with his nephew. "Where's your tuxedo?"

"Very funny," answered Justin Lawson, who was dressed in khaki pants and a collared tee-shirt. "Don't be giving Mom any ideas."

"You've got quite the crowd here. These are all friends of yours?"

The boy moaned and rolled his eyes.

He's beginning to look like his father, thought Yakabuski: a dimple in his chin, a recent growth spurt so he stood over six feet, his hair a summer blond.

Just like his father . . . Yakabuski wondered if that was going to be a problem. Tyler Lawson died a disgraced man, a thief and money launderer, a gangster — it was not unfair to describe him that way — and there were many in Springfield who would never forget or forgive. Sadly, for Justin Lawson, the sins of the father are easier to pass on to a son who's a mirror image.

Although Yakiabuski's sister – who was already running the most successful real estate office in Springfield when she married Tyler Lawson – had nicely survived the scandal, so maybe he was over worrying.

"I have half-a-dozen friends here, Uncle Frank, and I had to fight Mom to get that," the boy said, turning his gaze back to Yakabuski. "The *mayor* is here. My *principal* is here. I tell you . . . it's embarrassing some days."

"And other days, it's charming. Your mother will never change, so you may as well accept it," Yakabuski said with a smile. "Justin, I'd like you to meet Rachel Dumont."

The boy extended his hand. "Rachel *Dumont*. Are you Gabriel Dumont's . . . ?" his voice tapered off as he seemed to realize this was a question a polite person wouldn't ask, but the question was half-way asked, so there followed an awkward silence.

" . . . Daughter," said Rachel, finishing the question for him. "Yes, I am. You've heard of my father, Justin?"

"Gosh, who hasn't. He's famous."

"For all the wrong reasons, I can assure you."

"Yes, of course," said the boy and then he stood there, shuffling his feet until Yakabuski rescued him.

"I dropped your present off on my way here," he said.

"Awesome!" the boy shouted.

"Didn't get a chance to wrap it. Hope you're all right with that."

"More than all right. Thank you, Uncle Frank. "

The boy gave Yakabuski a hug. It lasted long enough to make him uncomfortable, make him want to disentangle the boy from his chest, but Justin was family, so he kept patting him on the back and saying he was welcome, no need to thank him again.

"Maybe we can go out this weekend," Justin said, straightening out of the hug.

"I'd love to, but I can't this weekend. I have some work that needs to get done. But we'll get out before the end of the season."

"Promise?"

"Promise."

"Great." Justin smiled and turned to Rachel. "It was nice meeting you, Ms. Dumont."

As the boy was walking away, Rachel said, "It seemed like he knew what your birthday present was."

"He does. He's been pestering me for one since he was ten."

"What did you get him?"

"A canoe."

The first course of Justin Lawson's birthday dinner was steamed oysters, served ten minutes after an announcement came over the country club's PA system, informing the guests that dinner would commence in ten minutes. The wait staff entered the ballroom like the first wave of soldiers onto Juno Beach.

Punctual, proficient, slightly excessive, but when all was said and done, rather memorable — the dinner was Trish Lawson writ large. Her family sat with her at the head table, smiling and elbowing each other, as if in on a joke you needed to be called Yakabuski to get. Which, maybe you did.

"Your sister has outdone herself tonight," Yakabuski's father said, eyeing his oyster fork with suspicion. "Have you seen the cake, yet?"

"Is that what's behind the curtain over there?"

"Yep — eighteen layers. It's taller than Justin. Can you believe that? And it's completely fake, just going to be used for photos. Real cake is in the kitchen. Trish says the baker is here too. Have you had a chance to talk to her?"

Rachel nodded while picking up her napkin and dabbing at her lips. "Your daughter? Yes, we talked on the terrace. Not for long. She seemed in a hurry, which was understandable given she probably had a million things to do."

Yakabuski, sitting between his father and Dumont, chuckled. "The day you see Trish and she's *not* in a hurry, you better let me know, because there will be something dangerously wrong with her."

"Dangerously wrong?" said his father. "Check to make sure she's breathing. Although you're the same way, aren't you Rachel? From what Frank tells me there's no moss growing beneath your feet."

"I hope not. That might require a fungal cream," she said. "Although I quite like walking barefoot on moss, so maybe it wouldn't be that bad. What else has Frank told you?"

"Well, you're as pretty as advertised."

"Really? He told you that?"

"Don't listen to him," said Yakabuski, feeling heat traveling up his neck and face. "He's just trying to get me into trouble. He takes perverse pleasure in doing that."

"What, you never told me she was pretty?"

"What I said was, and don't get the wrong idea, Rachel, we don't sit around talking about you . . . "

"Because there are enough people in Springfield doing that already?"

"That isn't what I— "

"She's not wrong, Frank."

"*Dad!*" he said, a little more forcefully than he'd intended.

"To hell with them, Rachel, you're smart enough to know that. Bunch of know-nothing gossips."

"Thank you, George. So — what else *has* your son said about me?"

"I better not answer. If he's denying saying you were pretty, then I don't know what . . . "

"What I said, Dad, and shoot me for saying it, but I said something about Rachel's eyes, one time, and that was — "

"What did you say about my eyes, Frank?"

"Well, they jump right out at you."

"I have bulging eyes?"

"No, no, it's the shade of blue, it's . . . your eyes are beautiful."

Rachel blushed, her cheeks turning a crimson colour that was almost as bright as the colour that had spread across Yakabuski's face. But far more attractive on Rachel's cheeks.

The oysters were followed by vichyssoise, followed by Roquefort salad, followed by baked char and steak, followed by fruit and nuts. By the time the cake was wheeled to the head table there were panicked looks around the ballroom from people who knew the appearance of the cake meant there was more they needed to eat.

Yakabuski's eyes scanned the room, taking note of the guests and wondering if anyone from the Mission Road Estates had been left off his sister's invitation list. The mayor sat with the local member of parliament next to the table that had the president of the Northland Bank and the president of Springfield Shipping and Trucking. The woman who ran the Springfield Little Theatre, of which Trish was a board member, sat a few tables over with the conductor of the Springfield Philharmonic, who had brought as his date a local television actress who no longer lived in Springfield but must have returned home for a non-winter-month visit.

The rich and want-to-be rich, entertainers and entrepreneurs, chefs and CEOs — his sister had called out Springfield's dinner-party A-Team to celebrate her son's birthday.

Given this, Yakabuski wasn't sure later why he was surprised when his gaze fell upon the table to the far left of the ballroom, the table next to the one bar that had stayed open during the dinner service. At that table sat a man who owned a forestry company and a man who ran a utility company.

A lumber baron and a water baron.

Tommy Coogan and Walter Crawley.

Who were laughing and tossing back highballs as though they were at a fraternity reunion rather than a teenager's birthday party at the Mission Road Golf and Country Club.

"What are you staring at?" asked his father.

"I'm not sure," answered Yakabuski.

16

THE NEXT DAY, Yakabuski tracked down two more men on Donnie Murphy's list. Ralph Kincaid worked for a trucking company on the north shore, a journeyman mechanic who never stopped working while Yakabuski interviewed him. He stood on a two-step ladder, his head under a Freightliner.

"Need to have this truck ready to go out this afternoon or my head's going to be on a pike," Kincaid said.

Yes, he'd dated Agnes McKenna. When he was working at Coogan's mill on Smoke Island. Two years ago.

Hadn't been to the Back Channel since he quit working for Coogan.

Murdered? Not surprised. Agnes was trouble looking for more trouble.

He was assaulted one night when Agnes told some big hulking brute at Dickinson House that he was bothering her. This, after he'd slept with her the night before and had burned through half his paycheque buying her shooters and blow.

Didn't touch that shit anymore.

Didn't touch women like Agnes McKenna, either.

"Can you pass the half-inch ratchet, pal? The one right by your foot, there."

The other man was Des McAdam, who worked at the O'Hearn sawmill in Springfield. Yakabuski had the shift supervisor bring him into the HR office for the interview. Before they started, McAdam asked if they could go outside instead.

"You can smoke the other side of the gates," he explained.

McAdam had been the most recent boyfriend, nine months ago, when he was working on the barge that hauled slag out of the Coogan mill on Smoke Island. He'd met her at a party in one of the trailers.

"Does the slag still get dumped in the river?" asked Yakabuski.

"Not supposed to," said McAdam, and he gave an exaggerated shrug of his shoulders; left it to Yakabuski to guess the correct answer.

"You met her at a party?"

"Yeah, at the trailers."

"Whose trailer?"

"Her brother's."

"Liam Burke?"

"Yeah. You must know him," and McAdam gave Yakabuski a slight, almost conspiratorial smile.

"Partying at a trailer owned by Liam Burke. You still using, Des?"

"Nah," McAdams said.

Yakabuski let a few beats pass. Some people don't like silence. They need to fill the empty spaces.

McAdams was one of those people. "Not really . . . on weekends, sometimes."

"You bought from Agnes?"

"You know about that?"

"She got it from her brother."

"Hey, I don't know anything about that. Don't be spreading around that story."

"You scared of Liam Burke?"

"Am I scared of Liam Burke? Why don't you ask me if I have any gawdamn common sense — you'll get the same answer."

"How did they seem to get along, Agnes and her brother?"

"Those two? Closer than seemed right."

"You're not suggesting . . . "

"Fuck no. Forget I said that. I was just thinking out loud for a minute . . . some people made that joke, when Burke was a hundred miles out of earshot, people kid around sometimes. But they were just close, man, that's all it was. I was sleeping with her — don't you think I'd know?"

Yakabuski answered with a shrug of the shoulders.

"No, I'd know. We talked a lot, when we weren't making out, a lot of times even when we *were* screwing, we'd talk, it's easy to talk when . . . "

A surprised look came to McAdam's face. He had suddenly remembered he was talking to a cop.

"When you're speeding," said Yakabuski, finishing the sentence for him.

"Yeah . . . when you're doing that. She talked an awful lot, sometimes about her brother, and they were close man, that's all it was. Any family that's been on the Back Channel as long as the Burkes — you'd have to be close. No one else around."

"She was a McKenna when she died."

"McKennas been up there as long as the Burkes. Bobby McKenna — now there was a basket case."

"Did you ever see them argue, ever witness a disagreement between the two of them?"

"Agnes and Liam? Never."

"They were selling drugs together, dealer and supplier," Yakabuski said. "That can be a tricky relationship. You never saw a dispute concerning the drugs they were selling?"

"Between the two of them? No."

"*Between the two of them*? Did you witness some other dispute?"

"These questions could get me in trouble, detective. And there's no reason to get me in trouble. I had nothing to do with Agnes getting killed. I haven't been to the Back Channel since I left, and why would I want to hurt her, anyway? She was always good to me."

"Then help me find her killer. Did you witness a dispute at the trailers involving Agnes or her brother?"

"If you're looking at Burke for the killing, I just don't see it. He adored Agnes. I think you're wasting your time."

"Did you witness a dispute, Des? Yes or no?"

"Yeah, I witnessed a dispute. Some guy came into the trailer one night, all hopped up, wanted to front some crank from Agnes, but she wouldn't do it, said he already owed her money, and no more blow till the slate was clean. Guy got pissed, and Burke had to chase him off."

"How did he get rid of him?"

"By sticking the barrel of a Colt pistol up his nose and telling the guy the only thing going up his nostrils that night was the bullet chambered in *this here gun*. That's word for word what Burke said, I'll never forget it: 'the bullet chambered in this here gun.' Like he was in a movie or something.

"Guy turned white as a sheet and then Burke dragged him across the room and threw him out the door. There was blood at the bottom of the outside stairs when I left the next morning. Guy must have hit his head."

"Describe him."

"Big fuckin' guy. Long grey hair. Grey beard."

"Burke call him anything?"

"Dumb fuckin' asshole."

"A name, Des. Did Burke call him by his name."

"He did, but I can't remember what it was. Started with an M, I think?"

"Could it have been Murphy?"

" . . . Now that you've said it, maybe it *was* Murphy. Yeah, it was Murphy. Sure as I'm standing here."

17

LIAM BURKE CAME half-way down the stairs and looked around the ladies-and-escort side of the Shamrock tavern. It was Friday and the tavern was crowded; late afternoon, so many of the men still wore their dark-green factory pants and work shirts, although the women sitting at the bar had their hair piled high and Burke could smell hairspray from where he stood. The turnover from late afternoon clientele to evening clientele had begun. The women, a little ahead of the men.

Burke stood on the stairs, gazing down upon the heads of his patrons until he spotted Yakabuski. The cop was standing by the front door. Watching him. He was a big enough cop, thought Burke, as he motioned for Yakabuski to join him at the bottom of the stairs.

Burke didn't like being watched. Didn't like that Yakabuski had spotted him before he'd spotted Yakabuski. There was an annoyed look on his face when he shook Yakabuski's hand a minute later.

"Detective."

"Mr. Burke. Thank you for seeing me."

"Didn't know I had a choice. Is that something new for you guys?"

"I'm investigating your sister's death, Mr. Burke, as I explained to you on the phone. I would think you'd welcome the opportunity to help."

"Glad to help — just don't want to be thanked for doing something I had no choice about doing. Let there be no false words between us, Detective Yakabuski. How does that sound?"

"Sounds fine."

"Good. Come with me."

Burke turned quickly and went back up the stairs. Most of the customers in the Shamrock had their eyes on Yakabuski as he followed. The Shamrock was one of the oldest taverns in Springfield and while it wasn't a den of thieves like the Shiner-owned Silver Dollar, or a last-resort dive like the Alexander, there were plenty of customers in the Shamrock who wouldn't want to speak to a cop. When Yakabuski disappeared through a door on the second floor, several men paid their bar tabs and left.

Burke had purchased the Shamrock from the Clancy family. The family first opened the tavern in 1891. That was what most people thought, anyway, even though the deed to the tavern, and all the business documents, were still in the name of Sam Clancy. Ten years ago, Burke had come to the tavern, moved into the second-floor office, and Sam Clancy was never seen around the Shamrock, or Springfield, again.

Police *believed* Burke bought the tavern. There may have been a different business arrangement.

The office had no windows and no overhead lights. There was a floor lamp in one corner that must have had the lowest wattage light bulb on the market, as it cast a pale-yellow glow that didn't travel more than two feet. There was a desk lamp that did a better job, but Burke's office was still more shadow than anything else. Although they sat in comfortable chairs, it felt to Yakabuski like they were standing on a dark corner, talking beneath a streetlamp.

"So — what do you need to know?" Burke asked.

Cutting right to the chase, thought Yakabuski. After the warning about false words, now we're dispensing with any pleasantries, any build-up or foreplay. My time is precious. Just want to screw.

We can do that. "How long was your sister dealing drugs for you, Mr. Burke?"

Burke gave Yakabuski a look as stone cold as the Springfield Escarpment in February. "I hope you have other questions, detective."

"A few."

"Would you like a drink?"

"Beer would be nice."

Burke picked up his cell phone and punched a number. He ordered two pints of Algonquin lager, then put the phone on his desk and began spinning it. Clockwise. Counter-clockwise. The desk was black metal, polished to a fine sheen, and the phone spun easily. Burke tilted his head and watched his phone. "I cared about my sister a great deal."

"I've heard that."

"Now you're hearing it from me. I never took advantage of my sister, as your question implied."

Yakabuski looked at the spinning phone and wondered if this was a habit of Liam Burke's, or did it indicate something else? Stress? Worry? A desire to surround himself with visual distractions so he could disappear when needed, a magician's nervous tick?

"When was the last time you saw your sister?"

"Last month," answered Burke. "I have a few places in Port Henry that I rent out. Need to go up sometimes to check on them."

"Your rental properties — trailers?"

"That's right."

"You're a good landlord. That's a six-hour drive, there and back."

"I try."

"So, you rent them out. Does that mean someone else's name is on the paperwork for those trailers?"

"I have leases, that's right."

"Is your name on any deed, or tax roll?"

"In Port Henry?"

"Anywhere."

Clockwise. Counter-clockwise. Burke kept spinning his phone. A lazy twirl. No urgency to it. "I fail to see how these questions will help you investigate my sister's death, detective."

"She was assaulted, Mr. Burke. You're in a violent business. These aren't coming-out-of-left-field questions I'm asking you."

"How I conduct my business? You find that relevant?"

"I do."

"Left field, right field, I don't care where these questions are coming from, I'm going to ask you to stay on point. You're here to talk about Agnes."

A knock sounded on the door and both men went silent as a waiter came in with their pints of beer. They stared at each other across the desk, like fighters in their respective corners, waiting for the bell.

When the waiter was gone, Yakabuski said: "Thought we were done with false words, Mr. Burke. Isn't that what you said downstairs?"

"I don't see the relevance of your questions."

"How can you not? Did your sister's death have anything to do with your business? Anything to do with her selling drugs?"

"No comment."

Yakabuski gave him a hard stare and took a sip of his beer. "All right — can you think of anyone who might want to hurt your sister, to get back at you?"

It was as though a light bulb suddenly flicked on above Burke's head. "I see what you're asking. No, detective, my life is clean and serene these days. No drama, no enemies lurking around the corner. It's almost a bore."

He stopped twirling his phone and took a sip of his beer.

"No business disagreements?"

"None."

"*Clean* and serene. You're not cranking anymore?"

"Again, no comment."

"What about your sister?"

"You know the answer to that, detective."

"Guess I do. Why didn't you try to help her?"

"I did. In ways you wouldn't understand."

"Getting her to sell drugs for you? How was that helping?"

"Are you wearing a wire?"

"Want to check?"

"Yes, I do. Stand up."

Yakabuski stood and waited for Burke to come around the desk and pat him down. After a few seconds had passed, Burke waved at him to sit. They drank their beer for a minute and then Burke said, "Agnes never had as much money as she needed, detective. My sister was always a dollar short, no matter the month, no matter the cause. What can you do, when you love someone like that? You help them as best you can."

"What you did for her; I don't see how that's helping."

"Then you never had to live on the Back Channel. You take joy where you find it, detective. And you don't ask a lot of questions when it comes around."

"Sounds like a junkie's credo," said Yakabuski. "I thought you were smarter than that."

"Did you think I was talking about drugs?" replied Burke. "I thought you were smarter than that."

The two men smiled at each other. Burke kept spinning his phone. Clockwise. Counter-clockwise. Yakabuski finished his beer and left. On his way down the stairs, he noticed the Shamrock tavern had about half as many customers as it had when he'd arrived.

18

CHIEF BERNARD O'TOOLE worked in the same office his grandfather had once worked. And his great-great-grandfather. He was the third one in his family to be chief of the Springfield Regional Police Force. The second one named Bernard.

A daguerreotype of the first Bernard O'Toole sat on a shelf in the chief's office, a group photo of the four men who had canoed up the Springfield River in 1847 in search of Peter Aylen, an Irish bandit who had taken control of the nascent village of Springfield, which at that time sat on the edge of the known world.

Not an exaggeration. No maps existed of the country upriver from Kettle Falls. No surveys had been completed. None had been attempted. The land to the north of the falls was shown on maps of the day as a grey overlay, with diagrams of sea monsters.

O'Toole and the other three police officers came to the edge of the known world, but they never caught Aylen, who fled across the river, then south into the States as soon as the cops arrived. But those four men had been the start of the Springfield Regional Police Force.

That he possessed that daguerreotype photo and was able to display it in the office of his great-great-grandfather — someone who was *in* the photo — was a source of considerable pride to O'Toole. Even the most casual of visitors to his office — a secretary dropping off files, a repairman working on the perennially broken-down radiators — could get the full history of the Springfield police force and the role played by the O'Tooles, simply by noticing the photo.

Although maybe not today, thought Yakabuski when he entered the office. O'Toole was speaking on the phone; the handset cradled between his ear and shoulder. He was signing papers his secretary was putting in front of him. A man stood beside her, a leather portfolio in one hand, his other hand in the air, one finger pointing up, so that Yakabuski knew Rory Farrleton, the chief's executive assistant, needed only a minute of O'Toole's time.

Yakabuski sat down. When the chief's secretary and executive assistant had left the room, and after O'Toole had taken two more phone calls, he looked up at Yakabuski.

"Not going to have much time for you today, Yak."

"I can see that."

"Anything new I need to know about?"

"Mounties say they're ready to arrest Warren Sempler for wire fraud. They have a meeting with the crown attorney this Thursday."

"Any chance the crown will balk?"

"With Clarice, there's always a chance, but they have wire taps and a Caymen's account that can be traced right back to him. Mounties are surprised he didn't do a better job hiding the money, being a banker and all. I've seen the evidence. They have a strong case."

"When are they doing the arrest?"

"If all goes well in the meeting with the Crown, Friday afternoon."

"He'll spend the weekend in the cells."

"That's the plan."

"Sempler won't know what hit him. What's the latest on your Back Channel murder?"

Yakabuski told O'Toole about the interviews with McKenna's ex-boyfriends, none of whom made a good suspect. And he updated him on the autopsy results. No doubt Agnes McKenna had drowned. No doubt she had been assaulted and was unconscious when she entered the water.

"Her daughter last saw her Friday morning, when she left their home to gather fiddleheads. Newton has time of death as that day, sometime between late morning and mid-afternoon. It would fit the timeline if she'd been killed not long after she left the cabin. The killer might even have been hiding nearby, watching her."

"You believe this was a premeditated murder? Why?"

"No sexual assault, no robbery that we know of, and her toxicology results were damn near clean; she could have passed a roadside sobriety test."

"No indication of a spontaneous crime, that's what you're saying."

"That's what I'm saying."

"Makes sense. What else you got?"

"Haven't been able to interview Walton Murphy. He may be hiding from us. I'm not sure yet."

"You still expect him to be at the market?"

"I do. We'll catch him there. He's looking like our best suspect. One of the ex-boyfriends saw him attack McKenna at a party. It was at her brother's trailer."

"I don't recall reading anything about a brother."

"He came up during the interviews. Meaghan McKenna, the victim's daughter, lied about having no other family. I'm hoping to talk to her at the market as well. Here's a file on the brother."

Yakabuski slid a file folder onto O'Toole's desk.

"The brother has a file?"

Yakabuski didn't bother answering. Waited until O'Toole opened the file folder and looked at the top page.

"Liam Burke! That's the victim's brother?"

"Yes."

"My lord, when did we find out about this?"

"Two days ago."

"That opens a dozen possible avenues of investigation. This might be a straight drug hit by someone who has a grudge against Burke."

"I agree. Although right now, there's no evidence of that. I interviewed Burke yesterday, and if he knows who killed his sister, or has any suspicions, he did a fine job of hiding it."

"Well, he would, wouldn't he?"

Yakabuski shrugged. "The market is this Saturday. I should have a better idea where we stand after that."

"I wonder what that market is like these days. Been a long time for me."

"You'll find out when I file my report."

O'Toole nodded. "You know what else I haven't done in a long time, Yak? Play a round at the Mission Road Golf and Country Club."

Yakabuski stared at O'Toole for a few seconds before asking, "Were you playing last Saturday?"

"I was."

"Thought I saw you on the fifteenth fairway. Wasn't sure."

"That's funny — while I was getting ready to shank a shot on the fifteenth fairway, I thought I saw you on the terrace. Wasn't sure."

"It was my nephew's birthday party."

"Also thought I saw Rachel Dumont sitting with you. Wasn't sure about that, either."

Yakabuski felt a tightening in his chest. "She was there."

"Do you think that was a wise move? Rachel Dumont is a member of the Travellers."

"That happened when she was born. She never asked for it."

"As true as that may be, it doesn't change the fact that she *is* a member of a criminal organization."

"One that protected her family when we weren't up to the job."

"If you're starting to make public service announcements for the Travellers, then I really am worried about you."

"Just reminding you of what happened. It was starting to

sound like you forgot part of the story."

O'Toole gave him an annoyed grunt and sat straighter in his chair. "Rachel Dumont has more criminal affiliations than a wing at the Wentworth Pen. You run the criminal investigation department of the Springfield Regional Police Force. Surely you see the conflict."

"I don't. Rachel Dumont has never been charged with a crime; has never committed a crime to my knowledge. When did we start judging people by their last names?"

"You're being deliberately obtuse, and you know it. Do you really think it's wise to be dating Rachel Dumont, to be seen in public with her at the Mission Road Country Club for heaven's sake!"

Yakabuski gave O'Toole a hard look. He was disappointed and angry with his old friend, trying to keep at least one of those emotions in check.

"Rachel was a guest at my nephew's birthday party," he replied. "I brought her. We're not dating. As for whether it's wise to be seen in public with her, I wouldn't know about that; I'll leave it to other people to decide how wise or stupid I am. What I *do know* is that it would be unwise, in the extreme, for people to mention Rachel Dumont to me again unless it was to give her a compliment."

Yakabuski stood and strode out of the chief's office, leaving O'Toole's sitting at this desk with his mouth agape.

19

EARLY SATURDAY MORNING, Yakabuski and Griffin headed back to Port Henry. They took separate vehicles and made good time, not much weekend traffic on the highway, the fog burned off early, most of it before the sun had risen. It was going to be a hot day along the Back Channel.

Yakabuski was still annoyed with O'Toole, although his temper had cooled somewhat. He still thought the police chief had been out of line with his questions about Rachel. But he regretted storming out of the office. Even if O'Toole hadn't intended to be rude, he had been out of line. And that left him disappointed with the chief in ways he never thought possible. The two men had worked together for almost thirty years, considered each other friends, yet O'Toole had practically reprimanded Yakabuski about what a chattering public might say regarding him taking Rachel Dumont to his nephew's birthday party.

As if it mattered. When had the chief become so concerned about appearances? And just as worrisome, to an investigative cop — how had he missed it?

Yakabuski considered the problem as he drove along the Springfield River, watching the sun rise above a treeline of spruce and pine, the shadows on the highway shrinking and then disappearing, as though fleeing into the woods.

Shortly after 8:00 a.m. he reached the *Welcome to Port Henry* sign. He drove another three miles and arrived at the market.

There had been a market in Port Henry since the first days of the settlement, the first one held the same year the government stopped working on the colony road. It was still an informal affair, with no person or organization in charge and no vendors' fees for being there. You just needed to arrive on the south shore of the Port Henry harbour on the first Saturday of the month and set up a table.

It was a sad looking market if you saw it by the side of the road and didn't stop. Old pick-up trucks with their tailgates down and dirty boxes stacked in the bed. Carnival tents with denim patches and soot-stained ropes. Fold-out banquet tables with tattered coverings and other tables that weren't tables at all, just wooden crates shoved together. Every sign in the market was hand-written, usually on the back of flattened cardboard boxes.

If you stopped, though, and walked around, you would find a market as exotic as a Marrakesh bazaar. The men selling the fur pelts and the princess pine were all bearded giants with yellowed teeth and hands as gnarled as tree roots. The women selling the blueberry preserves and knitted shawls smoked tiny clay pipes and gambled at the three-card Monty tables set up in the midway.

The midway never had rides, except for a carousel that an enterprising man from La Toque brought in for a few years, charging a nickel a ride until one day a parent said they had been to Toronto, where a carousel in a city park cost nothing, and what sort of crook was the man from La Toque? After getting severely beaten, the man with the carousel never came back.

Most of the midway was a bingo game, a few Monty tables, a couple of tents where children threw balls at bottles and tried to catch plastic fish. For many years, there was also a tent that sold moonshine, first by Walton Murphy, then by his son, Donnie, who inherited the family business when his dad bought a tugboat and started deadheading, finding it easier work than running a still.

The wares sold at the Port Henry Market — right from the

start, when it was as much a way for settlers to find out who was still living along the Back Channel as it was a way to make money — were not the wares of manufacturing or cultivation. They were the wares of foraging and hunting, scavenging and stealing. You came to the Port Henry Market to buy forest herbs and fur pelts and planks of wood stripped from old barns, maybe a chicken or goat, maybe a hawk.

Yakabuski and Griffin parked side by side, just inside the entrance to the market. Yakabuski got out of his Jeep and stretched his arms overhead. He took a deep breath, smiling at the scents he was smelling.

"Are you serious about buying a hawk?" she asked, walking up to him.

"Why don't you start at the bingo tables," said Yakabuski. "I'll stroll around and see who's here."

"I saw the postmaster over there," said Griffin, pointing at a tent so badly faded it was anyone's guess what the original colours would have been. Yakabuski spotted Stinton Halliday standing nearby.

The postmaster was rotating his head from left to right, looking around and pretending he hadn't seen the cops. Yakabuski stared at him until the postmaster finally acknowledged their presence, his eyes going wide, as though in surprise. He gave them a barely noticeable, close-to-the-chest wave.

"He doesn't seem pleased to see us again," said Yakabuski.

"Is anyone?" asked Griffin.

"Good point. Let's meet by the cars in an hour. If you run across Walton Murphy, give me a call."

"Will do."

Yakabuski started walking toward Halliday. As he approached, the postmaster ducked into the badly faded tent. Yakabuski followed him inside, where the postmaster was lined up behind four other people. They stood in front of a table where an old lady in a shabby dress was slowly turning over Tarot cards.

"Mr. Halliday."

"Detective," said the postmaster, turning around to look at Yakabuski. "I'm surprised to see you here today."

"I noticed. You didn't think we were coming back?"

"Hadn't thought about it that much, to be honest. But here at the market, on a Saturday morning — don't you get days off?"

"I wanted to come. I used to come to the market with my father. Would have been thirty years ago. He came for the chaga mushrooms."

"You can still get those."

"Not sure if they did my dad any good."

"Sorry to hear that. They didn't do him any harm, I hope."

Yakabuski shook his head and the line moved forward.

"Want to know something I don't understand, Mr. Halliday? When I interviewed you last month, you spent a lot of time running down the victim. Do you remember that?"

"I recall answering your questions. Don't recall 'running down' anyone."

"Really? I'm being charitable when I use that expression, Mr. Halliday. It would be more accurate to say you bad-mouthed Agnes McKenna from hell to high water. You said she was a junkie, a payday whore who hung around Coogan's lumber-yard, and you called her an unfit mother — you remember saying all that?"

"I was merely answering your questions as fully and honestly as I could, detective," sniffed Halliday. "I didn't make anything up, if that's what you're implying."

"Not implying that at all. I know you told the truth."

"Then I don't know what your complaint is."

"Not complaining. I'm just surprised."

"At what?"

"That a man hell-bent on destroying a woman's reputation would neglect to mention that Liam Burke was her brother."

The postmaster stared at Yakabuski long enough to move

up another spot in the fortune teller line. "You never asked me any questions about her brother," he said.

"Right again, Mr. Halliday. But you offered up plenty of other details about the victim. Why did you draw the line at Liam Burke?"

The postmaster remained silent.

"Burke owns some trailers in Port Henry," said Yakabuski. "Do you know how many?"

"No idea."

"You're the postmaster, I thought you knew everything."

"He doesn't have a box."

"Weren't the Burkes one of the first families up here?"

"They were. The Burkes came the same year my family did."

"He'd have a box then, wouldn't he?"

"The Burke's grant is abandoned. If you leave the homestead, you lose the box."

"When did you last see Liam Burke?"

"Been a long time."

The line moved forward one more spot and it was Halliday's turn to have his fortune told. Yakabuski smiled at him and turned to leave. Just before the postmaster sat down, though, Yakabuski leaned in and whispered, "Here's a tip for you, Mr. Halliday; never get your fortune told by someone who can't afford a new tent."

Yakabuski was strolling toward the aviary when he saw Meaghan and Robbie McKenna sitting behind a table. They were selling fiddleheads and golden root, chaga mushrooms and princess pine, not getting much business it looked like.

"I didn't know you sold at the market," Yakabuski said, walking up to the table.

"My momma came to every one of them," she answered. "Rain, sleet, snow — she come to the market. The chaga and golden root I'm sellin' here — she picked it." Her voice cracked as she spoke, but then she crossed her arms and asked in a stiff voice: "How's your investigation going? Got my momma's killer yet?"

"If we did, you'd be the first person we'd notify."

"Want me to thank you for that?"

"I don't want you to — "

"Answer's no, then. Is that right?"

"That's right."

"You going to tell me these things take time?"

Yakabuski sighed. "I'm not going to tell you that, Meaghan, even if it's true. May I ask you a question?"

"Can I stop you?"

"I didn't know Liam Burke was your uncle. Why didn't you tell me that?"

"Why would I?"

"Because your uncle is well known to the police, and you're smart enough to know that. He's a drug dealer, and your mother benefitted from that. Those three facts open a lot of investigative avenues when it comes to the homicide of your mother. But it doesn't seem like you wanted us to know about it."

"That my mother was a weekend meth head? Gosh, I wonder why I didn't want you to know that."

"It doesn't help the investigation, when you keep things from us."

"Doesn't seem to help much when I tell you stuff, either."

Yakabuski continued walking around the market. He passed tables stacked with chaga mushrooms and golden root, several more with stones: mica, quartz, brightly coloured river pebbles. There was wicker furniture, rough-hewn pine work boxes, dowry chests, whirligigs, checker sets.

The Port Henry Market was big enough to be split into sections, with the traditional vendors — the trappers and hunters and quilters — in one section and the flea-market crowd in another. Yakabuski walked by tables loaded with smoked fish and salted game, dressing poles where fresh game vendors had hung moose and caribou quarters three days before market day, so the blood left in the carcass would blacken and begin to marble.

In this section were tables of baked goods and quilts hanging from tree branches. In the spring there were tables piled high with fur pelts: beaver, otter, fisher, and lynx. The aviary was still there, behind the dressing poles, with a wall of stacked bird cages. Inside the cages were pigeons and roosters and herons, the herons with their wings clipped so they couldn't fly, so they could be tethered to a pole in the marshes, where they would eat their weight in mosquitos and no-see-um bugs.

The flea market section made up most of the Back Chanel Market now. It didn't exist until the colony road to Port Henry was finally completed as a Depression-era infrastructure project. Once an umbilical cord to civilization was established, the junk started to arrive — second-hand car tires, used plastic toys, 78 rpm records, moth-eaten sweaters, rusted tools, eight-tracks.

Yakabuski remembered when the flea market took up no more than a half-dozen tables. Back then, the Port Henry Market was a rowdy, shambling, last-circus-on-the-rails affair, with cock fights and moonshine and late-night boxing matches held in the dirt under the glow of a starry sky and kerosene lanterns. He didn't miss the fights — animal or human — but felt a twinge of sadness when he remembered everything else.

He made his way back to his Jeep, where Griffin was already waiting for him.

"Well, there's consensus around the bingo tables," she said.

"What about?"

"It's a wonder Agnes McKenna didn't die years ago."

"Poor lifestyle choices?"

"You got it. And this opinion, it might be worth mentioning, came from women smoking Virginia Slim menthols and eating fried peanut-butter-and-cheese sandwiches."

Yakabuski laughed. "Holy Elvis."

"Yep. I noticed Meaghan McKenna was here."

"Already spoke to her," Yakabuski said. "No sign of Walton Murphy?"

"No one has seen him. No one I talked to anyway. Is his son here?"

"Over there," said Yakabuski, pointing at a table piled high with wooden carvings.

"That's right, my cardinal carver. Didn't he say his dad was going to be here?"

"He did."

"Selling logs that he pulled out of the river; do I have that right?"

"They're called deadheads, a log that's been in the river a long time, that got lost during some old timber run. If you're lucky, you'll find squared pine. Some of those logs have been underwater for two hundred years."

"And that's a good thing?"

"Crazy good. People with way too much money want squared timber. Open concept family room, stone fireplace, Napoleonic-era roofbeams. You watch big fancy real estate shows, don't you?"

"No, but I get what you're saying," Griffin said. "Have you spoken to Murphy?"

"Not yet. Maybe it's time we did."

"Haven't seen your dad yet, Donnie," said Yakabuski. "Thought you said he was going to be here today."

"He'll be here."

"Getting late, isn't it?"

"He'll pull the tug right into the harbour, have the deadheads tied up to the stern. He's got plenty of time."

"I heard a story about your dad assaulting Agnes McKenna at a party in one of the trailers. Know anything about that?"

Murphy gave him a nasty look. "Come all the way up here to roust my dad, did you?"

He'd been drinking. Not yet ten in the morning, and he'd already sampled the wares he sold out the back of his truck, the one parked in the woods behind his wood-carving table.

"I need to interview your dad," said Yakabuski. "If he doesn't show at the market today, I'm going to issue an arrest warrant for him. If you have any way of contacting your father, you may want to let him know that."

"You think he's scared of you?"

"I have no way of knowing. I've yet to speak to him."

"Well, he ain't scared of you. I'm telling you that right now. Just like he weren't scared of your dad, and he ain't scared of any other stinkin' cop, whether you're comin' from Springfield or High River or any other damn place."

He was gesturing now, wild swings of his arms that seemed to throw off this balance. He weaved and leaned, then stumbled, knocking some carvings to the ground after he grabbed the table to stop himself from falling.

"Are you all right, Mr. Murphy?" Griffin asked.

"I'm flippin' fine, *thank you very much*," he replied. "Just *flippin' fine.*"

As he was saying this, a couple pushing a three-wheel stroller approached Murphy's table. The man picked up a carving of a wood duck and showed it to the woman. Murphy straightened himself and gave Yakabuski an exaggerated salute.

"Excuse me," he said. "I have business to tend to."

20

AT TWO O'CLOCK, some of the vendors began to pack up and leave. The baked goods vendors, the ones who had nothing left to sell. The fresh game vendors, who needed to butcher what they hadn't sold.

Milt Foster looked at the departing vendors and thought about joining them. He still had fiddleheads left, and he should probably try to sell those because they would be no good to him tomorrow. But he had sold all his flowers, *most* of the fiddleheads, and none of the other items were perishable — the river stones, the quartz nuggets, the driftwood.

Maybe he'd leave. He was standing up, about to get the boxes from the back of his minivan, when he saw it.

Something white, in the reeds out in the harbour. He thought it was foam at first, churned up and trapped in the reeds somehow. He stared at the shape a long time before deciding it was too solid, too stationary, to be a bed of foam.

Paper? No, it would have torn by now. An animal? It didn't look like an animal. A plant of some kind?

Foster stayed with that thought. There were plants and trees growing along the Back Channel that didn't grow any other place on earth. It was the reason he drove to Heartbreak Bay once a month to buy golden root that resembled a small shrub. He had heard stories of a white pine so large, six men couldn't get their arms around the trunk, and wildflowers so rare they didn't have a scientific name.

The more he looked at the white shape, the more Foster thought it was a plant. A white flower of some sort. An orchid? There were new varieties of orchids being discovered every year. He had read somewhere that a single seed or shoot from a newly discovered orchid could be sold at auctions in London for six figures.

Six figures!

It was this last thought Milt Foster had running through his head as he waded into the river. The spring run-off hadn't been that bad this year. The harbour seemed fordable until several yards past the reeds. He made his way carefully across seaweed-stranded rocks and crayfish beds, his pants rolled up to his knees.

He had walked about forty feet, was within five feet or so of the reeds, when he let out a scream, stumbled backwards, and fell into the river. He splashed around, as though he were drowning, until he remembered he could stand. Then he got to his feet and ran to his minivan.

Yakabuski and Griffin waded into the harbour and pulled out the body. It was a man with long white hair and tattooed arms, a big man, dressed in denim overalls and a white fleece hoodie, the extra weight of the sodden fabric making it harder to heave the body out.

Finally, they got him ashore. They turned him over and saw his face for the first time. His right eye was swollen shut and a bone protruded from his cheek on the same side. His lips were split and his skin was discoloured. It looked like he'd been in the water for several days.

"Know him?" Griffin asked.

Yakabuski nodded. A crowd had gathered around the body and Yakabuski looked at who was there. He saw the postmaster and the McKennas, was still scanning the crowd when he heard a scream. He looked to the woods, where the scream came from, and saw Donnie Murphy running toward him.

"Papa, what have they done!" he yelled as he threw himself onto the ground. He started sobbing and wailing and running his fingers through the dead man's hair.

"Mr. Murphy, you have to get off him," yelled Griffin as she grabbed the sobbing man by the back of the jacket. She tried to lift him off the body but Murphy resisted, his hands continuing to grip onto his father. Griffin was still struggling with Murphy when Yakabuski walked over. Murphy looked up as Yakabuski approached and finally let go of his father.

He got to his knees and started punching the ground. Big swings that ended with a thud and what might have been the sound of bones cracking. Some of the people who'd gathered around winced when they heard it. Yakabuski grabbed his arms and said, "I'll put you in cuffs if I need to, Donnie. I swear I will."

"Put *me* in cuffs? What about the bitch that killed my dad. What about *her*?" Murphy struggled for a few seconds, but then his body went slack, and he began to cry. Yakabuski let go of his hands and stood up.

"I take it that's Walton Murphy we just pulled out of the harbour," said Griffin, catching her breath.

"The one and only."

Donnie Murphy was now writhing on the ground, rubbing his bloodied fingers over his face, flopping around like a boated fish. "I couldn't make out what he was saying," said Griffin. "I take it he doesn't think his father's death was an accident."

"He thinks it's murder. We probably won't be wrong if we think the same thing."

Just then, Murphy stopped rolling around, leapt to his feet, and lunged toward Meaghan McKenna.

"I'll fuckin' kill you," he screamed. "You and any McKenna bastard that's with you."

But his lunge was more of an off-balance, could-land-on-my-face-at-any-minute stumble and Yakabuski had no trouble catching Murphy before he reached Meaghan.

"You're in the cuffs now, Donnie," said Yakabuski. "I'll let you go as soon as you calm down and stop threatening people."

21

O'TOOLE LOOKED OUT his window at the steam rising from Kettle Falls. It looked like more water than usual was being pushed through the turbines of the hydro-electric plant. The steam was fifteen, maybe twenty feet higher than normal. The sound of rushing water echoed in the room, even with the windows closed.

"Could there be something to this feud?" he asked, turning back to Yakabuski.

"Might be something to it now. We had to restrain Donnie Murphy to keep him from attacking Meaghan McKenna."

"A seventeen-year-old girl?"

"He was drunk, but he was blaming her for his father's death."

"Again — a seventeen-year-old girl?"

"You need to meet her; I don't think there's much that would be beyond the capabilities of Meaghan McKenna."

"You seriously consider her a suspect?"

"Can't rule her out. But if this was retaliation for the killing of Agnes McKenna, I'd say there's another family member we should be looking at."

"Her uncle."

Yakabuski nodded. "If Liam Burke thought Walton Murphy had killed his sister, he'd go after him."

"Don't the Mounties have him under surveillance?"

"They do. I phoned the lead investigator this morning. Six days ago, Burke entered the Shamrock, and he wasn't seen again until closing time the following night."

"How much time was that?"

"Thirty-two hours."

"The Mounties think he gave them the slip?"

"They do."

"That's just great. Where is Burke now?"

"In Port Henry."

"What?"

"He drove up yesterday. He's at his sister's place. Looks like he's there to keep an eye on his niece and nephew."

"Because of Murphy threatening them?"

"That would be enough to make me move in," Yakabuski said.

"We need to bring Burke in for a proper interview."

"I agree. Griffin is going up there tomorrow. She should have a patrol car backing her — a two-constable patrol, if that can be arranged. She'll bring Burke in."

"I'll have a car waiting for her. What time is she heading out?"

"Five."

O'Toole nodded again. "Why aren't you going?"

"I want to get Newt's report on Walton Murphy as soon as it's ready. I also have an appointment with the doctor who screwed up the cause of death for Agnes McKenna. He asked if we could meet. He says it's important."

"Why not meet him in Port Henry?"

"He's already in Springfield."

O'Toole stopped asking questions and turned back to the window and the view of Kettle Falls.

When a minute had passed Yakabuski began to wonder if the meeting was finished. He was about to stand when O'Toole said, "The other day, when I talked to you about your nephew's birthday party — I was out of line. I want to apologize."

Yakabuski tried to recall if he'd ever heard O'Toole apologize before. Nothing came to mind.

"I appreciate you saying that, Bernie."

"I just hope you know what you're doing, Frank. For a man who never wanted a complicated life, you've made a strange decision."

"I haven't decided anything, yet."

"Well, you're walking a complicated path. Does that sound better?"

"You think Rachel Dumont would complicate my life?"

O'Toole started chuckling. He turned back to Yakabuski, and the chuckle had become a full-throated laugh by the time he asked, "My lord, man — don't *you* think that?"

22

LAUNDRY HUNG FROM ROPES inside the cabin. Meaghan pushed aside some bed sheets and her brother's jeans and made her way to the airtight. Opening the metal door of the wood stove, she added a log and stoked the embers. When it was burning well, she put on another.

It was good of Lizzie to hang the wash when she and Robbie were at the market. Would have been better if she'd hung it outside. Or remembered to light the stove.

It was like that a lot with her aunt these days. Half-steps. Half-measures. Half-a-thought. Like she was turning into a fraction.

Meaghan pumped some water out of the faucet, filled a tea kettle, went back to the front room, and put the kettle on the airtight. The steam from the kettle would add moisture to the room, making sure it took longer to dry the clothes, but she would probably re-hang them outside in the morning anyway, so it didn't make any difference. May as well put on the kettle and make some tea. She doubted if she'd be sleeping much tonight.

It had been tough, seeing the body of Walton Murphy. Tougher than she would have expected, given that she hated the man and had asked her uncle to kill him. She hadn't seen that many dead people in her life, and she supposed you needed to do that a lot – see dead people – before it didn't bother you any. Walton Murphy and her mother, those were the only dead people she'd ever seen, and she wished she'd never seen her mother.

Why was ID'ing a dead person so important to the people who ran things in this world? Why did they make that a rule? She could have done without seeing her mother on a metal shelf at the Food Town; done without seeing her face busted up and her hair tangled and brittle like winter branches of a thicket bush. Belly bloated. Mouth stiff and open. Did she die while she was still screaming? She'd never get that image out of her head. It had already burrowed in there and it weren't ever coming out.

They needed you to ID the body. That was the rule. And good luck trying to forget what you saw.

It seemed a sort of cruelty, but that's how most rules seemed to Meaghan, nothing more than ways for people who ran things in this world to be cruel and mean to people who didn't. Most rules didn't make sense to her. She couldn't think of one that had ever helped her.

Even that boy doctor seemed to know how cruel and stupid this rule was. While she was doing the "ID-ing," he'd looked at the floor, at the wall of stacked ketchup jars, at a mop and pail in the corner, any spot where her momma wasn't.

He couldn't bear to look at a dead body. What kind of doctor was he?

When it became obvious that he weren't gonna ask her the official question, Meaghan offered up the answer just so she could get out of there.

"That's her . . . that's my momma."

"Agnes McKenna?"

"Yes."

His only question.

He zipped up the sleeping bag, and they left the cooler.

She had thought there would be papers to sign, but there weren't. When they were back outside again, he thanked her for coming and extended his hand, but she'd already turned away to stare at some men working in Coogan's lumber yard. After an awkward few seconds, he said, "Well, I guess that's it."

"I guess it is."

He slid his hands into his pants pockets, walked away, and that was it: the official identification was finished.

The tea kettle whistled, and Meaghan took a cup out of the cupboard and dropped a teabag into it. She poured the steaming water into the cup. She didn't see her brother come into the room, didn't know how long he'd been standing there before she noticed his head peering around one of the hanging bed sheets.

"Hey, Sweet-Pea. Did I wake you?"

The boy stared at her but kept his thumb in his mouth. He had a blanket around his shoulders.

"Come here. You can sit next to me by the stove."

"There's room?"

"Yeah, there's room."

The boy came out from behind the sheet. He wore grey sweatpants and a sweater, three pairs of athletic socks.

"Cold night, ain't it Sweet-Pea? Come here. Let me warm you up. Lizzie forgot to light the stove."

"She couldn't find the matches."

"They're right here in the tin can. Like always."

"She said she couldn't find 'em." The boy as he shrugged his shoulders. His sister wrapped her blanket around him and rubbed his head. "Good thing she wasn't looking for me," he added.

"Yeah, good thing."

They stared at the fire. The first log she put on was about to break apart and become embers. The second was burning well. She thought of putting on a third, telling herself it was summer now and she didn't need to be as careful with the woodpile, but it was cold enough inside the cabin to make you forget that, and she'd seen it snow almost this late in the year once before.

"You're old enough now to light the air stove," she said. "You don't need to wait on Lizzie no more. I give you permission."

"To use the matches?"

"Yes."

"Thought you said I could never touch the matches. Said I'd burn the cabin down."

"I changed my mind. You can touch 'em now. If I'm not here

and you're getting cold, if Lizzie can't find the matches, then you go ahead and light the stove, Sweet-Pea."

"The cabin won't burn down?"

She rubbed her nose with the back of her hand. Looked down at her brother, who was only eight years younger than she was, not a baby anymore, and tried to say something. But her mouth went dry on her and the words came out like small, choking sounds.

"Are you cryin'?" he asked

"No."

"When is Momma comin' back?"

"She ain't Sweet-Pea."

"What do you mean, she ain't?"

"I mean she just ain't."

The boy thought about that. "Is that why I can use the matches?"

Meaghan turned away from her brother so he wouldn't see her crying.

When she had Robbie back in bed, she took her blanket and went to the porch, where her uncle sat in one of the wicker chairs.

"Boy OK?"

"He'll be all right. Just had a nightmare. Sure you don't want to come inside?"

"I'm good."

She looked up at the sky, which was awash with stars, and a quarter crescent moon that seemed to be hanging right above the cabin. "It's a nice night. Don't blame you. Want a blanket?"

"Maybe later."

"Thank you for comin' back. Donnie Murphy is almost as scary as his dad."

"He's a two-bit moonshiner. He ain't going to cause you any trouble, Meaghie."

"You can't stay on the porch forever."

"You think Donnie Murphy is going to be around forever?" Her uncle laughed. Then he leaned forward and took a four-inch roach from a seashell ashtray. He lit it and leaned back in the wicker chair.

"I sure don't think he's going to be around forever." Her uncle laughed one more time, offered her the spliff, and although she considered it, she shook her head.

"I'm going to play it straight for a few days, see how all this plays out."

"Hell, I can do that for you, Meaghie. Don't need to wait. It plays out with no more Murphys on the Back Channel."

"How many will you go after?"

"How many are there?"

She looked at her uncle and wondered if he was making a joke, then wondered why she was doubting him. Her mother had told her many "Uncle Liam" stories. She'd heard a few from other people, too. Like the time the Popeyes were trying to take over the meth business on the Upper Divide, which was Uncle Liam's business, and four bikers came to High River to explain the new business arrangement.

Everyone knew that story. Three of the bikers were found hanging from trees in High River Provincial Park. The fourth was rolled out of a car in front of the Popeyes' clubhouse in Springfield, a bomb strapped to his chest that was remotely activated once several bikers had run out of the clubhouse and gathered around what the coroner would later confirm was an already dead biker.

Punchline to the story was Uncle Liam strolling into that same clubhouse, that same night, with a dozen "business associates" from the Upper Divide. He informed Papa Paquette he'd start blowing up the Popeyes' bikes next, and the Popeyes' warehouses, and the Popeyes' homes. Wasn't going to stop at just blowing up the curious and the stupid.

Unless, of course, the Popeyes were willing to stay with their current business arrangement. Uncle Liam cooked the drugs. The Popeyes bought what he cooked.

Paquette said he was fine with the current arrangement — had Uncle Liam heard anything different?

That was one story. There were dozens more, all of them variations on the same narrative — her uncle had a brass pair. And he was crazy.

Or *coco* as they said along the Back Channel. One crazy, hell raising, damn-the-torpedoes, *coco* son-of-a-bitch. Dear Uncle Liam.

Who had never been anything but kind to her. Who had driven half the night to be with her now, because Donnie Murphy had threatened her. Who had just asked — as though wondering what would make the perfect cheer-up gift for his niece — how many Murphys she wanted him to kill.

"Donnie's got a son ain't half bad. Garland. He's never done nothin' bad toward me."

"I ain't interested in good Murphys, Meaghan. Who needs to go?"

"Now that Walton's gone . . . ? Just Donnie, I guess."

Her uncle nodded, the smoke from the spliff framing his face, his eyes half closed, to keep away the smoke, although maybe he was tired, she thought. He looked tired.

"I'm off to bed. Would you like that blanket?"

"Sure."

She went inside and got a faded Hudson's Bay blanket from a closet. It was the oldest blanket in the cabin, also the best, and her uncle smiled when he saw it.

"That'll do the trick."

"Are you sure you want to stay out here?"

"I already rigged up the cans. No sense being inside where I can't hear them."

She glanced at the pines surrounding the cabin. The starry night gave her a clear view of what on other nights would be a darkened forest. She could see the twine her uncle had wrapped around the trees, and the tin cans the twine had been threaded through.

"You want a rifle?" she asked. "Be better than that handgun you got."

"Handgun'll work fine. Get off to bed, you."

McKenna headed back inside the cabin. It was only as she was drifting off to sleep that she remembered she hadn't thanked her uncle for getting rid of Walton Murphy. She wondered, briefly, when he had found time to return to the Back Channel. And why he hadn't told her about it.

She thought about this only briefly, before sleep overtook her.

23

THE NEXT MORNING, Meaghan was awakened by the sound of tin cans clanking together. She looked at the clock on her nightstand, surprised to see it was after eight.

There was a loud knock on the front door.

"Ms. McKenna, are you inside? We need you to open the door."

She looked out her bedroom window and saw a police patrol car.

What in the world?

She grabbed a sweater off a hook on the wall and was heading to the door when she heard another shouted question: "Is you uncle inside the cabin, Ms. McKenna? Is Liam Burke in there with you?"

"No."

"His car is here, Ms. McKenna. I'm going to ask you again — is Liam Burke in the cabin with you?"

"And I'm going to tell you again — *no, he ain't!*"

"I need you to step out of the cabin with your hands in the air. Can you do that for me?"

"You want me to do *what?*"

"Please, Ms. McKenna, just do as I'm asking."

"My brother's in here with me. So's my aunt. You want them on the porch, too?"

"Yes."

"All of us with our hands in the air?"

"Yes."

Robbie was behind her, pulling on his sweater and wiping his eyes. Aunt Lizzie was coming out of her bedroom, lighting a cigarette.

"Put that out, Lizzie. They want us on the porch with our hands in the air."

"To hell with them. I'll smoke a gawdamn cigarette on my gawdamn porch if I gawdamn feel like it."

Meaghan gave her a concerned look. "Better let me go first."

Meaghan walked onto the porch with her hands in the air, followed by her brother, who had his arms raised, mimicking his sister. Aunt Lizzie came last. She had decided to put her hands in the air after all. Her Camel cigarette was clenched tightly between her lips.

Donna Griffin had her handgun drawn, not saying anything while two uniformed police officers walked into the cabin. In less than a minute they were back outside, shaking their heads.

"All right, you can put your hands down," said Griffin, as she holstered her handgun. "Where is he, Meaghan?"

Meaghan looked at the wicker chair where her uncle had been sitting the previous night. An ashtray on the armrest was overflowing with cigarette butts and marijuana roaches. The Hudson's Bay blanket lay twisted on the floor.

"No idea," she answered.

24

DR. PETER ATKINSON looked like he hadn't slept in days. The skin beneath his eyes was grey and puffy, his clothes were wrinkled, his hair was bunched into geometric shapes that sat atop his head like children's building blocks. The astringent smell Yakabuski remembered about the doctor was missing as well, as though Atkinson had been too rushed that morning to apply his skin cream. Or forgotten. Or no longer cared.

When the doctor contacted him, Yakabuski had suggested they meet at the Red Bird diner. He thought an informal setting, outside the police station, would be a kindness. When their coffee arrived, the doctor took greedy gulps, while stealing furtive glances around the diner, as though looking for hidden danger. "Did you know I've been suspended?" he asked.

"Yes."

"I wasn't sure. Your name isn't on the letter . . . do you *know* about the letter?"

"I was asked to sign it."

"But you didn't. You probably have more cause to be angry with me than anyone else. Why didn't you sign it?"

"Because I didn't think it would accomplish much. And it felt like piling on to me."

The letter had been written by Fraser Newton, head of the Springfield police I-Dent department. Newton had been outraged by Atkinson's error about the cause of death for Agnes McKenna. He thought the young doctor was incompetent, an embarrassment to the medical profession, and in desperate need of constant supervision by a medical group Newton referred to as, "the adults."

"You know who signed the letter?" asked Atkinson.

"I do."

The doctor groaned and hung his head. Newton had convinced more than a dozen people to co-sign the letter he had written, which asked the Ministry of Health to fire Atkinson.

"When was the last time you slept?" asked Yakabuski.

"Last night."

"How many hours?"

Atkinson shrugged. "Not many. I slept in my car." He stretched his arms overhead, his bones cracking. "Not the most comfortable place to sleep."

"You okay?"

"I'm okay." He leaned over his coffee cup and stared into it, as though the answers to all life's great questions were swirling around in the dregs.

"What did you want to see me about, Doctor?"

Atkinson looked up from his coffee with a startled expression. It was unclear to Yakabuski if it had been the question that startled him; or looking up from his coffee cup and finding himself in the Red Bird Diner talking to a cop.

"Yes . . . I wanted to see you for two reasons. First, I want to say I'm sorry . . . for what happened. I screwed up. I know that. I made assumptions, instead of following facts. I was careless and I created problems for many people. Missing a homicide — there aren't many mistakes a doctor can make that would be much bigger."

"I don't know if that's true. You didn't *cause* a homicide."

Atkinson, snorted. "Thank you for that, but I know you're being kind. It was a colossal blunder by me, and I need to apologize."

Yakabuski gave him a curious look. "Apologizing to those you've hurt. That sounds like step nine. I didn't take you for a drinking man, Doctor."

"I'm not."

"Have you spoken to any lawyers since you received the letter?"

"No."

"I can't help you with any liability problems you may soon be facing, Dr. Atkinson. No matter how many times you apologize."

"Oh, my god, that's not it at all! You think . . . " Atkinson covered his mouth with his hands, as though he was about to be sick.

"That's n-not it at a-all, detective," he stammered a minute later. "I've been t-talking to m-my dad. He says I need to apologize for what I've done, *before* any lawyers get involved. Say I'm sorry to those I've hurt. That's what I'm doing."

Sounded to Yakabuski like the doctor's father knew a thing or two about the twelve steps. Or maybe he was just a good father giving his son some good advice.

"Listen to your father," he said.

Atkinson nodded and they sat in silence for a while, watching people come and go. The early-shift waitresses were cashing out at a nearby table. The elderly woman behind the cash register was reading a copy of the *Springfield Sentinel* that had a photo on the front page of two teenagers diving into the Springfield River. It was the start of summer. Not much was happening.

Yakabuski motioned to their waitress to bring more coffee. When she had filled their cups, Atkinson stirred in some cream, his spoon hitting the side of the cup from time to time and sounding like a tiny bell.

"You said there were two things you wanted to talk to me about, doctor."

"Yes, there are. You should know that it never seemed important to me, the reason I didn't mention it at the time . . . it's only become apparent . . . in light of recent events . . . only now does it seem like something that might be worth . . . "

The look on Atkinson's face right then was one Yakabuski had seen many times. It was the look of someone who had been running from some awful truth they didn't want to confront — didn't even want to acknowledge — but the race was about to end, they were running out of track, and they weren't going to win.

"What do you need to tell me, Doctor?"

"You need to understand," he continued, "it's *important* that you understand . . . how this would have looked to me at the time . . . put yourself in my shoes. Can you do that?"

Yakabuski didn't answer.

"I'm not from here. That would have made a *huge difference* . . . if I'd had some way of knowing . . . "

Yakabuski stared at Atkinson until the doctor hung his head and finally said, in a tired, defeated whisper, "You need to understand . . . I thought people drowned up here all the time."

Yakabuski was back at the police station fifteen minutes later, telling the chief's secretary he needed to see him right away. Pull him out of his meeting.

He could have waited to tell O'Toole. There was no useful purpose, no urgent need for the chief to know what the doctor had gone on to tell Yakabuski. From an investigative perspective, it made no difference.

But it didn't seem right, waiting to share the news. Seemed to Yakabuski like it put him in the company of that boy doctor, putting people aside until it was convenient to notice them, or deal with them.

O'Toole walked out of the third-floor boardroom with a surprised look on his face. "Yak — if you're here about Liam Burke, I already heard the news. He's taken off on us."

"I'm not here about Burke."

"What then?"

"We have a serial killer on the Back Channel."

III

PAST HOPE

THIRD CLUE

Port Henry, 1866

The murder of Governor Angus Arnprior by his land agent shocked the government in York. A thousand-pound reward was soon offered for information leading to the capture of Patrick Adams. Later raised to two thousand. Later to five, an astronomical amount that far exceeded the lifetime wages of most working men.

At the same time, a company of British soldiers was dispatched to Springfield to search for Adams. The soldiers stayed until autumn, until the river was about to freeze and snow had already fallen along the Upper Divide, but they never found him. Nor any sign of him. No abandoned cookfires. No new trail through the woods. No hidden canoe.

While the soldiers searched, a Back Channel settler returned his land grant and the worry in York turned to panic. No settler, in the history of building colony roads in the New World, had ever returned a land grant. If other settlers were to follow, the Port Henry settlement would fail and the government's attempt to colonize the Upper Divide would become a political embarrassment.

Given the money already spent on building an unfinished corduroy road, more than an embarrassment. A political scandal.

The settler who'd fled was named Ambrose Guthrie and he had been one of the first to arrive on the Back Channel, getting his hundred-acre grant in 1860. Guthrie was also the first to realize, after five years of digging rock, that what his labors had produced was a thin, peat-like loam of soil that shriveled when exposed to the elements, that had the look and texture of desiccated spider webs.

And then it blew away.

The land was useless.

Even if something could be grown atop the rock, there was no way to bring crops to market. Not after the spring run-off, anyway, for the Back Channel was too low any other time of year. And there was no road. The promise of a colony road from Springfield to Port Henry had been another cruel deception, another government lie.

So disillusioned was Guthrie, before leaving Port Henry he burned his cabin and salted the land he had cleared. He told the harbormaster, who was the only government official in Port Henry, that people needed to be warned.

Don't come to this place.

He also gave the harbourmaster his deed, even though he was told there was no need. All the land grants were provisional, until improvements to the land had been completed and registered. Guthrie told the harbourmaster to keep the deed anyway. He wanted no reminder of his time on the Northern Divide, no "truck nor trade with a place this cursed." Then he boarded a down-river barge and was never seen again.

Steerage records show Ambrose Guthrie arrived in Springfield in 1860 with a wife and five children. The same records show he left in 1865 with no wife and two children.

So, he had endured some hardships, thought the new governor when he'd heard news of what Guthrie had done. Who hadn't? But to give back your land? Burn down your cabin and salt the earth?

The ungrateful bog. That's what you get for trying to help some people.

The new governor's name was George Winthrop. Guthrie's public renouncement of the land grant program had been such a spectacle, Winthrop felt he needed to do something about it. And so, in early summer of the following year, for the first time, a territorial governor of the Northern and Upper Divide came to Port Henry.

Winthrop stepped off the barge in full military regalia — red tunic, white belt and gloves, an infantry officer's sword. The sword was so long and the new governor so short, the blade bounced off the steps of the barge when he disembarked, making a clanking sound that scared away the birds.

Winthrop spoke to the settlers in front of Dickinson House, a rooming house not far from the remains of Guthrie's cabin. The rooming house was also a tavern on "barge days" — those days when a barge would arrive from Springfield. Given the historic importance of the governor's visit, the tavern had been open for two days.

The governor sat in the tavern for more than an hour before coming out and making his speech. He told the assembled settlers that Ambrose Guthrie had been, at best, a man who'd quit on his neighbours, quit on his family, quit on the prosperity that fate was soon to lavish upon him. At worst, he was a deranged and hateful anarchist — a man they were glad to have sent into exile.

The governor promised the settlers that the colony road would be completed within two years. Perhaps sooner. A procurement dispute with the Board of Ordnance needed merely to be resolved and then work would resume immediately.

"Post haste to Port Henry," he roared, and liking the sound of the phrase, and having imbibed several glasses of port at Dickinson House, the governor kept repeating the phrase. "Post haste to Port Henry! Post haste to Port Henry!" Doing this even though none of the settlers shouted it back; not even when he beckoned them to do just that, gesturing his hands toward them as though he were bringing babies to his bosom.

"Post haste to Port Henry! Post haste to Port Henry!"

Despite the lack of crowd participation, Winthrop considered the visit a success. No one had heckled him. No one had approached him, wishing to talk. And best of all, no one had threatened to give back their grant and salt the earth like that ungrateful bog Guthrie had done. He returned to Springfield a happy man.

Later that year, the dispute with the Board of Ordnance was settled, and 100,000 pounds sterling was sent to Springfield to pay for completion of the colony road.

The following year, construction was stopped. The colonial government told the provincial legislature that the land had proven too unforgiving, the task too arduous, for the project to succeed, despite all best efforts. After seven years of contracted work, and the expenditure of hundreds of thousands of pounds from the public purse, only twenty-two miles of corduroy road had been completed.

On the day the colony road was cancelled, the harbourmaster was painting a *Welcome to Port Henry* sign on the side of his house, which was the largest building on the channel, one made of brick, not wood like the others. He had just begun the job; had painted only "welcome to", and a capital P and a capital H, to get the alignment right, when he heard the news.

The next day, the harbourmaster lost his job. A barge from Springfield arrived, bringing a letter from Winthrop that said because the Port Henry colony was now a failure, the colonial government no longer needed a harbourmaster.

Upon reading the letter the harbourmaster — a timid man given to long bouts of melancholy and remorse for the decisions he had made in life —got drunk for three days. During that time, he tried to drown himself; set fire to several boats; proposed marriage to three teenage girls; and at some point — no one could later remember when — finished his sign.

The harbourmaster's home still stands. The faded letters of the town's original welcome sign can still be seen. In the days after construction of the colony road came to an end, every stranded settler along the Back Channel came to see the welcome sign, many applauding the harbormaster's work and wanting to slap him on the back, but he had already left the settlement.

His sign read:

Welcome to

Past

Hope

25

IT TOOK A MONTH to get all the bodies shipped to Springfield.
One of the families — the Byrnes — fought the exhumation,
the brother of the dead man telling Yakabuski, "Dead is dead,
son. Why you botherin' us?"

"Don't you want to know how your brother died?" asked
Yakabuski.

"Don't see how it makes any difference to Harold. Probably
best we leave him where he is." Three times Yakabuski visited Gerald Byrne, trying to convince him to sign the papers
that would allow for the exhumation of his brother. He only
succeeded the day Byrne asked him how much it would cost.

"For the exhumation?" Yakabuski said in surprise. "It won't
cost you anything, sir."

"You sure 'bout that?"

"Yes."

"It cost us nearly a thousand dollars to put Harold in the
ground, but you say it's going to cost us nothin' to take him
out? How does that work?"

By mid-June, the autopsies were complete. Yakabuski, Griffin, and Inspector Fraser Newton gathered in the basement
of the Water Street detachment, where I-Dent was located, to
discuss the results.

"Last one came in yesterday," said Newton, as he put six file
folders in the middle of the metal table that they sat around.
"Coroner told me he would rule Ennis a suspicious death, but
given what else we have, he says we'd be safe to consider her
a homicide as well."

"So . . . we have six homicides?"

The I-dent cop nodded. Griffin opened one of the file folders and said, "That doctor ruled *each of these deaths* an accidental drowning? Are we sure he even has a medical licence?"

"We're sure," Newton answered glumly. "Not for much longer, though, if I have anything to say about it."

There was a whiteboard set up in the room, and the photos of the six victims had been taped to it. The photos would have been considered poor quality even in the days before smart phones, back in the hey-day of the bus station photo-booth and the Kodak Instamatic.

The best photos were for Harold Byrne and Tobias Smith. Army enlistment photos. Crisp focus. Good lighting. The photo of Dorothy Ennis had been cropped from a group photo taken at a curling bonspiel. Peter Kelly was a twenty-year-old transit pass from Montreal. Agnes McKenna was a wedding photo, taken on the steps of the Springfield Registry office, also cropped. Walton Murphy was a fishing photo, Murphy kneeling beside an upside-down canoe that had a dozen trout displayed on top of it, a photo heavy with shadows, the trout more in focus than Murphy.

When you put them all together and clipped them to a whiteboard, they seemed like photographs you had pulled from a lost-and-found box. Abandoned. Misplaced. A hint of tragedy to each one, even if you didn't know the details of the tragedy. You were looking at people whose lives hadn't worked out the way they'd wanted. You knew it just by looking at the photos.

None of the victims were related. Ages ranged from thirty-eight (Peter Kelly) to seventy-seven (Dorothy Ennis.). Four men and two women. None were neighbours. None shared a religious or business affiliation. Two of the men had worked at the Coogan mill on Smoke Island, but not at the same time. Both women had been known to sell collectibles at the Back Channel Market, but not together, and for Dorothy Ennis, not in years.

You could have thrown names of people who lived along the Back Channel into a hat and you might have drawn the names of the six victims. That's the way it appeared. Random deaths, the victims having nothing more in common other than living in the same geographic area, in settler cabins or trailers on land their families had owned for generations, deep in the pines, or deep in the marshland. Nothing connected them. Nothing separated them.

"We're missing something," said Yakabuski, reaching for one of the file folders. "There has to be something that connects these people."

"Even if there is, we'd have trouble finding it," said Griffin. "Four of our victims didn't have bank accounts. None of them had a cell phone. None had a computer. The nearest CCT camera is eighty-seven miles away. It's in La Toque, by the way."

"Why did you bother checking that?" asked Newton.

"To see how fucked we are."

Newton blushed and Griffin quickly said, "sorry, Inspector, that just slipped out. But the things I've mentioned — bank accounts, cell phones, cameras — that's how you connect people these days. When you don't have that information . . ."

Griffin stopped talking. She looked momentarily confused. Then angry. "Not having that information is just *weird*. These people are like black holes. The stuff we know about them, it's embarrassing. We have more information on kindergarten kids in Springfield."

"Frustrated, are we?" asked Yakabuski.

"Frustrated, bewildered — I don't understand how people can live like that."

"Like what? Poor?"

"It's not that. Or it's *more* than that, I guess. These people seem lost to me. Like they've been kicked off the bus or something. I feel sorry for them one minute; the next minute I'm angry with them, and I don't know why. Maybe for not doing a better job of protecting themselves. Living in a place like the Back Channel — why would you do that to yourself?"

"You're assuming they had a choice," said Yakabuski. "I wouldn't make that assumption."

How do you separate people from place? Along the Back Channel, it was almost impossible. The land you stood on was part of your story, part of your family's story. There was no severing it. No parting ways with it.

On the other hand, Yakabuski understood what Griffin was saying. Bad land was bad land; God never seemed to feel any different about it, so why stay? There was no good answer, although if you lived on bad land long enough maybe it became home. The Algonquin had a parable for that; a story told to Champlain by a one-eyed chief during one of the French explorer's first visits to the New World. A story that became Champlain's story in many ways. Yakabuski tried to remember how it went, couldn't recall the exact details, then turned to Newton and asked:

"What are the differences?"

"Two of the men were beaten to death, the other two men were beaten, but were alive when they went into the river. They drowned. Agnes McKenna also drowned. Dorothy Ennis was asphyxiated."

"And then she was dumped in the river, right? All our victims went into the Springfield River?"

"The bodies were all recovered from the Springfield River, yes. Thought you were asking for the differences."

"The river intrigues me — why not bury the bodies where they'll never be found? What else?"

"Ennis was asphyxiated, so cause of death is inconsistent among the victims," replied Newton"

All right — what are our similarities?"

"Each body was recovered from the Springfield, like you said," answered Newton. "The facial bruising on the bodies suggests a left-handed assailant."

"Suggests?"

"I'd like to run some more tests to get a better handle on the damage done by the assailant, and the damage done by the river. Until I do that, I . . . "

"You're not in a courtroom, Newt. Do we have a left-handed assailant?"

"I'd say so. Yes."

"No signs of sexual assault or torture. All victims fully clothed. No signs of defensive wounds. Correct?

"Correct."

"Who was our first victim?"

"Difficult to say," said Newton. "The first body to be recovered was Peter Kelly. The next was Harold Byrne, six days later. Decomposition was about the same on both bodies. It would be one of those two, but I can't say with certainty which one."

"And the date would be . . . " Yakabuski reached for a file folder, opened it, read for a few seconds, and said, "June 14 of last year. That's for Kelly. So, almost exactly a year ago."

"That would be the timeline, yes."

"Murphy was a big man. Any indication there was more than one assailant?"

"No. Murphy died by blunt force trauma, a blow to the back of the head administered by a heavy object. No defensive wounds. That first blow likely killed him."

"Somebody snuck up behind him."

"Looks that way."

"Any doubts about what we're looking at here, Newt?"

"As I've already said, Ennis was asphyxiated, so cause of death is inconsistent."

"Didn't Agnes McKenna show signs of asphyxiation?"

"She did."

"But none of the men."

"That's correct."

"The women were strangled. The men weren't. How old was Ennis?"

"Seventy-eight."

"Maybe she didn't need a beating, Newt. Maybe putting hands around her neck was enough."

Newton nodded for a few seconds before saying, "That's possible. Although it's also possible that a different cause of death indicates a different killer."

"Do we have any evidence of a second killer?"

"No. Just something we can't rule out."

"Like life on Mars?" said Griffin, and after she'd said it, her eyes grew large, and she gasped. "I'm sorry, Inspector. I didn't mean to say that."

"Don't apologize," said Yakabuski. "You're in this room to give us your opinion, not to agree with everything we say. Life on Mars — you think those are the odds of these deaths being unrelated?"

"I do."

"And you, Newt?"

The inspector looked at Griffin and shook his head ruefully. "Are these deaths unrelated? I think the constable is right — there would be a better chance of finding life on Mars."

Griffin gave Newton an appreciative nod as Yakabuski gathered the file folders and stood. "I better go upstairs and let the chief know it's been confirmed," he said. "We're looking for a serial killer on the Back Channel."

26

THE WATER STREET police station was built in 1867, only twenty years after the first police officers had arrived on the Northern Divide. The station was built with two-foot-thick limestone blocks. Had oak doors nearly as thick as the walls. The holding cells in the basement had been carved out of a ridge of gneiss. It was a fortress to rival any military block house. Only thing missing was the gun slits.

O'Toole's third-floor office had portraits of former chiefs that hung at eye-level upon dark, wood-paneled walls. An oak-framed window had a sill that was half the size of the window. A steam radiator beneath the window had claw feet large enough to trip over. Like the rest of the detachment, O'Toole's office made you think there were people in the room that you couldn't see.

"You've had your meeting with Newt?" O'Toole asked, when Yakabuski was sitting in front of him.

"Just finished."

"And what do we have?"

"Six homicides."

"My lord. I was hoping it wouldn't be true."

Yakabuski updated O'Toole on the investigation. They had six homicide victims, all found in the water along the Back Channel, all beaten by a left-handed assailant, no apparent connection between the victims. None had been sexually assaulted. None were robbed.

The update was embarrassingly brief.

"Multiple murders taking place along the Springfield River — makes me think of the Shiners. Have we considered that possibility?" asked O'Toole.

"There's no Shiners living on the Back Channel."

"How can we be sure of that?"

"Shiners live in Corktown and think the Upper Divide is another country. They wouldn't even know how to get to the Back Channel. There's also no money to be made up there, so why would a Shiner bother?"

O'Toole snorted. "Yeah, you're right. No money, no sex, no motorcycle gang doing Darwin's work — these killings appear to be as random and pointless as killings get."

"There must be a connection between the victims. We just haven't found it yet."

"No doubts about a single assailant committing all six murders?"

"Given what we have, Griffin says the odds of these murders being unrelated are worse than the odds of finding life on Mars."

"Has she really run the math on that?"

"No. It's a gut feeling."

"So, we have a serial killer on the Back Channel, someone who kills without motive, started doing it about a year ago, and we have no clue who it might be — that's what we have here?"

Yakabuski did a quick tally in his head of the known facts of the case, considered theories and contradictory facts, then said, "That sounds about right."

"The RCMP have a profiler you should talk to. I'll set it up."

"All right," said Yakabuski and he leaned forward to pick up the file folders he'd put on the chief's desk. He didn't get up from his chair, though, and a few seconds later O'Toole asked:

"Anything else?"

"When you said we don't have a clue who the killer might be, that is literally what we have in this case. No clues. After two months of work, we don't have a single lead we can follow. With six victims, this can't be about a feud between the McKennas and the Murphys. With six victims, this isn't about Liam Burke or Agnes McKenna selling meth. This is a new investigation, and we should treat it as such. We need to re-examine everything."

"I see where this is going," said O'Toole. "You're not going to give it up, are you?"

"I don't think we're in a position to give up on anything, no matter how unlikely it may seem to us."

A tired smile came to O'Toole's face. He turned his chair around so he was looking out his window. "See that steam down there, Yak?"

The chief was pointing to Kettle Falls and the steam rising from its base.

"I see it."

"Walter Crawley controls that steam. Same way Walter Crawley controls the Springfield River and any other river within two hundred miles of us. Same way he gets to decide if your house gets flooded in the spring or freezes in the winter. Walter Crawley controls —"

"I know what a water commissioner does," Yakabuski said.

"And *I know* how much you enjoy poking powerful people in the eye. It's like a parlour game for you."

"Who has a parlour anymore?"

"You know what I'm saying, Yak. Why do you insist on kicking wasps' nests? Even ones that might not need to be kicked. Why don't you leave it alone? Have you ever done that before?"

"Leave a wasp nest alone?" Yakabuski said in a questioning voice. "Guess that depends on where I find it."

O'Toole chuckled as he swiveled his chair forward. "Be on your best behaviour when you talk to him, Yak. I don't want to spend the rest of my week unruffling that man's tail feathers."

27

BEING WATER COMMISSIONER on the Northern Divide was like being God's right-hand apostle. The job came with tremendous power and influence. More than what the fabled lumber barons of old possessed. More than kings and queens. More, even, than any saint — as saints needed merely to perform one or two miracles in their lifetime before being canonized. Water commissioners, on the other hand, could summon them daily.

A water commissioner made rivers disappear. Moved lakes from one watershed to another. Stilled waterfalls. Ended drought. They could also — best trick they had — create hydroelectric power. Which was raw power. Power as elemental and fearsome as power gets.

Saints were entry-level workers in the miracle department compared to water commissioners.

For Walter Crawley, the job was a family affair. His grandfather had also been the water commissioner for the Northern Divide. William Crawley Senior — or Big Bill, as he was often called — had held the job for thirty-two years, from 1920 to 1952.

Crawley rose and walked out from behind his desk when Yakabuski entered the room. "Detective Yakabuski, it's an honour to meet you."

"I appreciate you taking the time to see me, Mr. Crawley."

"Happy to do it. I have your book at home. If I'd known you were coming today, I would have brought it in and asked you to sign it."

Crawley was of medium height and build, with a receding hairline, coke-bottle glasses, and dark blue chin stubble that looked permanent. The chin stubble and balding head gave him the appearance of a downtrodden junior accountant, which was jarring when you first met him, considering everything else about Walter Crawley — his clothes, his office, the secretary who met Yakabuski at the elevator and escorted him into the inner sanctum — screamed money and power.

"I wouldn't be able to sign the book," said Yakabuski. "I didn't write it. A reporter from the *Sentinel* did that. I'm also working right now."

Crawley gave Yakabuski a bemused smile, the sort of smile rich and powerful people get once they've decided the person in front of them would make a dreadful dinner guest. "Well, it's nonetheless an honour to meet you, Detective Yakabuski. How may I assist?"

"I'm investigating some murders that have taken place around Port Henry. Agnes McKenna, Walton Murphy, Peter Kelly, Harold Byrne, Tobias Smith, Dorothy Ennis — do those names mean anything to you, sir?

The commissioner tapped his chin. "No, can't say that they do. Should they?"

"I wouldn't know," answered Yakabuski, flashing him a friendly smile. On the wall behind the commissioner was a map of the Springfield River from headwater to mouth, a topographical map showing the entire watershed. The map took up most of the wall. "Get out on the river much?" Yakabuski asked.

"Not as much as I'd like too," replied Crawley, turning to look at the map. "Far too much paperwork these days, but it's still part of the job, thank heavens, going out and inspecting the dams, the hydro stations. I like being outside. I started my career as a geological engineer."

"Good degree to get when most of your family works for the water commission. You were thinking ahead."

"You know your history, Mr. Yakabuski. Yes, my grandfather was Big Bill Crawley. He built the first hydroelectric stations along the Springfield. My great-grandfather had the contract to build the dam at Ferguson's Falls. Lucas Crawley. He owned a few dams on the Racine as well. It was only six years ago that the federal government bought the last private dam my family owned."

Yakabuski kept looking at the swirling grey and green lines of the topo map. The intricacy of the inkwork gave the map a splendor and beauty that went beyond the geographic. "Must be something, having control over the rivers," said Yakabuski. "How fast they run. How high they go. Those are super-hero powers."

"Just takes an engineering degree," said Crawley, laughing and patting himself on the knee. "But tell me — the deaths of these people you've mentioned, does it have something to do with one of our dams? I haven't received an incident report."

"No one drowned because of a water release. They were beaten and thrown into the Springfield. Some of them drowned, some were already dead. The first body was found a year ago."

Crawley looked at Yakabuski. No longer bemused. The mood had changed. The topic serious. He picked up on it effortlessly, a man who had been trained to read the room. "That's a bad way to go."

"Yes, it is. How familiar are you with the Back Channel, Mr. Crawley?"

"Not well. As you probably know, it's not navigable, not commercially anyway. There are no towns of any size, other than Port Henry. The Back Channel has never been an issue for the Commission. I've had no reason to visit or study the area."

Crawley picked away at some lint on his worsted suit. When a few seconds had passed, he added, "Although it's *odd* you should be asking me about this, because I *was* at Port Henry earlier this summer."

Yakabuski nodded. "That *is* odd. What took you up there?"

"I needed to see Tommy Coogan. I had a business meeting with him, at his yard."

"Coogan has offices in Springfield. Why not have the meeting here?"

"I needed to inspect some wood we're buying from him. Squared timber, if you can believe it. Know what that is?"

"I do."

"Yes, of course you would. Well, we still use that wood for locks along the French River. The exact same beams used to build Nelson's battleships. Coogan dredges for those logs and normally has a good selection. I was at Port Henry in early May, I think it was."

"It was. I was there the same day you were. You drive a Land Rover, don't you?"

Crawley gave Yakabuski an annoyed look. "I'm getting the impression this visit is less random than you led me to believe, Detective Yakabuski. You'll forgive me, then, if I jump ahead. Yes, I drive a Land Rover. Now — why are you here?"

Yakabuski returned Crawley's disgruntled look with another friendly smile. "In a homicide case you canvass the area around the crime scene, Mr. Crawley. You happened to be in the neighbourhood one of the days I was there."

"I see."

"I would have interviewed you that day, but we . . . *missed* each other."

"So, what would you like to know?"

"Did you notice anything unusual when you were in Port Henry?"

"Unusual in what way?"

"In an unusual way."

Crawley gasped. "That's a rather cheeky response, Detective Yakabuski."

"I didn't mean it be, Mr. Crawley. This is a routine visit. I interviewed Mr. Coogan the day you were in Port Henry. Several other people as well. If I'd bumped into you that day, I would have asked you the questions I'm asking you now. As I said, we just missed each other. Where were you when I was interviewing Mr. Coogan?"

"Must have been in the yard inspecting the wood."

"You did the inspection yourself?"

"I'm more than capable, detective."

"Of course."

Ten minutes later, Crawley's secretary came into the office and reminded him that he had a board meeting at the top of the hour. That's what she said: "top of the hour," like she was announcing an upcoming newscast.

Crawley asked if there was anything else he needed, and when Yakabuski said no, the secretary walked him back to the elevator. She wore high-heeled shoes and black stockings with a wide back seam.

As he rode the elevator down, Yakabuski wondered where you found stockings like that, and whether the secretary looked more like Jayne Mansfield, or more like Marilyn Monroe.

For most of the ride, though, he wondered why Tommy Coogan would let a water commissioner wander around his lumber yard like some DIY-er looking for two-by-fours.

That afternoon, Yakabuski received a phone call from Meaghan McKenna.

"Are ya the one holdin' my uncle?"

"Meaghan, nice to hear from you. How have you been?"

"Is that a yes or a no?"

"One of these days you should learn to be more direct. You have a bad habit of beating around the bush. Did you know that?"

"So, you got him."

Yakabuski sighed. "Meaghan, as far as I know, we have not detained your uncle. Where are you phoning from?"

"Payphone at the Food Town. What do ya mean, 'As far as you know?' Ya would know, wouldn't ya?"

"Yes, I would know."

"Then who's got him?"

Yakabuski considered the question. But before he could attempt an answer — the Mounties, maybe? The provincial police? — he heard a click and the call went dead.

"Nice chatting with you, Meaghan," he mumbled, and slid his phone back in his pocket.

28

IT TOOK THREE DAYS to arrange the call to the RCMP homicide division in Toronto. The profiler's name was Dawn Sullivan, one of the lead investigators on the Roger Wilson case. Wilson had been the commanding officer of an airbase near the American border. He had taken to crossing the border and killing prostitutes in rent-by-the-hour hotels in Detroit. It was Sullivan who told border guards on the Ambassador Bridge to pull over the General's car, not wave it through like they had eight times previously. His age and background had fit her profile of the killer.

Her photo had been on television and in newspapers so many times since Wilson's arrest, Yakabuski felt as though she were sitting in the room with him, even though they weren't even on a Zoom call. "I've only had a few hours to go through your material," said Sullivan at the start of their conversation. "I won't be comfortable making any conclusions."

"The timeline has been explained to you?"

"Yes. You've only just become aware that you may have a serial killer on your hands. The initial deaths were ruled accidental. There's been no build-up, and you're starting cold."

"That's right. With six victims. Anything you can offer us would be a huge help right now."

"I get that. It's the reason we're talking. I just wanted to warn you that I may not be as helpful as you're hoping. When do you think your first victim was killed?"

"Last year, right around this time. Body was recovered from the river on June 14."

"So, all your victims were killed within the past year?"

"Yes."

"And you have sent me all the information you have on your victims?"

"Yes."

Sullivan didn't say anything for a few seconds. "Detective Yakabuski, I can't do a profile for you," she eventually said. "Not with the material I have in front of me. I'd need to know a lot more about your victims, and a lot more about where the murders took place. I've never been to the Northern Divide."

"Would it help if you came up?"

"No time, I'm afraid. I'm due in court next month and that's where you'll find me until Christmas."

"The Wilson trial is starting?"

"You got it. The best lawyers in the country are going to spend five months trying to convince a jury that photos of a man wearing a dead woman's panties on his head aren't as damning and incriminating as they may first appear."

"Glad I'll be missing that one."

"Wish I could. Listen, even though I can't do a profile for you, maybe I can still help."

"I'll take anything."

"Why don't I tell you the many ways that your case *isn't* normal? For one, most serial killers are highly mobile, if not outright transient. It's why there are serial killers out there we haven't caught and may never catch. Moving from place to place is crucial to getting away with the crime. The location of your murders, they were all in Port Henry?"

"The bodies were found there. The killings likely took place farther upriver, but they all happened along a twenty-three-mile stretch of the Springfield River known as the Back Channel."

"So, one geographic location?"

"That's right."

"Right there, that's a real oddity. Port Henry makes no sense as homebase for a serial killer. The timing is just as odd. Six victims within twelve months. I had a quick look at the autopsy reports. An elderly woman was asphyxiated; the others were all beaten in what seems to be roughly the same manner. Do I have that right?"

"You do."

"That's *extremely* odd. There's normally a progression. Someone like Wilson, who kills because of sexual urges he can't control, that's a multi-year monster you're looking at. He may have started by stealing women's clothes. Maybe he was a peeping Tom. He would have committed some rapes, maybe *many rapes,* before he killed someone. The first killing may have been an accident, or it may have been planned, but it's normally a while before he kills again. The urges have been satisfied.

"There's also the fear of getting caught. But once they've convinced themselves they've gotten away with it, — hell, it was easy — they'll do it again.

"It ramps up after the second murder. That's a standard pattern for serial killers. But that's not what you have. You have six murders; all committed in a short period of time. Victims were assaulted in roughly the same manner. No signs of torture. You have men *and* women. There's nothing about your case that's normal."

Yakabuski laughed. "I see what you meant, when you warned me that this conversation might not be as helpful as I imagined."

"I'm sorry, detective, but there's not much I can tell you and feel confident about it. I don't like to speculate."

"I'm willing to risk some uncomfortable speculation right about now."

This time, it was Sullivan who laughed. "All right, I'll play along. Just this once. Let me tell you about some serial killers who tick none of the regular boxes. They started killing late in life. They killed a lot. They weren't driven by sexual urges, voices in their head, or any mental impairment.

"One of those cases was in San Francisco. Homeless men were being killed in the Tenderloin district. The killer turned out to be another homeless man. He'd killed one of his friends by accident, then taken the dead man's shopping cart. When he wasn't arrested, he started killing other men from the shelters and stealing their belongings.

"In another case that fits some of the facts in your case, the killer was a dishwasher. He killed his wife one night in a drunken fight, hid the body in their apartment, and when her disability cheque came in later that month, he cashed it. He kept cashing those cheques for six years.

"No one questioned it?"

"They had a joint bank account. No one questioned it. He went on to marry two other women, killed them both, and started cashing their pension cheques. He was finally caught when he killed a woman who lived in his apartment building. He killed her because he wanted her apartment. It had a better view. Dead woman's son came knocking one day, dishwasher answers, that's how he got arrested."

"How was he disposing of the bodies?"

"We found all four women dissected and wrapped in butcher's paper inside a commercial-size freezer he had in the kitchen of his apartment. He'd bought it from the restaurant where he worked."

"No one thought that was strange?"

"Makes you wonder, doesn't it? So, tell me — do you see common denominators in the two cases?"

"I'd say money was one."

"Very good. You can get a late-in-life serial killer — a killer with no history of violence, an evil monster who seems to have dropped out of the sky — if the motive is money. It will never happen if the motive is sexual, or some screwed-up power dynamic. Notice anything else about the two cases?"

Yakabuski thought a minute. "A homeless man and a

dishwasher? They're both poor."

"Now I *am* impressed," Sullivan answered. "Not everyone sees that. The common denominators in these cases . . ." and then she paused, long enough for Yakabuski to think something had happened at her end, someone had come into her office or what have you. He was about to ask, when she said, "I must caution you again, detective, these are *rare* cases. The two cases I've mentioned are the only ones I know about, and I know the case histories of *hundreds* of serial killers."

"If you're worried about this coming back to haunt you, it won't," said Yakabuski. "I've never once blamed another police officer for a case that went south on me, or blew up in so many pieces I couldn't figure out where it went. I won't be starting the habit now."

"Well, so long as we understand each other. The common denominators in these *rare* cases are that the motive is money; and the killer is someone who never had any."

Yakabuski tried not to groan. Every person on the Back Channel had just become a suspect.

29

THAT NIGHT, YAKABUSKI had dinner at Rachel Dumont's apartment. As he was barbecuing burgers on her balcony, he told her about his interview with the RCMP profiler, and his interview earlier in the week with the water commissioner.

"Doesn't seem like the case is going well," she said.

"It isn't. We have more victims that we have clues. Might be the strangest case I've ever worked."

"The profiler was no use whatsoever?"

"She tried. She didn't brush me off or anything. Poor people are getting killed by someone who's probably just as poor as they are, someone who has a plan to get rich by killing poor people. That was the takeaway."

"You sound angry."

"Getting there. Did you know a thousand men died while building dams along the Springfield River in the 1800s? A thousand men. But you won't find a marked grave for any one of them. Or any kind of memorial. They were immigrant labourers, and when they died, they got rolled into a trench, covered with dirt, and people forgot about them. If you're walking in the woods by one of those dams and you come across a mound of dirt, you're likely walking over a dead man.

"Always been that way. The Shiners ran Springfield for more than a decade after the dams were finished. There's no way of knowing how many people they killed. They'd steal timber cribs and drown everyone aboard. Wait for people outside the taverns on Water Street, mug them and throw them over Kettle Falls. Business competitors were shot right in their offices. The lumber barons weren't much better. No one was ever arrested for any of those crimes. "

"That was a long time ago, Frank."

"And what's changed? When I talk to someone like Gordon Byrne, who tells me it doesn't make a difference how his brother died — dead is dead, leave his body where it is — on worthless land out back of the worthless farm he spent his life growing old on . . . I get so tired of it all. Tired of people thinking this is the best they can get from life, and other people making sure that's all that ever gets offered."

"That's quite a speech, Frank."

"Sorry. I get carried away sometimes."

"Don't be sorry. You didn't do anything wrong. I've just never seen you this angry before."

"I try not to get that way. Doesn't do a person any good. I think I'm just tired tonight. It's been a long week."

Rachel looked at him another second, then went inside to set the table. Grace wasn't home. She had an extra-curricular event of some sort at school — she always had something: band, drama, junior yearbook. Rachel set the table for two. Yakabuski watched her work, moving around the table as gracefully as a dancer. He remembered what his brother-in-law had said about Rachel, when he had mailed her a hundred-million-dollars in stolen diamonds. He wrote that he was returning the diamonds because they had been stolen from the land, "and you belong to this land as surely as these diamonds and can best decide their fate."

Some people carry place inside them. The lucky ones, who are always standing right where they belong. Rachel Dumont was one of those people.

After dinner they washed the dishes, standing next to each other at the kitchen sink, Rachel washing and passing him the dishes. Yakabuski drying and stacking them.

Rachel kept smiling at Yakabuski, and when she had done that enough times, he asked, "What is it, do I have something stuck in my teeth?"

"No, I'm just wondering why you came to see me tonight. Is it because you needed to get angry and honest for a minute?"

"That might be possible. I value your opinion."

"Value my opinion," she said, and her smile grew. "Yes, it could be that. But it could be something else too, Frank. Those stories you told me earlier, about the unmarked graves, the people the Shiners killed, you're angry at how those people were treated. It makes you feel bad.

"You cheer for the underdog, Frank. Most people do, but it's some sort of mission for you. Sometimes, it seems like you're trying to rectify some past injustice, not just solve a case. Does that make any sense?"

"I'm not sure. I'd have to think about it some."

"Maybe it's even why you came over tonight."

"What do you mean?"

"You don't get it? That surprises me; you being such a great detective and all."

"Perhaps you should enlighten me."

"You came over so you can feel better. You came over because I'm good for you."

Yakabuski stood there in near shock. Her words had the clarity and brevity of a gunshot. A thing inescapable.

Simple words. Strung together in a simple declarative sentence. To express an inescapable truth.

Rachel Dumont was good for him.

Three chords and the truth. That's what he'd just heard, what he was staring at right then, what he could reach out and embrace.

As Yakabuski leaned forward to kiss her, he was already regretting the time he had wasted by doubting his emotions, by denying the truth of how felt about Rachel Dumont.

Promising himself he would never make that mistake again.

30

COOGAN FORESTRY PRODUCTS had their offices on Water Street, the first street to be named in Springfield. The street was originally a ring road around Kettle Falls, where the mills and log chutes were being built, and in the early years of the town it was a lively street, a hissing, steaming, cauldron of mechanical noise and human babble. Bawdy shouts came from the second-floor windows of the taverns, where the bedrooms were located. Piano-roll tunes and drunken laughter came from the open doors on the main floor. Out on the corduroy road, mule riders pulled sleds of timber to the mills, screaming for people to get out of their way. Voyageurs with fur pelts strung on high poles strolled up and down, yelling the price for each animal. Fires burned in banded barrels along the shore, and mill workers on their knees played dice games around every fire.

Today, there were no mills or dice players on Water Street. No lumber chutes or textile factories, either. The corduroy road had been converted into a boardwalk, crowded with food carts and tee-shirt vendors. None of the original wooden buildings had survived, although some of the red-brick warehouses and factories still stood. They had long ago been converted into restaurants and coffee shops and clothing stores.

The rowdiest that Water Street got these days was when a businessman on a three-cocktail lunch complained about the bill after the server had cut him off. Or a food-cart umbrella blowing away in a windstorm, a common enough occurrence atop the falls.

Yakabuski had mixed feelings about gentrification. He had difficulty feeling nostalgic about the past, about places and events that were probably hellish for the people living through them, no matter how fondly people remembered them today. For the people who worked and lived in Springfield in the 1800s . . . it must have felt like a penance. Statues and plaques commemorating those years would have struck them as wildly inappropriate.

But doing the opposite of honouring the past — loathing it, changing it, cleaning it up — seemed almost as bad to Yakabuski. An act of deceit and denial. Is that why all gentrified buildings and neighbourhoods looked tawdry and shameless to him? And why he felt a tinge of sadness whenever he saw a red-brick building that had been sand-blasted until it looked anemic. Then fitted with R-2000 windows that looked to him like penciled-on eyebrows.

Pick your devil.

Coogan Forestry had its offices on the top floor of the most sand-blasted red-brick building on Water Street. Although Yakabuski was not expected, Coogan agreed to see him, something that shocked the receptionist. "Yaka . . . ? I'm sorry, what was your name again?"

She had an earnest, imploring look in her eyes. She wanted to remember the important people.

"Yakabuski."

"Well, Mr. Yakabuski, he has a meeting starting in five minutes, but Mr. Coogan says you can go in . . . Will you be long?"

"I don't expect."

"This meeting has been scheduled for weeks . . . oh well, I guess you're a lucky man."

"I'm sorry?"

"No appointment, and he sees you right away? I've never seen that."

She smiled at him. Gave him another imploring look, no doubt thinking her facial expression looked different than what it was. A gaze of professional focus, perhaps. A stare of high-IQ attentiveness. Something like that.

Yakabuski wanted to tell the receptionist she needed a different definition for lucky if she thought it meant a private meeting with Tommy Coogan, but before he could give her that advice she was out of her chair, waving at him to follow her.

Coogan's office was glass and steel. No wood. Nothing that looked natural. It was a strange office, Yakabuski thought, for a man who owned a forestry company.

"Detective Yakabuski," Coogan said, as he stood and extended a hand across his desk. "To what do I owe the pleasure?"

"Just have a few more questions for you, Mr. Coogan."

The two men shook hands.

"About that woman who was killed in Port Henry?" Coogan asked.

"Not just one woman, anymore, I'm afraid."

"Not just . . . Please, have a seat. Gloria, can you bring us some coffee . . . You'll have a coffee, detective?"

Yakabuski nodded and sat in the chair Coogan was pointing toward. Coogan came out from behind his desk and sat on a settee across from him. Between the two men was a glass and chrome coffee table with nothing on it. No magazines, coasters, pamphlets or literature about the good work being done by Coogan Forestry. Nothing hung from the walls, either. Coogan's office looked like it had been delivered yesterday.

As they waited for the coffee, Yakabuski told Coogan about the six murders and the ongoing police investigation. When he was finished, Coogan said, "A serial killer on the Back Channel? I don't believe it . . . six homicides?"

"That's what we've confirmed. There could be more."

"Did any of these people work for me?"

"Two of the men did. Peter Kelly and Harold Byrne. Kelly was off-and-on in your bush camps. Byrne worked at your Smoke Island mill for nineteen years."

"Nineteen years? My goodness. What did you say his name was? Harold . . . "

"Harold Byrne."

" . . . I'm sorry, no. And the other man was Peter . . . "

"Kelly. Peter Kelly."

"Sorry, that's another *no*. Although there are more Kellys up and down the Springfield River than there are fish. Can't be expected to know every one of them." Coogan did not seem embarrassed, in the slightest, by not knowing the names of men who worked for him. Not even one who had done the trick for nearly twenty years. "So, your victims were men *and* women," he asked.

"Yes."

"These murders . . . they're not sexual, then?"

"They could be, having male and female victims doesn't rule that out. But you're right, they're not."

"How odd. I'm used to serial killers being . . . you know, perverts."

"This one is different."

"I see that . . . what can I do to help?"

"A homicide profiler for the RCMP told me many serial killers are transient. That got me to thinking — how many bush camps do you have around Port Henry?"

"Depends on the year. Depends on the price of softwood in the United States, the price of oak, the price of a new home in Peoria, the page-count of big city newspapers and whether there still *are* big-city newspapers. Depends on a great many things, detective."

"The last two years — how many camps?"

"Two."

"I'm going to need the names of every person who worked in those camps. When do they open?"

"November."

"Anyone there now?"

"This time of year, there'd be a maintenance crew."

"How many men?"

"Three, four, I'm not sure of the exact number."

"One for each camp?"

"No, the crew would work both."

"Put the names of those men at the top of your list."

"Hold it ... you think one of my men is the killer?"

"Don't know yet. I haven't run the names."

"Let me save you some time. I know these men. None of them is your killer."

"How would you know something like that Mr. Coogan?"

"How would I ... "

"Only one way I can think of to know something like that."

"That's not what I meant, and you know it."

"Of course I do. Same way I know you shouldn't be giving false assurances. Unless you were doing something else just now."

Coogan gave a half-snort, half-chuckle and leaned back in his chair. "When do you need the names?"

"I was thinking by the time I got on the elevator."

"Impossible. I'm already late for a meeting. I can have them for you by end of day."

"End of day would be ...

"Five."

Yakabuski looked across the glass table at Coogan's out-of-proportion patrician face and thought of asking him the other questions he had for him. Questions about Water Crawley and oak stands and absent tree markers. Decided he'd save those questions for another day. When he had more time.

"Five will be fine, Mr. Coogan. Appreciate your help. You can email the names. Here's my card."

31

MEAGHAN MCKENNA lay in bed, wondering where her uncle had gone. She had not seen or heard from Liam Burke in ten days. Ever since he gave the cops the slip, when they came to arrest him.

She had questions for him, and she was starting to get annoyed. How had he evaded the cops when they came to the cabin looking for him? His car was still parked out front.

How had he got rid of Walton Murphy, who was a giant of a man, twice the size of her uncle.

How had he done it?

And what was his plan now?

She felt she had a right to those answers. Her mother was dead, so she had skin in the game, and if her uncle was treating her like a child — if that's what was happening, protecting her in some misguided, I'm-a-man-and-know-what's-best-for-you sort of way — she would be furious.

As she lay in bed, her mind asking question after question, she heard a sound from outside.

Ca-ruuuuu-mp.

Must have been a raccoon, she told herself. Or a goose that had got itself lost and was flying around out there. She'd heard some geese that morning, which meant the birds were starting to move again, and a northern goose is just about the dumbest bird God ever invented. It'd be just like a goose to be honking in the middle of the night.

A comforter was pulled tight beneath her chin but there was enough of a chill in the room for her breath to come out as wisps of mist.

Yes, probably a goose. If not that, a racoon.

That the noise hadn't sounded like either animal meant nothing. She had, after all, been falling asleep.

And there it was again.

Ca-ruuuuu-mp.

Now she was wide awake.

Throwing off the comforter, Meaghan got out of bed. The sound had come from outside, by the front of the cabin. She tugged on the winter boots she'd left beside the bed and grabbed a brown cardigan from the back of the door. It wasn't a goose. She knew that now. Some other animal. One she wasn't familiar with.

During the spring floods there were all kinds of animals that got mixed up and moved around. There'd been a polar bear in Port Henry once, and strange birds were always showing up . . . "Accidentals," she'd heard them called, and accident seemed a good way to describe showing up in Port Henry if that wasn't your intention. The logger who knew about accidentals told her they weren't migratory birds neither, just birds from the other side of the Pole that got blown over sometimes in bad storms.

She didn't know if that was true. But there were strange animals moving around in the woods along the Back Channel, she knew that much.

She stretched out the sleeves of the cardigan, so they covered her hands, blew air into them and stood by the front window. It was the darkest time of night, well past midnight, a time when not even a starry night and a full moon would have shown her much of anything.

She tried to pick out objects as best she could. The lighter shade of black would be the laneway, beyond that the road leading to the river. The darker black would be the trees.

Ca-ruuuuu-mp.

She held her breath. There it was again. But the sound had shifted, calling out from a different location. This time, behind the cabin.

Like it was circling.

She took a step backwards, an exaggerated, high pantomime step. The sound had also been muffled, restrained, as though the animal was making a sound it didn't want to make.

There weren't many animals that did that.

She backed all the way into her brother's bedroom, cupped a hand over his mouth and shook his shoulder. "Be quiet," she whispered, when his eyes shot open. "There's someone outside the cabin."

The boy stood next to her, on his tiptoes, trying to peer out his bedroom window. "Should we get Lizzie?" he asked.

"No, we'd just get her all worried. Let her sleep."

"Don't you think she should be here?"

"Lizzie won't be any help to us, Robbie."

"What are we gonna do?"

"You ask too many questions. I need you dressed and ready to help."

"Help with what."

"Don't rightly know. Whatever comes up."

"Why do I have to get dressed? Why can't we stay inside?"

"You know what you do when someone's chasin' you, Robbie? When someone's coming after you?"

"N-n-no," the boy stammered.

"You chase back."

"But who's chasing us?"

"Don't know and it don't matter. You fight back. That's all you gotta know, Robbie. Now, go put on some clothes."

Meaghan wished she still had the shotgun. Her aunt had sold it at the market last summer, for a hundred dollars and some bushels of beets and potatoes that stayed in the root cellar for most of the winter. A good deal at the time. Not so good now, Meaghan thought, as she took the .22 calibre squirrel rifle from the front room closet.

"You stay inside by the front door and wait for me, Robbie.

His eyes welled up, and his lip started to quiver. She drew him into a tight hug. "Don't you start crying. Don't you dare start crying on me."

"Where you goin'?'"

"Outside to see what's there. Don't you follow me. Stay here."

She opened the front door a crack, peered outside, then opened the door a little wider and slipped through. She kept close to the walls of the cabin, where it was dark and shadowy, and made her way to the back. When she got there, she swore under her breath.

Dammit! Lizzie hadn't taken in the wash. The bed sheets had frozen and looked like white marble columns. Three rows of them. Giving a bright, ambient light that shone better than a full moon.

She would be easily spotted. If there was something out there, she'd be seen the second she stepped away from the cabin. Meaghan considered what to do, was still doing that when she saw a shadow pass in front of a sheet. The silhouette of a person. She could see it clear as day. See it better than hand puppets on a wall, which it half looked like, the shadows you'd see on the wall of a darkened room after you shone a flashlight behind your hands.

There was someone standing in front of Lizzie's bedroom window. They had something in their hands. She couldn't make out what it was.

Looks like the sheets won't be a problem after all, she thought, as she raised her rifle and took aim at the silhouette. Looks like they might even be a help. Bad news to good news in the blink of an eye. Don't see that too often.

She fired.

They stood in a small circle, staring at the ground.

"You got it, Meaghie."

"If I got it, it'd be laying here, Lizzie."

"Can't you see the blood?" her aunt asked.

"I see the blood. What I don't see is a body. Lord, I wish you hadn't sold that shotgun."

The old woman gave Meaghan an annoyed look and tightened the drawstring on her house coat.

"But you hit it," said Robbie. "Whatever it was, it won't be botherin' us any now."

"You can't let a wounded animal run around in the woods, Robbie. You got to put it down."

"*Was* it an animal?" asked her aunt.

Meaghan looked at the blood stains on the ground and didn't answer. She'd taken two shots, dead centre on the silhouette, and why there wasn't a body lying there, she didn't understand.

"You need to go back inside, Lizzie. Push furniture in front of the door. Get Robbie to help you."

"Furniture in front of the door? What kind of an animal do ya think ya wounded, girl?"

"Just do it, Lizzie! Please!"

Her aunt grabbed Robbie's hand and went back inside the cabin.

Meaghan headed into the forest, moving easily around the towering pine, even though it was so dark she couldn't see past the end of her fingers. She knew the pattern of old growth forests, the space there would be between the trees. She could tell by the feel of roots beneath her feet how far away the base of a tree would be, and what the pitch of the land would be five steps ahead.

She had a pen flashlight in the pocket of her cardigan and was tempted to use it. She was having trouble following the blood trail, but she didn't know if the person she was chasing had a gun. She hadn't seen one. And there had been no return fire.

Odds would be in favour of the person not having a gun. She might be taking no risk, by turning on the flashlight.

She might also be lighting herself up like a shooting range target if she was wrong about the gun. A gun was a bad thing to be wrong about. Odds worked differently with guns.

She was still debating whether to use the flashlight when she came out of a gully and saw car headlights in the distance. She fell to the ground. Stayed rock still for several minutes.

Eventually, she lifted her head and took another look at the lights. The car wasn't moving. She couldn't hear a motor, either. She waited a few more minutes, then began crawling toward the lights. When she was fifty feet away, she saw that the car was a Honda Civic. Headlights on. Motor not running.

When she got to within twenty feet, she yelled, "Whoever's in that Honda, you better come out. I got a rifle pointed right at ya."

No answer. She waited another minute and then stood, keeping her rifle pointed at the driver's side of the front windshield. She took slow steps until she reached the car, then carefully opened the driver's door.

A man fell out. Covered in blood. She took her pen flashlight from the pocket of her cardigan and clicked it on. The brutalized face of Doctor Peter Atkinson popped out of the darkness.

Behind her, she heard her brother say, "Gosh, Meaghie, how many times did ya shoot him?"

It was mid-afternoon by the time Yakabuski reached the McKenna farm. By then, the laneway leading into the cabin was lined with patrol cars and unmarked police vehicles. Yellow crime scene tape ran around the cabin and down toward the river.

There was an ambulance parked beside the cabin, but Yakabuski didn't see anyone inside the vehicle, or inside the perimeter.

"Glad you're here, Yak," Griffin said, walking up to him. "Don't know if I could have held them off much longer. The inspector says he's got to get going in the next twenty minutes or he'll lose the light."

"I was in court all morning, couldn't get away. Where is the inspector?"

"He's inside the perimeter, behind the cabin, by the car. You can't see him from here."

"Anyone with him?"

"No, just him. Like I said, they've been waiting for you."

"What about the ambulance?"

"First on scene. Didn't get the memo, so they drove right up to the cabin. The inspector already yelled at them. They're over there, if you want to talk to them." She pointed toward two ambulance attendants, who quickly looked away when Yakabuski turned his head. "The inspector says they went into the cabin and took one walk down to the car, so not much time inside the perimeter. He thinks you're OK."

"Did he say anything else?"

"Yeah, he said you're not going to like the car."

Yakabuski walked inside the tire ruts the ambulance made when it drove up to the cabin, careful not to step on any footprints. The car was about a quarter mile from the cabin. When he got there, he took some plastic baggies from the pocket of his coat.

"Glad you could make it," said Newton.

"Been in court all day."

"So I heard," the inspector replied. "Well, just need you to do your magic, and we can get started here."

The ground was muddy and there were footprints everywhere. Yakabuski could see two sets of studded boot-prints, another set that looked like running shoes, another set that didn't have much in the way of tread. Dress shoes of some sort.

"Let me see the bottom of your shoes, Newt."

The inspector raised his left foot, then his right. Florsheim's. There were the dress shoes.

Yakabuski walked around the vehicle and saw the doctor's

body. It was half in, half out of the car. The head was almost touching the mud. The right foot still touched the gas pedal.

"Have you looked at the doctor's shoes?"

"Dry as a rock. He never got out of the car."

Yakabuski looked toward the cabin. While he did that, he began taking bent pieces of cardboard from one of the baggies. The pieces were different colours and had numbers stenciled on them.

He put a piece of blue cardboard, with the number one on it, inside the running shoe print. He then took a piece of yellow cardboard and placed it inside one of the boot prints. He began walking toward the cabin, putting down pieces of cardboard as he went.

"Call the paramedics down here," he yelled, and Newton took out his cell phone.

As he made his way to the cabin, Yakabuski pulled green pieces of cardboard from another baggie and put some of those down as well.

"You've seen this blood trail?" Yakabuski yelled.

"I've seen it. Goes from the car to the cabin."

"But the doctor never got out of the vehicle?"

"He's still wearing his seatbelt."

Yakabuski pushed some bed sheets out of his way and walked to the rear window of the cabin. He knelt and examined the ground beneath the window. He put down some red and white pieces of cardboard, then stood and took a photo of what he had done. He put the baggies in his pocket.

When Yakabuski returned to the Honda, the two paramedics were waiting.

"Let me see your boots," he said.

"You want us to take them off?" one of them asked.

"Just need to see the soles. Inspector Newton has already explained crime scene rules to you gentlemen, is that right? I don't need to do it again?"

"No, sir," the paramedics said, as they shook their heads and raised their feet.

"Good. I won't bother with a report this time. But don't let me see this sort of mistake again."

Yakabuski looked at the soles of their boots and pulled out his cell phone. "Keep them there, I need a photo."

Once the paramedics were gone, Yakabuski showed Newton the photo he had just taken, then the photo of the ground beneath the rear window of the McKenna cabin.

"Yellow will be the paramedics," he said. "I'm betting green is Meaghan McKenna. She found the body?"

"She did."

"Green is Meaghan McKenna. Red will be the boy. White will be Lizzie McKenna."

"And blue?"

"That's our killer. Looks like a size 11 Nike."

32

THE PARAMEDICS MOVED the doctor's body to the ambulance and were gone thirty minutes later. The patrol cars left the same time as the ambulance. Newton and another I-dent cop began working around the car, and along the blood trail leading to the cabin, taking photos and collecting evidence. They didn't speak as they worked and it suddenly seemed oddly peaceful, the woods around the McKenna cabin, no longer the frenetic, police-running-everywhere scene that had greeted Yakabuski two hours earlier.

He sat on the front porch of the cabin with Griffin and Meaghan. Robbie McKenna was inside the cabin, playing a game on Griffin's phone. Aunt Lizzie had gone to bed. Newton and the other I-dent cop were too far away to be seen, although you could hear their voices from time to time.

"I don't understand what happened," said Meaghan. "I shot someone. I know I did. The doctor didn't look shot. Not from no squirrel rifle."

"He was stabbed to death. His death had nothing to do with you, Meaghan."

"But I followed his blood right to his car after I shot him."

"I don't think you shot anyone."

"I ain't a bad shot, Detective Yakabuski. And the person I shot was lit up bright as day. No way I missed him."

"He was behind the bedsheets, is that right? That's what you mean by bright as day, you saw his silhouette through a white bedsheet."

"That's right."

"Come here, I want to show you something"

She followed Yakabuski to the back of the cabin. He talked

as they walked. "A silhouette is a distortion. It's never the actual size of the thing you're looking at. It's like the shadow that follows you down a street."

They were standing in front of the rear window. Yakabuski pointed at two small holes that were about three feet above the top of the window frame. "Those will be your bullets. They went well above the person, unless they stood eight feet tall. I'm guessing you were aiming for the head?"

The girl kicked at some dirt and didn't answer right away. Eventually, she said, "Can't rightly remember."

"I thought you were a great shot."

"'Parently not as good as I thought. Never knew 'bout that silhouette trick. But the blood — I must have hit something?"

"It's the doctor's blood. It goes from his car right to this window. Whoever was out here last night must have killed the doctor, gotten some of his blood on their clothes, and that was the blood trail you were following."

"Why was the doctor here?"

"I don't know for sure, but if I had to guess, I'd say he came out to apologize to you."

33

MEAGHAN MCKENNA was upset. She was almost screaming at Yakabuski.

"I ain't leavin'. Not me, not Robbie, not Lizzie. This is our home."

"Meaghan, it's not safe to stay here."

"This is the Back Channel. Safe got nothin' to do with anythin'. Never did."

"You won't be gone long, Meaghan. This killer . . . we'll find them."

"Yeah, when? When are you gonna catch this freak?"

"You're right, I can't say how long it will take. But someone likely tried to kill you tonight, Meaghan. It was only the doctor showing up unexpectedly that saved you. We can't take any more chances. You and Robbie, Aunt Lizzie, we need you all to leave."

"To go where?"

"We'll arrange accommodation for you and your family in Springfield."

"Ain't happenin'. Ain't gonna be chased from my home."

"Meaghan, we don't have the manpower to post police officers in front of your cabin. You need to come with us to Springfield."

"Never asked you for no cops. I can take care of myself. Can take care of Robbie and Aunt Lizzie just fine, too."

"This isn't about self-reliance, Meaghan. It's about protecting yourself. Why won't you let us help you?"

She didn't reply. Gave Yakabuski a look that let him know she had said everything she intended to say. She was done. A teenage girl who didn't over-talk or over-protest.

Yakabuski was staring at a unicorn.

Who was staring back, her arms crossed, and her chin thrust forward. Griffin walked up behind him and said, "Yak, can I talk to you a minute?"

They stood beside their vehicles, Yakabuski thinking about what Griffin had just proposed. Meaghan was still on the porch. They were just out of earshot.

"You sure you want to do this?" he asked.

"Solves a few problems, doesn't it?"

"Detaining the McKennas as material witnesses would solve just as many."

"Think a judge will give you an order for all three? Only the girl witnessed anything."

"When I explain the situation, there's a good chance."

Griffin started to laugh. "Good chance? Is that what I just heard? Didn't I get advice from you once about what 'good chance' means? Same thing as ninety-five percent guaranteed, if I remember right."

Yakabuski chuckled. "Ninety-five-per-cent guaranteed means not guaranteed."

"And good chance means only a chance. Why don't we at least see what she thinks of the idea."

"All right. Let's go talk to her."

Meaghan gave Yakabuski a suspicious look. "She wants to stay here? Why would she want to do something like that?"

"To protect you, Meaghan. Because she's a police officer who wants to help you.

"Where would she sleep?"

"I don't mind sleeping on the porch," answered Griffin. "I won't be taking anyone's bed."

"A cop living in my house? Shit, my mom and dad would

be rollin' in their graves. It ain't gonna happen."

"The other option, Meaghan, is to have a judge declare you and your family material witnesses. Then you'd have no choice. You'd have to come with us."

"You'd do that?"

"In a heartbeat."

"I'd run away."

"Then you'd be a fugitive. Makes my job easier. No problem hanging onto you after that."

"If you catch me."

"Meaghan . . . we'll catch you. You'll be creating a lot of trouble for nothing. It's a dumb risk. And dangerous for your family, too. Do you really want your brother to be on the run? The smart move would be to let Constable Griffin stay with you. It's a compromise solution. We can protect you. And you get to stay in your home."

The arms stayed crossed. The jaw stayed clenched. But a minute later, Meaghan said, "She gotta bring her own food. I ain't feeding her."

34

LIAM BURKE HAD STAYED in the woods around his sister's cabin after eluding the police. He was comfortable in the woods. Could go for weeks with only an army knife and a bed roll. He also had an abandoned cook-shed less than a mile from his sister's cabin, with provisions inside.

Burke knew if the cops had come all the way to the Back Channel to arrest him, they would find him as soon as he returned to Springfield. Or to one of his trailers in Port Henry. He needed to disappear for a while.

He kept watch on his sister's cabin while in hiding, as that seemed a smart thing to do. Until he figured out who was killing people along the Back Channel, his niece and nephew could be in danger. He was in the woods behind the cabin when he heard a man screaming. In the distance. Not from the cabin.

So, he stayed where he was, and twenty minutes later a man passed him, no more than twenty feet away. Burke followed the man to the cabin, was getting ready to tackle him, when his niece came around the corner and fired two shots at the man, who quickly turned and ran.

Burke nearly lost him after that. Hadn't been expecting to follow someone hightailing it into the woods. But the man proved easy to track, even on a dark, almost starless night.

He carried a red gas can.

As soon as Burke saw the can, the man was as easy to track as a transmitter-tagged wolf. He kept his distance, not wanting to confront his quarry right away, curious to know where he was heading, and whether there might be others waiting for him.

Not sure, even, if it was a man he was tracking. That was an assumption, he reminded himself, and you don't make those, not if you wanted to stay one step ahead of the game, not if you want to stay *in the game*.

Keep your distance. Control your curiosity. You have plenty of time.

Burke followed his quarry through the woods, a zig-zagging path that made him wonder several times if the person had lost his way. They ended up on an old logging road, where a car was parked. The person threw the gas can in the trunk, jumped into the driver's seat and started the motor.

Burke strode onto the logging road, pointed a pistol at one of the car's front tires, and fired.

There was a loud bang when the tire exploded. Burke pointed the gun at the car's windshield.

"Next one's headin' your way, my friend. Get out."

For several seconds, nothing happened. The car engine continued rumbling, two strong headlights continued shining through the forest, illuminating and distorting the trunks of giant pine, and the winding dirt road.

Then the engine stopped, the lights went out, and a car door opened.

Never make assumptions. Never be surprised. Those lessons had been drilled into Burke as deeply and profoundly as a deep-hole gusher into the hardpack outside some dirt-poor Texas town.

Never make assumptions. Never be surprised. Lessons learned and defended long ago, and yet, right then, all Liam Burke could do was stare in disbelief at the person who had stepped out of the car.

"On your knees, hands behind your head."

The person did as Burke demanded. The car door was open, and Burke pushed a button on the console to pop the trunk. Took out the gas can and gave it a shake.

"This is full. Were you going to burn down my sister's cabin?"

The person stared at Burke but didn't answer.

"My niece and nephew live there."

"So does your aunt," the person said. "You don't care about the old lady?"

There was no fear in the person's voice. No tremor or hesitation.

"She's not my aunt," Burke answered.

"Right — she's not your blood. I forgot. That matters a great deal on the Back Channel, doesn't it?"

"You would know."

"We all know."

Burke stared in wonder at the person kneeling before him. There was a crooked, joyful smile on their face, a smile as humourless and threatening as any Burke had seen, and he had seen many in his life. Like the twisted, soulless grin the chief bull at C Block had on his face whenever he took a new inmate to the boiler room of the Wentworth Pen. Where handcuffs were already dangling from the pipes and a hidden toolbox contained whips, butt-plugs and other instruments of torture and degradation.

Burke considered himself a bad ass, someone you should cross the street to avoid, but ever since doing a five-year stint at Wentworth, he had known there were people on the planet who made him look like a choir boy. Pure evil that had taken human form.

People like that C-Block guard operated on a different level of sin and depravity and even when you think you're tough and capable and ready for anything the world can throw at you — you're not.

"What did my sister ever do to you?" Burke asked.

"Nothing."

"So, why did you kill her?"

"She was an instrument. Like the rest of us. Nothing is

personal here, Liam. How could it be?"

"Instrument? What's that supposed to mean?"

"We all need to be useful, Liam. You understand that. If we're not useful, then we're just taking up space. Free will, on *the best of days*, is merely the right to decide how you're going to be useful."

"How was my sister useful to you?"

"By dying."

Burke's skin tingled and turned cold right then. As though he had walked through a spider web.

"How did you benefit from my sister's death?"

"Ahhh . . . that's the mystery, isn't it? Don't think I'm going to help you with that one."

The person began to laugh, a low guttural sound that became a maniacal, high-pitched scream, one that reminded Burke of feral animals baying at night.

When the laughing stopped, Burke said, "You're insane. I had no idea. You've hidden it well."

"You give me too much credit. This is merely the first time you've noticed. If you'd paid more attention, you might have seen it too."

"Seen what?"

"What's been happening along the Back Channel. And what's *about* to happen."

You think you're ready for what the world can throw at you, but you're not. At least, not in any practical or useful way, not in any way that might change the outcome. Maybe it hurts less when the end comes. If you had faith. If you had confidence in your abilities. But who knows? No one has stuck around to tell the tale.

Never make assumptions. Never be surprised. Those were the thoughts Liam Burke had rolling through his head when he noticed the person kneeling on the dirt road in front of him no longer had their hands clasped behind their head.

35

TO MEAGHAN'S SURPRISE, it wasn't that bad having Constable Donna Griffin living with them. She helped with the chores — kept the airtight burning, weeded the vegetable garden, minded Robbie. Her little brother was normally a flight risk, but he followed Griffin around like a runt puppy. Which he was, in a sad, truthful way, so maybe that made sense.

The cop was good with Lizzie, too. Which wasn't easy. Her great-aunt was quarrelsome and confrontational on her best days, mean and nasty on the bad ones, yet Griffin had her laughing and playing cards, forgetting the rules of cribbage every game. Griffin patiently re-explaining — "fifteen two, fifteen four, double-run is eight, you have twelve points, Ms. McKenna." Then they'd play another game, and Aunt Lizzie would forget how to count. Or how to peg. Or that she was playing cards.

Maybe her brother and great-aunt gravitated to Griffin because she was competent. If you lived on the Back Channel, you were familiar with the opposite — with plans that always failed, promises that were never kept, appointments that were never remembered, work that would be done tomorrow.

It was different with this cop. If Griffin said she was going to do something, she did it. Not a lot of fuss about it, either. She didn't talk about it, or make sure you knew what she was doing, the way her father had. When he was living with them. Any work that got done by him, he made a point to brag about it. To let them all know how "difficult" it had been. Like by doing this chore or that job meant they owed him something. Something that good men — good husbands and fathers considered as part of their duty to their families. But not her father.

Not Bobby McKenna.

It was different with this cop. She didn't seem to be playing anybody. Meaghan had worried about that when Griffin had first arrived. That she would be here under false pretences, not protecting them but spying on them. Snooping around. An undercover cop, almost, living in the cabin and when she had that thought she imagined her father being told this and she laughed.

Did life keep getting stranger as you got older? Or did it plateau at some age?

Meaghan thought about Griffin's question.

"I ain't scared," she answered eventually. "Maybe I'm worried . . . a little."

"Someone attacked you. Anyone would be scared right now."

Meaghan looked away. Clouds hung low in a grey sky, pushed down by a band of heavy air that you could actually see, a huge patch of sky sitting above the clouds, riven into different coloured bands of black and grey, a sky that resembled sheets of shale.

"That ain't it," she said. "I don't know what's happenin' any-more."

"That's what has you worried?" asked Griffin.

"Yeah."

"None of us know that, Meaghan."

"Well . . . I thought I did. When Momma was killed, I thought I knew what was happenin' and what I needed to do. Thought I was going to stay a few steps ahead of the game. Now . . . I ain't got a clue what game we're even playing."

"Meghan, you've lost me."

Meaghan looked at Griffin and knew it was time to decide. Trust a cop or not trust a cop — she couldn't dance around it anymore. Couldn't waste time thinking about it. She imagined her dad sitting with her right then and what he would tell her —

"Trust no one, Meaghie, that's how you stay safe in this

world; how you stay protected. Don't let the bastards near you and they can't hurt you. People living downriver — they're all bastards. Remember that girl. Cops ain't any different. She's no different. Listen up, child. It's good advice your daddy's givin' ya."

But maybe he was wrong. Maybe there was a different way of looking at the world.

First time that thought had occurred to her.

"I thought it was Wally Murphy who killed my momma," she said. "I was going to do somethin' about it, too, but then he goes and gets himself killed, so now . . . I know nothin'. That's what scares me."

"What do you mean, you were going to do something about it?"

Meaghan didn't answer.

Griffin reached out and gave the girl's shoulder a gentle squeeze. "Well, I'm glad you didn't. But why did you think it was Walton Murphy?"

"'Cause I seen him and Momma arguin' a couple weeks 'fore she went missing.

"Where?"

"Port Henry. We saw him in front of the post office. Momma told me to go wait in the car, but they were yellin' at each other for a few minutes, so they were easy to hear. Momma even gave him a shove."

"What was the argument about?"

"Money. I went to see him the day I seen Momma's body. At his trailer. Asked him straight up if he'd done it."

"My gosh. What happened when you did that?"

"He started chokin' me. Might have killed me, I guess, but then his daughter and grandson walked in on us, and he stopped."

"Meaghan! What were you *thinking*?"

"I was thinkin' someone needed to pay for killin' my Momma."

"Why didn't you *tell us* any of this?"

"'Cause you're cops."

"Oh, sweetheart," said Griffin, and she leaned in and gave Meghan a hug. "You can trust us, honest you can. You mentioned something about money — can you remember what else they said?"

"Momma said he owed her money, and he better get it to her soon, or there was going to be all hell to pay. Wally said he'd have her money soon enough 'cause he was 'bout to be rich. Momma gave him a shove and called him stupid, but he kept yellin' at her, sayin' he was goin' to be rich, he'd have plenty of money. Momma would have plenty of money, too."

"About to be rich — were those his exact words?"

"Well, there was a bunch of swearin', too, but he did say he was about to be rich. That's what he said."

"What did your mother say when she got back in the car?" Griffin asked.

"She said Wally Murphy was trying to con her, and it'd be a cold day in hell when a Murphy got one over on a McKenna."

"That's it? Nothing specific?"

"Nothin'. Although on the way home she did somethin' strange. We were halfway up the Channel when she suddenly turned around and we went back to Port Henry, to the post office. She told me to wait in the car, and she went inside, must have been gone ten minutes or more. We'd already collected the mail, so I don't know what she was doin' in there. She didn't come out with nothin', neither, so, you tell me."

"About to be rich. I wonder what he meant by that?"

"I got no idea," said Meaghan. "Did you find anythin' at his trailer?"

"The I-dent department spent a week going through that trailer. They didn't find anything."

"Nothing 'bout my momma?"

"No."

"What about his hidey-hole? What did you find there?"

"His what?"

36

GRIFFIN DROVE DOWN the laneway, then onto the logging road that would take them to Port Henry. The sun trickled through the tree canopy and fell like flakes of sunshine on the forest floor. Grey jays chirped and flew through the trees, and whenever the river came into view, when they were atop a hill, or when there was a sudden clearing in the forest, it was a curving ribbon of slow-moving blue water.

There was a beauty to the Back Channel that Griffin hadn't noticed until she began living at the McKenna cabin. A freedom, too, the sort that comes from living on land no one else wants and possessing nothing that another person would ever covet.

Maybe people living along the Back Channel weren't as crazy as everyone thought. As crazy as *she* had once thought.

There was something about the Back Channel that set it apart, that made it special in some strange way, as though it ran parallel to the rest of the world, kept different time, lived under a different sun, watched different stars appear in a different sky.

Now, the outside world had come calling and the Back Channel had its first serial killer. Someone who was keeping a deadly secret, in a place where people knew how to keep secrets. After all, secrets were one of the few things people on the Back Channel were allowed to own.

A hidey hole. *Why hadn't they thought of that?*

Walton Murphy's trailer sat on a knoll on the edge of the trailer park. It had been painted a bordello red, a colour so bright you could see the trailer from the tip of Smoke Island, even on the foggiest of days. Meaghan told Griffin that Murphy used to boast about his home being a navigation buoy, and how he threatened many times to put a Kelly-green trailer next to it, so he'd have a proper pair.

Although he was never drunk enough to carry through with the idea. Just drunk enough to paint the first one.

Griffin parked in front of the trailer. It had aged badly, perched on a knoll the way it was, and the bright red had faded long ago. The trailer looked brittle and old and vaguely like a rusted pop can. Like something you could step upon, and you'd be doing it a favour.

"Where should we look?" she asked, turning to the girl.

"It'll be outside," answered Meaghan. "Next to a tree, under a rock, it'll be marked somehow."

"You think it will be buried?"

"More'n likely. Most of 'em are."

"All right, do you want to split up?"

"Why don't we see where that trail goes, first."

Griffin looked to where the girl was pointing. "What trail?"

"You don't see that?"

Griffin kept staring. She leaned forward, so her nose was almost touching the windshield. "You see a trail through those trees?"

The girl rolled her eyes. "You better follow me."

Meaghan found Walton Murphy's hidey-hole twenty minutes later. It was under a flat rock, inside a hackberry bush. You couldn't see the rock until you were practically standing on top of it. The girl had gone straight to the bush as soon as they started the search.

It took both of them to turn over the rock, it was that heavy. Beneath it they found a tin-metal box, rectangular in shape, looked like one of the boxes some of the vendors at the market used to hold their money.

The clasp on the box was badly bent and Griffin struggled to open it. Didn't seem like Murphy used his hidey hole all that often. They finally got the box open, and Griffin poured the contents onto the ground. There was a roll of money. An old pistol. A framed photograph of a man and woman standing on the steps of a church. And an unsealed manilla envelope.

Griffin took some papers from the envelope.

"What are they?" asked the girl.

Griffin read for a few seconds, then looked up at Meaghan. "It's a newspaper story."

"About what?"

"The Port Henry Colony Road."

IV

SCREAMING AT GOD

FOURTH CLUE

York, 1866

The notary wore a wig that had seen better days. Grey and mottled, in need of a cleaning, a sad looking hairpiece that not even the dim light of a windowless office could disguise.

The agent sat the other side of the notary's desk. He had come late in the day and looked tired. His face was creased and weathered, his skin as dark as the bookcases in the office.

The notary said, "You shouldn't have come, Patrick. You must know that. I can be arrested merely for talking to you."

"There is no grand achievement in that," the agent replied. "In this colony, you can be arrested if your name is Allan and the governor outlaws the name Allan."

The notary laughed, a deep baritone laugh that turned into a hacking cough. The walls of his office were hewn stone, and although it was late spring there was still a winter dampness to the room.

"You're right about that, my friend. And your name has been outlawed. Are you aware how badly the new governor wants to find you?"

"Five thousand pounds."

"A princely sum. I should try to collect it myself. I could use the funds. And I need only say where you are. I need not confront you."

"Tell the new governor about this meeting and you'll be confronting me soon enough, William."

The notary gave the agent a hard look but couldn't hold it. He shook his head and blew out a frustrated breath. "I thought you were dead, Patrick. Everyone thinks that. Everyone except the governor, I suppose. It is good to see you. Where have you been hiding?"

"Port Henry."

"The settlers knew you were there?"

"Some did, yes, they gave me shelter."

"With a five-thousand-pound bounty on your head, people as poor as church mice did that for you?"

"Yes."

The notary had a doubtful expression on his face. Like the agent, his skin was worn and creased, and it would have been difficult to guess his age. He stared at the agent a while before asking, "Why did you do it, Patrick?"

"It needed to be done. To do nothing . . . it mattered too much."

"What did?"

"The truth about what has happened on the Back Channel of the Springfield River, what the government did to the people they sent there, how the people fought back — the story matters."

The notary gave him a puzzled look. When the agent saw this, he knew more was needed. For what he was asking of his old friend, there should be more.

"If you don't have a truthful record, William, what do you have in this world? Without that, we are living in a fantasy created by men who hide in their gilded homes, sitting back in their comfortable leather chairs, sipping whiskey and soda, looking at maps of the world, and believing God has given them licence to rule it all."

He set his satchel on the desk. "A true story is the only way people like you and I can fight back."

The notary looked at the satchel. It was old, the leather burred and cracked, the colour a weathered grey. "You did more than fight, my friend."

"I don't see it that way."

"You are the only one, then. Are there declarations in that satchel?"

"Fifteen. You need only notarize and register them. They have already been witnessed."

"Register declarations taken under warrant of a wanted man?"

"I was not a fugitive when I took then, William. You'd be breaking no law by registering them."

"I've been told there were no improvements made to the land. No cash crops. Not even hemp."

"That's correct."

"Cattle?"

"Cattle would starve. Any domestic animal would starve. The land up there ... God created it for predators, not for cows and goats."

"What is the improvement, then?"

"Fences."

"Pardon?"

"They have built fences from the rock the government granted them. The fences run for miles. They are some of the most remarkable things I have ever seen."

"You are asking me to affix my seal to rock fences?"

The agent looked at the notary and knew more was still needed. "The Indians along the Upper Divide tell a story of how this land was created. Have you heard it?" he asked.

"I pay no heed to Indian tales."

"The story was told to Champlain the first time he visited the New World, during a grand feast held in his honour. It is the oldest story this land has."

"I pay less heed to the tales of Frenchmen."

"This one is worth a listen. Let me tell it to you."

Three brothers once lived in paradise. One day the brothers decided to leave paradise and see the rest of the world. Day after day the brothers travelled and saw wonders they had never seen nor imagined: Animals with fur as thick and lustrous as moss, who could swim as well as they walked. Trees that altered *colour with the alteration of the seasons. Fish that grew longer than most men.*

They had been travelling many days when God suddenly appeared before them and asked, "Why have you left paradise?"

"We wished to see the world," the brothers answered.

"Then return home. I have given you everything you will ever need. It is a sin to spurn my grace. Return to paradise."

After saying this, God left, and the brothers debated what to do. They soon decided to defy God and resume their journey. The anticipation of new wonders, new worlds, was like a fever to them.

The next night a vengeful, wrathful God reappeared and smote the eldest brother, turning him into a giant white pine. "Return to paradise," God roared. "Do not defy Me again."

Fearful and trembling, the remaining brothers began the journey home. But although they mourned their eldest brother, and feared God, they were soon marvelling again at the wonders around them: birds with tail feathers that furled and unfurled as easily as a fan. Rivers with islands of cool, dark forests — too many islands to count. A moon as red as the embers of a late-night cook fire.

So enthralled were the brothers, when they reached paradise, they walked right by it. Did not even notice. The next night an angry, vengeful God re-appeared and smote the eldest brother, turning him into a granite boulder.

"How dare you defy Me," God roared at the last brother. "You are banished from Paradise. Remain here and live with what you have wrought."

The youngest brother did as God demanded. He stayed in this new world of pine and rock. After many years of struggle and solitude, a woman came to him. With this woman he fell in love and had many children. Their children had many children.

When he was an old man God returned, and God was pleased. "You have learned obedience. Your banishment is ended. You may return home. Paradise is waiting."

Upon hearing this, the last brother looked around at the world his brothers had created: at the dark green forests and high-cliff rivers, the rugged trails and ragged lakes, the hard, unforgiving land where he and his family lived. When he had taken it all in, he turned back to God and yelled, in anger and in awe: "No! It is you that must leave, my Lord! I am already home!"

When the agent finished his story, neither man spoke. Eventually, the notary ran his fingers through his wig and asked, "Why have you told me this, Patrick?"

"Because you know what the Back Channel is like. You have been there, have you not?"

"I helped survey the colony road."

"Then you know what's been done to these people. You know the injury."

"The injury?"

"Is that not a fair word?"

The notary shifted his weight uncomfortably in his chair. "I do not understand the story."

"The settlers on the Back Channel have claimed that cursed land as their home. This is the least we can do for them."

"Giving them title to useless land; this is doing them a favour?"

"That's not what you'd be doing, William."

"Then, what would I be doing, Patrick? What is it you are asking of me?"

"I'm asking that you let them scream at God."

In the silence that followed, the shadows in the notary's office grew long, the air chilled, and the din of the busy street the other side of the stone walls became intermittent, then distant, then disappeared altogether. The notary leaned forward and pulled the satchel toward him. He undid the buckle and removed a stack of papers.

He counted out fifteen sheets, then lit a candle beneath a wax pot, opened a drawer in his desk and removed a brass seal. He waited until tiny bubbles appeared on the surface of the wax, then inserted the seal, took it out, and pressed down upon a sheet. He returned the seal to the wax pot, set aside the paper with the melting wax to the other side of the desk and reached for another sheet.

Neither man spoke while the notary worked. When he was finished, he blew out the candle, and although it had not provided much light, when the flame went out the room turned dark.

"You should leave," the notary said.

"When will they be registered?"

"Tomorrow. I'll do it when no one is in the office . . . tomorrow afternoon. It will be done by then."

The agent stood and extended his hand. The notary stayed seated. "You were never here, Patrick. I wish you safe travels."

37

EDMUND MONK HAD his office in what most people in Springfield called the Arts Tower, although its formal name was the Dorothy Hendricks Centre for the Humanities. It was the tallest building on the campus of Springfield Valley Community College. Also, the tallest in Springfield, if you excluded the rent-geared-to-income apartment buildings on the North Shore, which most people were willing to do.

Monk's office was on the twelfth floor of the Arts Tower, but the wrong side of the building, with a north-facing view of Highway 7 and the truck yards on the edge of town. The south-facing side had a view of the Springfield River.

The professor was a small man, with a grey-and-black ponytail, thick glasses, and a way of swiveling his head when he got excited that reminded Yakabuski of a curious mouse. He kept waiting for the professor to turn his hands upside down and hold them close to his mouth, but it never happened.

"I have your book at home," Monk told him after they had shaken hands. "I haven't read it yet, but I intend to. It's in my to-be-read pile of books on my nightstand. You should see my stack, almost as tall as me. But that's a good sign — making it to my nightstand — means it's going to happen."

The professor wore sweatpants and a tee-shirt from a local ice cream shoppe. *Licks and Scoops*. He nodded vigorously and said again, "It's going to happen."

"I didn't write the book, professor. It was a reporter with the *Sentinel*. I'm sure he appreciates your interest. Reason I'm here — your name has come up in a homicide investigation."

"*What?*"

"A newspaper article was found among the possessions of Walton Murphy. Mr. Murphy was killed recently. His body was found in the Port Henry harbour last month."

Monk took the newspaper from Yakabuski. "I remember this story. It was written because of the commemorative plaque the city put up last year in honour of the Colony Road."

"I recall the ceremony. As you can see, your name is underlined a few times."

"Yes, I see that."

"Do you know why Mr. Murphy would have kept this newspaper article? He must have considered it important. He kept it in a safe place, along with some of his valuables."

"Murphy, you say; that's the name of your murder victim?"

"Yes, Walton Murphy. He lived in the trailer park in Port Henry. Most people called him Wally."

"Give me a minute."

The professor started typing on his computer. Then he leaned forward, lifted his glasses until they were perched on his head, and read what was on his screen. "I thought the name sounded familiar. I talked to Mr. Murphy this spring. I have it in my calendar."

"You had a meeting with him?"

"No, he phoned. Although we scheduled a meeting after that. We chatted for nearly an hour. Long enough for me to put the call in my daily logs. Walton Murphy. From Port Henry. Yes, I remember."

"Why did he contact you?"

"He had questions about that newspaper story. He kept it with his valuables, you say? You mean a safe?"

"A Back Channel sort of safe. What questions did he have?"

"Quite a few. His family was one of the first to settle along the Back Channel. The Murphys got their land grant in 1860. I found our talk quite fascinating. I had as many questions for him as he had for me."

"Colony roads are an area of specialty for you, is that right, Mr. Monk?"

"Nineteenth-century colonial history and economics — that's the specialty. Colony roads are an important component to that field of study."

"You seem to have a low opinion of colony roads. Judging by the newspaper article."

"Oh, absolutely. They were an utter fraud. The territorial governments of the day were all corrupt. They used the goal of "interior settlement" — that was the phrase that got you cash — to extract millions of dollars from the public purse. The money was ostensibly to build colony roads, although much of the money simply disappeared. The colony roads were all failures. Not a one was completed.

"Most of them, like the road to Port Henry, never even came close. The roads failed because they went to places where the government wanted settlement — where there weren't people — but why weren't people living there? Most of the time, it was because the land was crap.

"It was a cruel deception, settlement of this country; cruel for the people who had their land stolen, and cruel for most of the people given the land grants. The ones who administered the grants and built the roads, those people got rich. The people who came *for the land?* They got rock, and swamp, and deprivation that is almost unimaginable to us today."

"This includes the Port Henry Colony Road?" asked Yakabuski.

"Perhaps the worst of them all. It made no sense trying to get settlement along the Back Channel of the Springfield River. All the commerce was on the main channel. You were cut off from everything. And you couldn't build a corduroy road. It's all bog up there.

"You would have needed to elevate the shoreline two or three feet to get a road built. Or to get boats and logs down the channel. The lumber companies learned that the hard way."

"Lumber companies?"

"Yes, the white pine stands along the Back Channel are spectacular, some of the largest old-growth trees you'll find anywhere in the world. When they were building the Colony Road, timber rights were sold to O'Hearn, Coogan, Gillies — they all bought rights. Only to discover they couldn't float logs down the river to their mills in Springfield. The channel was too shallow. The lumber barons lost millions.

"Everything about Port Henry was a disaster. Some bureaucrat in Toronto saw the back channel of the Springfield River, saw no people were living there, and penciled in a colony road. That is honestly what happened. The government of the day spent nearly 200,000 pounds on a corduroy road that travelled about as far as the bus stop outside this building."

Monk started laughing. He was enjoying himself. "Maybe a little farther," he admitted. "But not much. It was an impossible task, and the government likely knew that before the road was even started."

"The people given the land grants were mostly Irish, were they not?" asked Yakabuski.

"To my knowledge, they were *all* Irish. That's how the land grants worked. The agents recruited from the same area, over in Europe. With your last name, detective, I'm willing to bet that your family is from High River."

"We are."

"And that's because in the 1850s and 1860s, the land agent for the Lower Divide did most of his recruiting in Kashubia. You've heard of this place?"

"My sister had her wedding reception at the Sons of Kashubia Community Centre."

"There you go. For the Port Henry colony road, the land agent worked in Belfast. His name was Patrick Adams."

"The newspaper published a separate story about him."

"Yes, a side-bar story — I believe that's what they're called

— I thought that was rather smart of the newspaper. That little story nicely illustrates how corrupt and incompetent, what utter folly the colony roads were. I mean, Adams *murdered* the colonial governor. The land agent became a wanted *fugitive!*"

"I didn't know the story of the land agent until I read the newspaper article. What happened to Adams?"

"No one knows. He was never caught, despite a 5,000-pound reward offered for his capture, which is a gob-smacking amount of money for those days. No one knows why he did it, either. Killing a colonial governor made him a folk hero to some people along the Back Channel, although just as many hated him. Adams had convinced them to come to Port Henry, after all, and the government abandoned them after that.

"There were sightings and rumours about Adams for years after the killing. He was helping to build a railway out west; he fled the country and was helping to build a canal somewhere. With a five-thousand-pound reward on his head, a lot of people went looking. He is a controversial and mysterious figure in the settlement story of the Back Channel, is Patrick Adams."

"And Murphy was interested in the land agent?"

"Yes, he asked several questions about Adams, although he had many questions, and not just about Adams, and not just about the Port Henry Road. He was quite interested in other colony roads, how successful they'd been, what sort of improvements were done to the land before the deeds were registered. None were registered in Port Henry, of course, anyone still living on an original grant is a squatter.

"I remember him asking if I thought the settlers along the colony roads had been mistreated. I told him he was being polite. The settlers got seriously screwed, and everyone in power knew about it."

"What was your impression of Mr. Murphy when you met him?"

"Don't have one. He didn't keep our appointment."

38

THE FOLLOWING DAY Yakabuski returned to Port Henry. After a wet spring and a slow start to the summer, as though the season were afraid to commit, the weather had finally turned. High cumulus clouds floated above the Springfield River. The sun shimmered off miles of white pine, making the crowns look like they had been wrapped in tinsel. It was warm enough to be comfortable outside in only a tee-shirt, and the horizon was in the far distance, not in-your-face the way it was during winter. The day was so clear, the Northern Divide looked stamped onto the horizon like a tin relief.

There were many places where the Divide was hard to see, and Yakabuski once read that it petered into flat land when it crossed the Great Lakes and made its way into Minnesota. The Springfield Valley was not one of those places. In most parts of the valley, the Divide was the dominant geographical feature, a ridge of high land that cast early-evening shadows and sent rivers flowing north or south. Sometimes the same river turned on itself and flowed both ways; had different channels flowing in different directions.

There were rivers like that around High River, and the places where the water ran in circles were marked with red buoys and warning signs that told boaters: *Caution: Dangerous Undertows.*

Despite the signs, people drowned every year. From time to time, the High River Town Council would debate whether to change the signs. Perhaps different words would save lives. The debate normally happened after someone had drowned.

But the signs never changed. When the debate was finished, the councillors always decided Dangerous Undertows said everything you needed to know about rivers along the Northern Divide and saying anything more was being unnecessarily chatty.

Dangerous undertows also seemed the right words to describe this case, thought Yakabuski. Nothing about it was obvious or out in the open. There was something dangerous swirling beneath the surface, although even that was an overly optimistic assessment of the case because what was the surface? What could pass for normal, as your baseline for multiple homicides that did not seem to have sex, or money or power as a motive?

Dangerous undertows? That seemed about right.

"Why was your dad interested in this story?"

Donnie Murphy glanced down at the newspaper clipping on his kitchen table. He let out an annoyed, why-are-you-wasting-my-time snort. "Already told you, I don't know."

"Take another look," Yakabuski said.

Murphy shrugged and began to read. While he did that, Yakabuski looked around the trailer. Murphy's wife was washing dishes at a nearby sink, her back turned to them. She didn't run the faucet, or make much noise at all, while her husband was speaking. Spying in plain sight. Seemed a useful skill to have if you were the wife of Donnie Murphy.

Garland wasn't in the trailer, and Yakabuski wondered what teenage boys did on the Back Channel when they weren't in school and weren't working. Counting the days until they could flee, he supposed.

Yakabuski had set out for the Back Channel early that morning, long before the sun was out, had caught it clearing the treeline when he was no more than thirty minutes away. Murphy wasn't happy about getting a dawn wake-up call, but the newspaper story was the first solid clue in this case, and

Yakabuski was anxious to reinterview people.

If he had time after the interviews, he was thinking of going to an O'Hearn bush camp on his way back to Springfield. None of the names Coogan gave him had set off warning bells — no worker had a history of violence, beyond some barroom fights that didn't even get weekend detention. None had appeared at a camp for the first time last year.

It seemed like a dead end. But if he had the time . . .

"All right," said Murphy, pushing the newspaper clipping back to Yakabuski. "I've read it twice. Dad ain't in the story. I ain't in the story. I have no freakin' idea why he kept it."

"He had this story in his hidey hole. He also phoned this man," Yakabuski put his finger on a photo of Edmund Monk, "and talked to him for nearly an hour. Why would your dad do that?"

"Not the foggiest. If that's what you came to ask me, you can shove off now. Your work's done here."

Murphy gave him a nasty look, and while still tapping on the photo of Edmund Monk, Yakabuski said, "Your dad thought this story was important enough to hide, to keep in the same place where he had $947, his birth certificate, a German Luger, and a framed photo of your grandmother and grandfather. Why did this story matter to him?"

"That luger was my granddad's. He took it off some Kraut he killed on Juno Beach. It belongs to me."

"Seems like your dad was keeping secrets from you, Donnie. I thought you two were close."

"We were plenty close. You sound like a jack-shit idiot when you talk that way. Everyone knows we were close."

"Either you know why your dad kept this story and you're lying to me; or your dad kept secrets from you."

"He wouldn't do that."

"Can't be both, Donnie. Want me to explain how that works, two things being contradictory?"

Murphy thrust his lantern jaw forward a couple inches, crossed his arms, and Yakabuski knew the interview was finished. He wasn't going to get anything more from him. And judging by how Murphy looked right then, Yakabuski doubted he had anything useful to say. He didn't look furtive or guilty, wasn't trying to keep the conversation going — which was always the sign of a grifter hoping to gain an advantage — he just looked angry.

His dad hadn't told him anything. Yakabuski folded the newspaper story, slipped it back in his shirt pocket and got up to leave. As he was heading toward the door, Murphy said, "Did you say you found more'n nine-hundred dollars at my dad's trailer? That money is mine."

Yakabuski had parked beside the post office when he'd arrived to speak to Murphy. Dawn was breaking and he wanted to see the sun sitting low over the river, feel the dew on his hands as he ran them over the bullrushes beside the causeway, smell the spruce and the pine, trees that always smelled strongest in the early morning, when the needles were wet.

He would be busy the rest of the day, but he'd taken his time about walking to Donnie Murphy's trailer. It was important, Yakabuski thought, to have a few minutes every day when you weren't running around thinking that everything requiring your time and labour was urgent; that it succeeded or failed based upon your immediate participation.

He thought early morning was the best time to steal those moments.

He was on his way back to the post office, walking at a much faster pace, when he saw a Jeep Rubicon pull out of the lumber yard. The Jeep turned right, as though heading out of Port Henry, then it slowed, stopped, and reversed until it came abreast of Yakabuski. The front passenger window slid down and there, leaning over the passenger seat, his hand still on the wheel, was Tommy Coogan.

"Detective Yakabuski, you're back. I'm beginning to think you should rent a place up here, save yourself some driving."

Yakabuski put a hand upon the roof of the Jeep and stared down at Coogan. "I don't mind driving, Mr. Coogan. You must feel the same way, or you wouldn't be up here right now. What time did you set out?"

"Five, little after. It's an enjoyable drive if you have the right vehicle, isn't it? Did you ever make it to the bush camps?"

"May stop in at Rainy River on my way back. But your men have been checking out fine."

"I knew they would. They're all good men, been with me for years. I think I'd know if I employed a psycho killer. The person you're looking for lives somewhere out on the Back Channel."

"You'd know if you were paying a psycho killer, Mr. Coogan? That's quite a trick. How would you do that?"

Coogan gave him an annoyed look but didn't answer. "How's the price of oak these days?" Yakabuski asked. "First time I saw you in Port Henry, that's why you were here. Still the reason?"

"Yes, oak is doing quite well, thank you, although I hardly need a reason to come to one of my lumber yards, detective. I get up to Port Henry quite regularly."

"Is that so? I got the impression it was a rare occurrence."

The annoyed look turned flat and impassive. Like Coogan had suddenly sat down to a poker game. "Who told you that?"

"One of your workers, first time I was here. It hardly matters. You tell me you're here regularly, then you're here regularly. I'm easy to please."

"I doubt that."

Yakabuski took his hand off the Jeep and backed up a step. He thought about asking Coogan if the water commissioner also had regular business in his Port Henry lumber yard, but decided against it. He was going to save his questions about Walter Crawley until he had some decent follow-up questions.

"Before you drive off," said Yakabuski, "one more question: Do you have any theories about these murders, Mr. Coogan?"

"You mean, who killed these people?"

"That would be a theory, yes."

The annoyed, how-dare-you look returned to Coogan's face.

"I haven't the foggiest, Detective Yakabuski. How could I?"

Coogan put the Jeep back into drive and rolled up the window. Yakabuski watched the vehicle until it crested the berm and disappeared into the marshes. *Right. How could you?*"

Yakabuski walked into the post office, where Stinton Halliday was slotting mail into the general delivery boxes. Yakabuski took out the newspaper story and showed it to him.

"Have you seen this before?"

"Sure, I remember that story," answered Halliday. "Everyone in town read that story. What about it?"

"Walton Murphy had this story tucked away with his valuables. I'm trying to figure out why. Did he ever talk to you about it?"

The postmaster gave him a suspicious look. "Why would Wally do that?"

"No idea, Mr. Halliday. I'm just asking questions. Did you hear *anyone* talk about this story?"

"Well, heavens, like I said, everyone knew about it, so everyone talked about it. How could you not? Port Henry in the newspaper? Three whole pages! 'Course those newspaper people tried to make it a more interesting story than what it was, putting in that stuff about the land agent, and the governor getting himself murdered. It was a three-page story 'bout an unfinished road. That's all it was. I laughed when I saw it."

"The story seemed to matter to Mr. Murphy."

"Can't imagine why."

Halliday kept working while he answered Yakabuski's questions, putting letters, and the occasional package, into the mail slots. The boxes were numbered. He had finished with the general delivery mail.

"Did Mr. Murphy get any unusual mail recently?" asked Yakabuski. "Anything that he didn't normally receive. I'm betting most people's mail stays the same: same bills, same birthday cards coming in at the same time of the year. Did Wally Murphy get anything out of the norm?"

The postmaster thought about the question for a few seconds, tilting his head and half closing his eyes, to let Yakabuski know he was taking the question seriously.

"Nothing comes to mind," he finally said.

"What about Agnes McKenna?"

"Nothin' but her government cheques."

"How did she cash those? She didn't have a bank account."

"Food Town cashes cheques. Lot of people just sign the cheques over to 'em. Where else you gonna spend money up here?"

Yakabuski asked the postmaster about the other victims and got the same answer. Nothing unusual had come in the mail. Nothing ever came in the mail for those people, other than government cheques and Christmas cards; old lady Ennis got the occasional letter as well. For everyone else, nothing.

Yakabuski was leaving the post office when he stopped and asked, "What about Coogan? Did the lumber company receive anything unusual in the past year?"

Halliday thought longer about this question. He stroked his chin while he stared first at Yakabuski, then at the floor, then out the window. He was a diligent man, thought Yakabuski, and the lumber company — you could tell by the lengthy pause — received more mail than anyone else.

Eventually, the postmaster said, "Can't think of anything. Sorry."

39

YAKABUSKI WAS HEADING HOME. Forty-five minutes out of Port Henry. Still a fine summer day, the sky stuffed with feathery clouds and the Springfield River running flat and slow. Through the open windows of his Jeep, he listened to the call and response of two grey jays, who must have been flitting out of the woods at the same speed as the Jeep, for he had been listening to them for several minutes.

The weather changed so often along the Divide, you took nothing for granted. A fine summer day — you didn't say that until the sun was on its downward arc and shadows had come again to the physical world.

Still, that was what Yakabuski was thinking when he was forty-five minutes out of Port Henry. It was a fine summer day. Only later did he wonder if being premature about saying that was the reason for what happened next. Like he needed to be taught a lesson.

His phone rang. When he answered, he heard a gruff voice say, "Where are you?"

It was O'Toole. A phone call from the chief was unusual enough for Yakabuski to sit straighter. "Been in Port Henry for the day. Just heading back now."

"You need to go to Pirate Bay Marina. How far out of Port Henry are you?"

"Forty-five minutes."

"You could be there in, what — an hour, hour-and-fifteen?"

Pirate Bay Marina. A private marina an hour north of Springfield. "I can be there in an hour. What's happened?"

"Couple fisherman found Wally Murphy's boat this afternoon.

It was abandoned. They found it twirling around in Horseshoe Bay. It's one of those old CIP tugs."

"I know the boat."

"Good, you'll have no trouble finding us then when you get here."

"You're going to be there?"

"Thought I'd have a look. I'm told there's no doubt the boat is a crime scene."

"I'll want to have a look at that. But why are you heading up"

"I'm told that boat is more than one crime scene."

"What does that mean?"

"Don't want to tell you over the phone, Yak. I also want to see it myself, before I talk about it. See you in an hour."

And there it was. The end of a fine summer day.

Wally Murphy's boat was a former tug from the Canadian International Paper Fleet, which at one time was the second largest freshwater naval fleet in North America. It was a CIP tug that used to be on the back of the Canadian dollar bill, towing a raft of logs past the cliffs on Parliament Hill.

The company started selling the boats when it began closing its pulp-and-paper mills. Murphy bought his nearly twenty years ago and used it for deadheading, along with some dredging in the spring, when debris and junk flowing down the Springfield got stuck on the shoals along the Back Channel.

The decommissioned tugs were well known along the river. They had a distinctive hull and sheer line, the bow rising out of the water like a high curveball, the stern sitting low enough to make you think the boat was dragging anchor. On this day, the tug was even easier to spot.

Two patrol cars were parked at the foot of a finger dock. At the other end was Murphy's tug. Also parked near the finger dock were two ambulances, an I-dent van, O'Toole's Lincoln Navigator, a Transport Canada van, and half a dozen SUVs Yakabuski didn't recognize but that were probably police or government vehicles of some sort.

On the boat itself were more people walking around than had probably ever been on a CIP tug. There were uniformed cops from Springfield, a couple of Mounties, a woman wearing the light-brown uniform of a Transport Canada officer. Fraser Newton was there as well, sitting on the transom, talking on a cell phone.

As Yakabuski pulled into the marina, two I-dent cops were stepping out of the cabin, wearing latex gloves and N95 masks. They removed their masks and leaned over the gunwale, taking in large breaths of air. They looked seasick.

O'Toole got out of his car and was walking toward him as he parked.

"You made good time."

"Getting used to the highway. What's going on here?"

"Boat's a crime scene."

"It's where Wally Murphy was killed?"

"That's not one hundred percent confirmed. Looks that way. There's blood in the cabin that's probably his. It's on the wheel and on a jacket that looks like his. Big enough to be a sail, so it's his."

"When will Newt let us know?" asked Yakabuski.

"He says end of day."

"If it's not one hundred percent confirmed that Murphy was killed on his boat, how can you be so sure it's a crime scene?"

"Ahhh, good question. You should be one of my detectives. Come on, I'll show you."

O'Toole turned and walked toward the tug. He moved so quickly it took Yakabuski a few strides to catch up and they were on the boat before he could ask another question. As he walked past Newton, the I-dent cop cupped his hand over his phone and said, "You'll want a mask. There's a box by the door."

Yakabuski put on a mask and followed O'Toole into the cabin. The windows had been left open, the door propped open as well, but the stench inside the cabin was still strong enough to make Yakabuski's stomach turn. A complete roll. Like it was doing a somersault.

Even with the mask, Yakabuski cupped a hand over his nose and narrowed his eyes in the hope they wouldn't water. The cabin smelled like an overflowing outhouse, mixed with the odors of a back alley, the spot near the garbage cans where customers from a nearby nightclub came to puke.

In the middle of the cabin was the reason for the stench. A pool of urine and vomit that had congealed and hardened. The pool lay beneath the body of a man hanging from a crossbeam. The man hung not from rope or fabric, but from steel wire, the kind of wire once used on trolling reels.

The wire had nearly decapitated him. The man's head lolled to one side, attached to his body by a stretch of skin that looked fragile enough to break at any moment. It was hard to look at the body and not imagine that happening.

"Recognize him?" asked O'Toole.

Yakabuski nodded. "It's Liam Burke."

40

YAKABUSKI PHONED GRIFFIN an hour later, as he was leaving the marina. He told her why he had stopped at Pirate Bay, and before he could give her the full story, she said, "Give me a minute. I'm going to step outside."

When Griffin came back, her voice was low and hard to hear. "Meaghan seems curious. These cabins are *soooo* small and the walls are paper-thin."

"Try raising a family of ten in one of them. How's she doing?"

"She seems all right. Don't know if I'm going to have the same answer for you when she hears what happened to her uncle. Are you going to tell her?"

"There are things I need to do in Springfield tomorrow. Can't get back up there for a couple days."

"So — we don't tell her?"

"I don't think it's right to keep it from her. And somebody needs to ask her some questions; see if she has any idea who might have killed her uncle."

"You want me to tell her?"

"Yes. And do the interview. The way Burke was killed — it looked personal."

"You think he lacked enemies?"

"It would be a hell of a coincidence if he were killed now and his death had nothing to do with the murders we're investigating."

"And there's no such thing as coincidence, right? A detective told me that once."

"Sounds like a wise detective."

"You might know him. I'm trying to remember the rest of his advice about coincidence."

"If he were truly wise, he might have told you that coincidence is a secret you don't know about yet, something that's being kept hidden from you, or something you don't fully understand because you haven't been paying attention."

"Or, because you're stupid."

"I believe that's the full lesson. I doubt if there's anything about Burke's murder that's going to change the course curriculum."

"All right, when should I tell her?"

"Soon as you can. What time does Meaghan's brother go to bed?"

"Around eight."

"After that. Let me know how it goes."

At ten that evening, Griffin phoned Yakabuski.

"How did she take the news?" he asked.

"Not well. I'm getting kicked out."

"What?"

"She wants to talk to you."

Meaghan came on the line. She was crying and screaming, and it took a few seconds before Yakabuski understood what she was saying.

"You killed him . . . you bastards killed him!"

"Meaghan, what are you talking about? We had nothing to do with your uncle's death."

"I tried to help you once, and all it did was get my uncle killed. My dad was right. Never trust a cop."

"Meaghan, you know that's not true. If you calm down for a minute and think this through . . . "

"Calm down! My uncle got chased out of my home by you bastards, *by her!* He couldn't go home, couldn' go to any of his trailers. Cops were huntin' him, keepin' him outdoors, and now he's dead. How *dare* you say you got nothin' to do with his killin'."

"Meaghan, I'm sorry for what happened to your uncle, but you're making a . . . "

"I ain't helpin' you no more. And I ain't lettin' her stay in my cabin. She's gone. You hear me! *Gone!*"

The line went dead. Not seeing how a phone call from him would improve the situation any, Yakabuski didn't bother calling back. Ten minutes later, his phone rang.

"Where are you?"

"Sitting in my car," Griffin answered. "I'm at the end of her laneway. I tried to stay parked in front of the cabin, but she came on the porch with a rifle, so I thought I should split."

"Good call."

"She wouldn't even let me pack. She said I could pick my stuff up at the post office in Port Henry."

Yakabuski thought back to the first time he'd met Meaghan McKenna, when she stormed out of his office because she didn't like the questions he was asking, questions she didn't think he'd be asking a girl from the Mission Road Estates. He remembered her indignant, outraged face as she marched through the detective squadron, her head just inches above the cubicle partitions.

"She has a temper," said Yakabuski. "It's a shame; I thought you were helping her."

"I thought so, too. So, what do you want me to do?"

"I can use your help here in Springfield, Griff. I was already thinking about bringing you back. Meaghan's tantrum may have been well timed. I'm going to post a patrol car at the end of the laneway. Wait until it arrives, then come home."

"A patrol car at the end of her laneway? She's going to freak."

"She can complain all she wants, but there will be a patrol car on that road until we catch our killer."

"How long 'till the car's here?"

"Four hours. Less if I can dispatch a car that's already on the road. I'll ask. Get some sleep when you get home. I don't want to see you in the station before noon."

"Sentencing me to eight hours sleep on a real bed? I can do that time. What work do you have for me?"

"The kind you excel at."

"Ahhh, sitting in front of a computer. Tomorrow is looking better, and better. What will I be looking for?"

"Phone me when you get to the station."

41

THE NEXT MORNING the sun rose without a cloud in the sky. An undiminished, unobstructed sun that seemed to grow above the treeline as though it were a balloon being inflated. Yakabuski watched it while he lay in bed, amazed by the beauty of what he was watching. Sunrise over the Springfield River.

Sometimes the best things in life, the things worth having, are the things that were bestowed upon you. You don't need to work to get them, don't need to be lucky or rich or competitive. Just need to notice.

As he showered and got dressed, he wondered if this was a convenient argument to justify his relationship with Rachel Dumont. "Look at that. Right under your nose!"

Then he wondered if the mere fact that it was a convenient argument made it untrue. Why couldn't it be both: a valid argument that said it was all right to have passionate feelings about the daughter of one of the greatest gangsters to ever plunder his way across the Northern Divide.

More than all right. An act of grace and gratitude — noticing the beauty that was right in front of him. Taking the time to do something like that.

By the time he reached the police detachment, Yakabuski had honed his argument so finely it could have cut someone.

As Yakabuski was walking past the reception desk, one of the civilian dispatchers waved him over. "Yak! I've got a message for you."

It was unusual, in the age of digital communications, to have a message at the reception desk. What was once part of his work-day routine, something he did every morning and every afternoon, Yakabuski couldn't remember the last time he'd checked for messages at reception.

"Walter Crawley called a few times looking for you," she said. "He sounds upset."

"A few times *this morning*? It's not even eight-thirty yet, Sandra."

"I know. Last time he called, he told me to have you phone him as soon as you got in."

"Told you?"

"Well, . . . it wasn't an ask. Do you need his number?"

"I have it."

"Do you want me to toss this?" She held up the yellow slip of paper.

Yakabuski nodded, and the receptionist crumpled it up and threw it in the wastebasket. "Good luck."

Yakabuski went to his office and checked his email, his voicemail, his texts, and his WhatsApp messages — the way he got his morning messages these days — then he picked up his phone and called the Springfield Valley Water Commission. He told the receptionist he would be there in fifteen minutes.

"Sir, you can't just book an appointment with the commissioner. If you give me your name again, I will pass your request on to his executive assistant, and she will see if there is anything we can . . . sir? . . . sir?"

Walter Crawley looked like he hadn't slept in days. There were bags under his eyes big enough to need a porter. His brush cut had grown out and was now spiked in geometric shapes that reminded Yakabuski of a speed belt. The biggest change, though, was his voice. The lilting, bemused, languid drawl Yakabuski remembered, was gone. The water commissioners now spoke in clipped sentences, his voice low and raspy.

"Mr. Crawley, you wanted to see me," said Yakabuski, once

he was seated in front of Crawley's desk.

"Thank you for coming by. Although a phone call would have sufficed."

"I'm right down the street."

"Yes, of course. "

"How can I help you?"

"I hear ... I hear there's been another murder."

"Liam Burke. A press release is going out this afternoon."

"Liam Burke? That name sounds familiar. Isn't he a ... he's a ... "

"He was a big-time drug dealer."

"That's right. I've read some news stories about him. Wasn't he related to that woman you were asking me about when we first met. A McKenna woman, I believe."

Yakabuski nodded but didn't answer. The men stared at each other long enough to make it seem like it was a contest. Eventually, Crawley said, "Detective, I know you've been exhuming bodies of people who have died recently in the Port Henry area. Would you be so kind as to update me on your investigation?"

"May I ask why the change of heart, Mr. Crawley? Last time we spoke, I got the impression this case held no interest for you."

"What makes you say that?"

"Your general lack of interest."

Crawley's head snapped back. He wasn't used to being reproached. "No, you misunderstood me, Detective Yakabuski. People getting killed along the Springfield River, I'm the *water commissioner* for heaven's sake, how could I not care?"

"When I interviewed you, Mr. Crawley, you said anything that happened along the Back Channel had nothing to do with you. What has changed?"

"You really did get the wrong impression, Detective. The last time we talked I may have wondered how I could help you. After all, the Water Commission has no dams along the Back Channel . . . I may have mentioned that to you."

"'Nothing to do with me.' Those were your exact words."

"Well . . . I misspoke."

"You misspoke?"

"Yes, people do that from time to time."

Yakabuski flashed a smile he hoped was smug enough to annoy Crawley. "Misspoke is a funny word, don't you think? What does it even mean? When someone says they misspoke, does it mean they lied? Or does it mean they said something they wished they hadn't? False statement or unintended statement? What kind of misspoke did you make, Mr. Crawley?"

The water commissioners gave him a haughty look. "I'm not interested in playing word games with you, detective. I contacted you to see if the rumours were true, and you have told me they are. If they were true, I was going to offer my assistance. I don't much feel like doing that anymore."

"What kind of assistance were you going to offer, Mr. Crawley?"

"Well, . . . If you're conducting any sort of search in the area . . . for the killer, or another body . . . I have men at the Smoke Island Dam who can help with that."

"Offering to help in a ground search; that's why you were trying to reach me this morning?"

Crawley gave him a tired smile, one so weary and unsure of itself the corners of his mouth barely curved upwards. "I think we're done here, detective. I'll have Chantal show you out."

Yakabuski stood and said, "May I ask you a question before I leave, Mr. Crawley? I'm wondering — what has you so scared?"

"What? Wherever did you get such a preposterous idea? I can assure you . . . "

"I don't know what you're scared of, but I know a scared man when I see one."

"Are you comparing me to some of those people in your book? Some of *those* . . . "

"I'm not comparing you to anyone, Mr. Crawley. I'm just telling you that you're scared of something and you're not hiding it too well."

Crawley opened his mouth to object, to say something he hadn't had time to think through, maybe to misspeak one more time, but then his head jerked back, as though he had just remembered something. He closed his eyes and inhaled deeply.

"Mr. Crawley, why don't you let me help you deal with whatever's troubling you? Trying to outrun it — that never works."

"I don't need any help. Nothing is troubling me," he said. But his eyes remained closed. The words sounded like a mantra. Like something he was trying to will into existence.

"I recognize people in trouble as easily as I recognize people who are scared. They're usually the same people. You're in over your head, Mr. Crawley. You're involved in some3thing you no longer want to be a part of, that you no longer control. You should let me help you," said Yakabuski.

But Crawley didn't respond. He sat in his chair with his eyes closed. Yakabuski turned to leave, his eyes landing on the map of the Springfield watershed. The length and breadth of Crawley's domain. It seemed a mocking tribute that morning.

At 12:05 that afternoon, Griffin walked into Yakabuski's office.

"After twelve," she said, setting a take-out cup of coffee on his desk. "So, what's the job, boss man?"

"You're too late, Griff. Had to give it to someone else."

She punched him in the arm. "You gave a computer research job to someone else? Yeah, right. What do you have for me?"

Yakabuski glanced through the open door of his office, to the desks in the detective squadron, craned his neck for a few seconds, as though looking for someone, then said, "I don't see him. All right; I'll give the job back to you. Maybe that's only fair, since it started with you."

"Ahhh, making me curious. Nice touch. Ditto for twisting your head around and pretending to be looking for someone. You go all in when you tease me, don't you?"

"Only when it's a slow day."

"Started with me, you say. I'll bite. What started with me?"

"The water commissioner being part of this homicide investigation. Started with you taking that picture of him leaving Coogan's lumber yard. I'd like you to check and see if there's any connection between those two men."

"Crawley and Coogan?"

"Yes."

"What sort of connection?"

"Thought I was quite specific about the parameters of your search."

"You said to find any connection . . . oh, I see."

"That's right — anything. If they both shop for groceries on a Thursday night, I want to know about it. If they use the same snow-plow company or order the same coffee at the drive-thru window, I'll take it."

"What if they both floss their teeth?"

"If it's the same brand of floss, it goes in your report."

"Wow, you're serious."

"Like a heart attack, Griff. Those two are up to something. We need to find out what it is. Maybe it has nothing to do with our homicides, but they're stirring the water somehow, and I don't think this case gets solved until we find out how and why."

"I'm on it."

As Griffin was leaving the office, she turned and said, "I thought you had things to do today. Reason you couldn't make it back to Port Henry."

"Later today. It's a family thing."

"Another one of your sister's galas? How many of those does she organize every year? I can't keep track."

"Me neither. But no, nothing to do with my sister. Just keeping a promise to my nephew."

42

THE FIRST OF THE EVENING shadows were appearing on the north shore of the Springfield River wshen Yakabuski pulled into the Horseshoe Bay parking lot. Rachel Dumont sat in the passenger seat.

"We won't have much time," she said.

"We'll have a couple hours. He'd be happy with twenty minutes. He's quite smitten with you. Don't know if I've told you that."

"You *haven't* told me that, and I don't believe you. Your nephew is a teenage boy. I must be an old woman in his eyes."

"You're thirty-six."

"Exactly."

Yakabuski was still chuckling when he began unbuckling the straps that harnessed a canoe to the roof of his Jeep. Dumont was helping, unbuckling straps on her side. It took no more than a minute for the canoe to be off the Jeep and on Yakabuski's shoulders. He began walking toward the boat launch, where his nephew and father were waiting. Dumont walked beside him with a cloth cooler on her back, a tackle box and two trolling rods in her hands.

"Ready to test out your birthday present?" Yakabuski yelled, as he lifted the canoe off his shoulders and placed it sideways on the ground, next to another canoe.

"I've already taken it out on the Springfield, Uncle Frank," said Justin Lawson, pointing at the second canoe. "Took her through Boar's Head Rapids. She handled beautifully."

"Better not let your mother know what you've been doing with my birthday present, or she'll never let me give you another one. Thought you said going out tonight would be your first time in the boat?"

"First time *fishing.*"

"Ahhh, fair enough. I'll get you to help me with your grand-dad."

"Sure. He's going in your canoe?"

"I want to get his advice on a few things. You all right going out with Rachel?"

Justin Lawson glanced at Rachel and his face turned red so quickly it might as well have been a traffic light. "Sure . . . if that's the best way to do things . . . sure . . . no problem."

"You all right with that, Dad?"

"Long as I catch a laker, I don't care whose canoe I'm in." He stuck his arms out and said, "Ready when you are."

They lifted Yakabuski's father out of his wheelchair and sat him on the front seat of the canoe. Yakabuski gave his father a paddle, then he and Justin hefted the canoe and walked it into shallow water. When the boat was afloat, Rachel handed Yakabuski the tackle box and trolling rods.

"I was here at the start of the season and caught my limit," he said, stepping into the canoe. "Caught them all beneath the cliffs on the east side. I was making passes of between fifteen and twenty feet. Probably be deeper this time of year."

"Hasn't been that warm a spring" said his dad. "Wouldn't surprise me if they're still at that depth."

"Well — let's go find out," said Justin, lifting his own canoe and carrying it into the water. He carried it easily, not even bothering to put it on his shoulders. It was a birchbark canoe made by a master boat builder from the Kesagami Reserve near Cape Diamond. Lighter than Kevlar, but sturdier and easier to control. A canoe Justin could pass on to his children, thought Yakabuski. If his nephew stopped running the Boar's Head Rapids.

After he had stored his tackle box and trolling rods, Justin extended his hand to Rachel and asked, "Can I give you a hand?"

Rachel smiled at him. The boy blushed once again. Then she gave Justin's arm a playful slap, leaned down, grabbed the gunwale on opposite sides, and hopped into the canoe. Her legs curled beneath her while she was still in the air, so that she landed neatly in the front of the canoe while already in a seated position.

It was the kind of athletic trick you might see a street busker perform, after they'd already juggled balls with their feet and climbed ladders that didn't have any support.

"I think she's good," yelled Yakabuski, and he started paddling toward the cliffs on the east shore.

Yakabuski's father counted line as it went out his Penn trolling reel. He had already calculated the angle. "You're running at fifteen?" he asked, looking over his shoulder.

"Fifteen."

"I'm going to try twenty-five." The line continued to spool off the reel and into the water. A few seconds later there was a clicking sound, as the release lever was locked. He looked over his shoulder one more time. "Is the fish-finder showing anything?"

Yakabuski glanced at the Garmin fish-finder he'd attached to the gunwale. He shook his head.

"You say you caught your limit here? When was that?"

"May. Right after the long weekend."

His father grunted and turned around. He gave his fishing rod a quick snap. There was a suspicious look on his face. It is the look all anglers have before they catch a fish — expectant but resigned to bad fortune. Confident, but willing to bet against the endeavour. He snapped his fishing rod a few more times. "So, what did you want to talk to me about?"

"The killer I'm looking for on the Back Channel; I've been at this for two months now, and I don't have a solid lead I can follow. I'm missing something."

"Well, you haven't arrested anyone, so, I'd say you must be missing something. That's not saying much, Frank."

Yakabuski rolled his eyes. He valued his father's opinion, considered him one of the best police officers he'd even known, his dad had come a lot closer to capturing Gabriel Dumont than he ever had.

But there was a cost for George Yakabuski's advice, and if Yakabuski couldn't put up with some teasing, he didn't have the going rate.

"I've worked plenty of cases that didn't have an arrest after two months," Yakabuski continued. "But I had suspects. I had leads to follow. With this case, there's nothing." Yakabuski took some long paddle strokes, then took his fishing rod out from under his leg and let out more line. "We've found another body — Liam Burke."

His father snapped his fishing rod a few times. "All right, that's saying something."

"The way he was killed, it's different from the other homicides. And his body wasn't found on the Back Channel. He was found fifty miles downriver, at Pirate's Bay Marina, but he was found on Wally Murphy's boat, and it seems likely his death has something to do with the other murders."

"How was he killed?"

"Stabbed to death. Then someone strung him up with steel wire, just to make sure. Damn near took his head off."

"Does your girl know?"

"Griffin told her last night."

"How'd she take it?"

"Not well. She's furious about what happened to her uncle. Blames us for it. Griffin had been staying with her, because of the attack at her place, the one where the doctor was killed, but Meaghan threw her out last night."

"She's in that cabin without any protection?"

"I've got a patrol car parked at the end of her laneway. We're keeping an eye on her as best we can."

Yakabuski's dad looked up at the cliffs his son was paddling past. The evening shadows were growing longer, marking lines upon the stone, making the granite look like shale. Making it look like something it wasn't.

"The doctor doesn't fit the pattern," he said.

"Because he surprised the killer," replied Yakabuski. "That's the working theory, anyway. The killer went to the McKenna cabin to kill the girl; maybe to kill all of them; but the doctor showed up, and the plans changed. The doctor probably saved her life."

"You suspect he was going there to apologize to her?"

"I do."

"Good working theory. I buy it. What does that tell you about Burke's murder?"

Yakabuski snapped his fishing rod a few times. "He surprised the killer as well."

"I'll buy that too. If you track Burke's movements in the days before he died, you may find a suspect."

"That won't be easy. We were looking for him when he got himself killed. So were the Mounties. He'd been missing for weeks."

"Do you know why Burke was on Murphy's boat?"

"No."

His dad turned to look at his son. "I'd say you were missing more than *something*, son. Sounds like you're missing *everything*."

Yakabuski gave his father another half-annoyed, half-bemused smirk. "Can't thank you enough for your support and assistance, Dad; it's overwhelming some days, truly touching."

George Yakabuski laughed. "I need to catch a fish. I'll be in a better mood once that happens. All right, your core case, the Back Channel murders, run that by me one more time."

For the next forty-five minutes, Yakabuski did just that. Told his father every known detail about the deaths of Agnes

McKenna, Walton Murphy, Dorothy Ennis, Harold Byrne, Peter Kelly, and Tobias Smith.

No fish was rude enough to interrupt.

He told his father what little they knew about the victims, and about seeing the water commissioner in Port Henry with Tommy Coogan; how both men had lied to him numerous times. He told him he had Griffin looking for a connection between them, although where that would take him, even if she found one, he had no idea. He was probably wasting her time.

He told his dad about his interview with the RCMP profiler, and how the Back Channel murders were the exception to every rule she had. This case had none of the motives you typically find with a serial killer. There was no sex, no deadly wielding of power, no identifiable hate crime being committed against an identifiable group.

And while many serial killers were transient, or committed their crimes across a wide geographic area, that wasn't the case here. No one was catching a plane in and out of the Back Channel. No one was hopping on and off the bus. On the small list of known, verifiable facts about this case, that one was near the top.

Their killer lived on the Back Channel.

When Yakabuski finished, his dad gave a few snaps of his fishing rod, before saying, "You have a real mystery on your hands, don't you?"

"That's it?" Yakabuski said, incredulously. "*I have a real mystery on my hands.* That's what you have for me?"

"I'm fishing, son. Which is another mystery to me at the moment. Yes, that's all I've got for you. Sorry."

Justin did better than his uncle and grandfather. Two lake trout that were worth keeping, two that he threw back. Rachel caught one as well, smaller than Justin's, but still a respectable size. Four pounds at least, thought Yakabuski, when he saw it.

He cleaned the fish right there, on a large flat rock near

the boat launch. While he did that, Rachel took the birchbark canoe out for a solo paddle. She told Justin she knew Nigel Whiteduck, the man who had built the canoe, and had long admired his work. She couldn't pass up an opportunity to put the canoe back in the lake and see how it handled.

When Rachel got in, she didn't sit on one of the canoe's thatched seats but knelt in front of the rear one. She kept her paddle to the left side of the boat, every stroke coming from that side, never once switching. When she had paddled forty feet from shore, she began taking small, circular strokes, moving her arms so quickly the water churned.

While she was doing that, she leaned back until most of her weight was on the heels of her feet. The bow of the canoe rose out of the water as steadily as though there were a hydraulic pump hidden beneath.

When the canoe was at a forty-five-degree angle, Rachel switched to a J stroke and the boat darted forward. She kept the canoe in a straight line for a while, the bow sitting at forty-five degrees, looking for all the world like a dragon boat. Then she must have altered her stroke, because the canoe began zigzagging to the left and right, the bow staying in the air.

"Will you look at that!" yelled Justin in awe. "She has that canoe jumping around like a water bug. How is she *doing that!*"

Yakabuski's dad was back in his wheelchair, and he rolled over to his son. "My God, she can really move that canoe. Did you know she could do that?"

"Had no idea."

"She out-fished you today, too. You better pick up your game, son, or you'll lose a woman like that."

Yakabuski looked down and tried to remember when he had seen a larger smile on his father's face. He turned back to Rachel. She was rowing to shore now. She was almost at the boat launch when his dad said, "I've been thinking about your victims. It's funny, but I feel like I know them."

"How would you know them?"

"I said it *feels like* I know them. I don't, but their names, I know their names. McKenna, Murphy, Ennis, Byrne ... "

"I'm not following you, dad."

"Floyd Byrne owns a fishing lodge on Smoke Island that's been in his family for generations. Ennis Falls is just downriver from Byrne's fishing lodge. There's also a Byrne Lake, and a Kelly Lake. Your victims — they have *old* names."

Yakabuski thought about that. "You're right."

"They're also Irish names," his dad continued. "There's a lot of Irish along the Back Channel. Like Poles in High River."

"Because of the land grants."

"I suspect."

"The victims — they're descended from the original settlers."

"I'd bet money on it.

43

YAKABUSKI WAS AT the police station early the next day. He wanted to see O'Toole before the chief started his daily meetings. Get promoted high enough and you stop working for a living and start talking.

The detachment had that early-morning quiet you find in commercial buildings. Hallway lights were dimmed or turned off. You could hear the hum of electric motors — printers, coffee machines, a 1990s-era fax machine — sounds that were normally buried under the din of a busy building. No phones were ringing. No doors were slamming. No people were coming and going.

Despite the early hour, when Yakabuski reached the detective squadron he found Griffin sitting at a desk, staring into a computer screen.

"You're here early."

"Couldn't sleep."

"How's your search going?"

"Just told you — couldn't sleep."

Griffin rubbed her eyes and pushed her chair back from the desk.

"If there's anything there, I'll find it. But no luck so far."

Yakabuski sat on the edge of her desk. "Why don't you give me a quick sit-rep."

"All right — the Water Commission has a dam on Smoke Island, where Coogan also has a mill. That's a connection. I spent most of yesterday afternoon working that angle, seeing if I could make it grow into something more."

"Like a motive for killing six people?"

"That would have been nice. But the search went nowhere."

"What were you looking at?"

"I started with the minutes of the board meetings for the Water Commission. The public record and the in-camera sessions."

"You can get in-camera minutes for the Water Commission?"

"Oh, please. Don't try to cheer me up. But there was nothing there. The Commission agreed to raise the water level between the Ferguson Falls Dam and the Smoke Island Dam by two-and-a-half feet next year, so they can generate more hydroelectric power. Riveting stuff."

"Did Coogan attend any of those meetings?"

"No record of him being there. And no record of Coogan Forestry Products ever being discussed at one of the meetings."

"Coogan is a publicly traded company. You went through their minutes?"

"Soup to nuts," answered Griffin. "I found no mention of Walter Crawley or the Springfield Valley Water Commission. And there is a lot of public information out there on Coogan Forestry. Annual reports, environmental filings for its mills and bush camps, property records for its buildings, the timber rights they own or lease, vehicle information on their trucks. A ton of stuff, and none of it mentions Crawley or the water commission."

"So, there's no obvious business connection between Coogan Forestry and the Water Commission."

"Nothing so far."

"Maybe there's a personal connection?"

"I've started that search. They're both members of the Mission Road Golf and Country Club, but there's no record of them golfing together. They have similar tastes in vehicles, both own expensive SUVs, but you can say that about half the men in Springfield."

"The ones that don't drive pickups."

"Sadly, yes. I'm going backwards now, to see if there's any

historical connection between them, but nothing so far."

"If there's anything there, you'll find it," said Yakabuski, and then he gave Griffin his own sit-rep. He told her about fishing with his father and what his dad had said about the names of the homicide victims.

"The original settlers — damn, I should have thought of that," said Griffin. "You drive by Kelly's Landing on the way to Port Henry, and there's road signs for Byrne Lake. Do you want me to work that angle?"

"No, stick with Crawley and Coogan. There might be nothing there, but let's confirm that before we move on. You need some coffee?"

Griffin held up an old, battered thermos. "Not for an hour or two. Got the coffee situation covered, boss man."

Yakabuski left her there, staring into her computer screen.

O'Toole was already sitting behind his desk, banging away on his keyboard. Yakabuski wasn't surprised to see him. The chief was normally at the detachment early. Yakabuski wondered sometimes if he was the one who turned the lights on in the morning; or was that an automatic thing, set up with timers, for when he came marching through the rear doors?

O'Toole glanced up from his computer screen and waved Yakabuski into his office. "Early start for you. Should I be worried?"

"Don't think so," said Yakabuski, as he walked into the office and stood in front of O'Toole's desk. "No more than normal, anyway."

"Situation normal, is that what you're telling me?"

Yakabuski shrugged and O'Toole let out a half-snort, half-chuckle. It was a rumbling, bear-stretching-in-the-woods sort of sound. He leaned forward and grabbed his coffee cup. "Tell me why you're here."

"We have our first good clue in the case."

That's all you needed to say around the Springfield police station for people to know that you were talking about the serial killer lurking somewhere on the Back Channel. The case. Nothing more needed.

"What do you have?"

"Our homicide victims, the ones that got pulled from the river, they're descended from the original settlers."

"What do you mean original settlers?'"

"The families that went up there in the 1860s, when they were trying to build the colony road. That's the connection between our victims. You can see it right here."

Yakabuski set a photo on O'Toole's desk.

"What am I looking at?"

"The land grants that were issued in the 1860s. You can see the hundred-acre parcels running off the Back Channel. Where those fence lines are, those are the grants."

"Are those rock fences?"

"They are. This parcel here is where Agnes McKenna lived. The one over here belonged to Peter Kelly. This one is Dorothy Byrne. Everything is within five square miles."

O'Toole studied the photograph. "I thought some of our victims lived in the trailer park in Port Henry."

"Three of them. But they still used the grants. They had hunt cabins on them, or docks where they moored a boat. The Murphys did that. They have a dock and a hunt cabin . . . right here."

O'Toole looked to where Yakabuyski was pointing. "That's right next to the McKenna property."

Yakabuski nodded and O'Toole resumed studying the photograph. After a few minutes he slid the photo back towards Yakabuski. Leaning back in his chair, he took a sip of coffee. "And this takes us where?"

"The 1860s" answered Yakabuski. "Before you ask, I have no idea why."

44

YAKABUSKI CLOSED THE DOOR to his office and set the Google Maps photo on his desk. He stared at it for ten minutes, setting a timer on his watch before he started. He stared at the criss-crossing lines of rock fences. The shoreline of the Springfield River. The stands of white pine towering over the fences, which in the satellite photo looked like drifting black clouds.

Somewhere in this photograph lay his answer. Or a path to his answer. If not that, then the path to the next clue, which would lead to the next clue, and once that started happening it was only a matter of time until he discovered the clue that would lead to the killer.

Somewhere in this photograph.

If he could just see it.

If he could just . . .

His watch timer beeped. Yakabuski considered setting the timer for another ten minutes but then slid the photo to the edge of his desk. He'd try the visualization trick again that evening. When he was at home.

Maybe a math exercise would be a better use of his time. To Yakabuski, most murder cases were like geometry problems, or algebra problems. You were looking for the missing piece that would complete the pattern, or the equation. The pieces were verifiable facts. Those were your building blocks. You just needed to gather enough of them.

An hour later, he gave up the math exercise. He didn't have enough pieces to make it work. The verifiable facts in this case were so meagre, they didn't tally up to even the beginning of a pattern. He had lines but no shapes; facts, but no patterns. He needed to find more clues.

Just then, as though she had been waiting stage left for her cue to walk on stage, Griffin appeared in his doorway.

"Tell me you've found something," said Yakabuski.

"You're going to be happy. You were so damn right — Crawley and Coogan are in bed together. I don't know what the game is, but we've got them."

Griffin placed her open laptop on Yakabuski's desk. On the screen was a photograph of a house perched on a cliff. It was overlooking a lake, or a wide river, you couldn't see the far shore.

"Our water commissioner has a cottage on Big Bear Lake. It's under his wife's name. His wife's *maiden* name."

"Is that what I'm looking at?"

"Yes."

"That's a cottage?"

"Not bad, right? Four bedrooms, five bathrooms, *two* hot-tubs. Why in the world does anyone need *two* hot-tubs. What's the logic behind that?"

"I wouldn't know. I don't even have one."

"You and me both. Well, this little fixer-upper was purchased two years ago by Crawley's wife. No money down, zero percent interest, a balloon payment once a year that doesn't seem to have been paid yet, amortized over *50 years.*"

"Where do you get a mortgage like that?"

"Not from a chartered bank. The mortgage is held by this company."

Griffin tapped on the trackpad and the screen changed from the photo of the cottage on Big Bear Lake to an Excel spreadsheet. The spreadsheet was titled Springfield Mortgage and Loans.

"Springfield Mortgage and Loans is a mortgage broker," she said. "Company appears legit. They've been around for twenty-two years. Have an A+ rating with the Better Business Bureau. They make their money by charging fees to home-buyers who have been turned down by the banks. Fees aren't cheap, but the company usually manages to get a mortgage for their customers.

"Doesn't sound like the sort of service Walter Crawley or his wife would ever need," said Yakabuski.

"They don't. I've been through Crawley's financials. He's rich. The Crawleys stick out like a sore thumb on the company's client list, and not just because of their net worth. They also have a one-of-a-kind mortgage."

"No interest and a balloon payment that doesn't need to be paid; you're talking more one-of-a-kind than that?"

"You tell me. Springfield Mortgage and Loans normally gets its mortgages from corporations — co-ops, trust companies, insurance companies that do mortgage brokering as a sideline. These companies don't mind a little more risk than the chartered banks feel comfortable with.

"What Springfield Mortgage and Loans does not arrange, typically, is a private equity mortgage. They don't deal with retail investors. But that's the kind of mortgage the Crawleys have."

"Someone gave them the money to buy the cottage."

"One-point-seven million dollars. And the mortgage broker went through a lot of effort to try and hide the identity of the investor." Griffin tapped her trackpad again. "Before the money reached the Crawleys, it was moved through three shell companies and the personal accounts of two Springfield Mortgage and Loans executives, including the CEO. But this is where the money came from."

Griffin pointed to a line on the spreadsheet.

Yakabuski leaned closer to the screen, then he snorted and shook his head. "Good work, Griff. I'll have Mrs. Crawley picked up. We might as well bring her husband in, too."

45

WALTER AND SUNNY CRAWLEY were never brought to the Water Street Police Detachment. They avoided that embarrassment.

An hour after sending two patrol officers and a detective to arrest the couple, Yakabuski received a phone call from the detective.

"Yak, I'm at the Crawley's house. I've got a situation. You need to come down here."

"What sort of situation."

"A suicide situation."

Yakabuski got there within twenty minutes. By then, three patrol cars were parked in front of the Crawley's Tudor-style home at the Mission Road Estates and yellow crime-scene tape was stretched across the curving, flag-stone pathway leading to the front door. Neighbours had gathered at the end of the next-door driveway.

The neighbours would later say in police interviews that they were surprised by the Crawleys' deaths. He was the water commissioner, after all, and she threw the best parties in the Estate, the perfect hosts, the perfect neighbours, really, although . . . And then they would lower their voices and look around as though someone might be eavesdropping . . . Lately they'd observed some odd things . . . peculiar . . . out of the ordinary for a couple like Walter and Sunny Crawley.

Walter hadn't seemed himself. Hadn't *looked* himself, truth be told. His suits were wrinkled, his hair grown long, or long for Walter Crawley, at least. Then, just last week, he had driven his Land Rover over his front lawn. It was late at night, he had missed the first curve on the winding driveway and must have decided to keep going, because the ruts in the grass led directly to the four-car garage. Ran right over a lovely rhododendron bush. You don't want to say drinking and driving, give the man the benefit of the doubt, but now that he was dead — well, what else could it have been?

Then, a few days after that incident, Sunny had cancelled her RSVP acceptance to the Raftsmen's Ball, which was the kick-off gala to the Holiday Season, an event she herself had hosted many times. The Crawleys, you see, owned a home that could host such an event, having a ballroom large enough to make a Rockefeller green with envy.

It was in that ballroom that they killed themselves.

The couple were still hanging from a chandelier when Yaka-buski arrived. It would be several hours before Newton said the bodies could come down. Walter Crawley died while wearing dark blue pyjamas with white piping down the sleeves and legs. A well-worn pair of leather slippers were on the floor beneath his dangling feet.

His wife wore a thick, white waffle-knit robe — the kind you see in high-end spas — cinched tightly around her waist. Her hair was wet. Newton would later confirm that the last thing Sunny Crawley did before stepping off an Ottoman with an electrical extension cord wrapped around her neck was to have a shower.

The things people cared about at the end; it was a constant source of wonderment to Yakabuski. When he was a young patrol officer, he was called to the suicide of a young man with terminal cancer. He'd jumped from the eighth floor of the hospital. But not before he had taken off his hospital gown and gotten himself dressed in the white suit he'd worn at his high school graduation three years earlier. He'd asked his mother to bring the suit to the hospital.

When she'd asked why, he told his mother the suit made him happy. Just looking at it. She didn't ask any more questions.

Wanted to believe that was true.

A white suit. As though it made any difference what he was wearing after he landed.

There were people going in and out of the ballroom and up and down the circular stairway and it took Yakabuski a few minutes to find the detective he had sent to arrest the Crawleys.

"Have you been through the house yet?" he asked.

"It's a lot of house, Yak," answered the detective, "but I've been through the ballroom, their bedroom, his study, what I'm guessing is her study."

"Nothing?"

"Nothing yet."

Of course there wouldn't be a suicide note, thought Yakabuski. Nothing about this case had followed a normal pattern. Why would you expect anything different?

46

MEAGHAN MCKENNA sat on her front porch, trying one more time to figure out who was killing people along the Back Channel. At first, she thought her mother had been killed by Wally Murphy, but then ol' man Murphy got himself killed, and then other people got themselves killed — even her uncle got himself killed, something the girl once thought was impossible — and now she didn't know what to believe. Didn't have a clue.

Didley, as her father used to say. That's what she knew. Jack-shit didley.

Which was one of the worst feelin's in the world, thought Meaghan; not knowin' what was goin' on around you, being ignorant and helpless, stuck waitin' for some bad thing to catch up to you 'cause that's what happens when you're not payin' attention, when you're standin' around being ignorant and helpless. You get caught.

Why was her mother killed? Why all those other people, *and* her uncle? She had been tryin' for days to find something that connected them and other than all of them livin' on the Back Channel, and all of them gettin' killed on the Back Channel, she had nothin.' She didn't think she'd ever pondered somethin' so long and come up so red-faced, ain't-you-a-loser, empty.

Nothing made sense to her anymore.

All from the Back Channel. All murdered along the Back Channel. Her daddy used to say there was no place on earth like the Back Channel — not that he'd been all that many places, hell, not that he'd been *anyplace* — but he always said there was something special about the Back Channel. Government census workers who came up every ten years, the only regular, returning visitors the Back Channel ever had; they said the same thing, according to her daddy. This place was special.

"These census people been everyplace in the gawdamn country, Meaghie, and the Back Channel just blows 'em away."

Though not in a good way. Her daddy always left that part out of the story. The census people were blown away by the Back Channel because it made their jobs impossible. There were cabins in the bogs and bays of the Back Channel that had never appeared on a map, never been counted. The government had to use hover boats and drones to try and find them all, and of course they couldn't, not all of them. One of the census men even wrote in a report to the Ministry of Northern Development that, "Our work in the Port Henry vicinity is similar to the task of counting ants. Without knowing where the ant hill is located."

Ants. People from the Back Channel had been called worse, she supposed, so it was hard to get too upset. Maybe the census man who wrote the report even thought he was doin' a kindness, being civil, by not usin' other words.

Ants, after all, sounded better than rats.

Born on the Back Channel. Murdered on the Back Channel. What was the connection?

Her dad also told her the census people got tricked every time they came up the river, were made dupes in a grift that everyone played.

It was the government, right? So — screw 'em.

"They ain't got a clue what's really goin' on," her dad would say. "They can call us whatever the hell you want, s'long as they keep sendin' the cheques."

Her dad would laugh so hard after saying that, he'd end up having a coughing jag that didn't stop until he lit a cigarette.

Then he'd explain to his daughter that the information the census men collected in their once-every-decade trip to the

Back Channel was used to calculate government benefits. Like the child bonus, disability, old age security, even some of the new stuff, the climate and carbon-tax stuff; all the math started with the census.

So, during the two weeks that the census men worked the Upper Divide, children were moved from cabin to cabin. Middle-aged men aged overnight.

"Gawd," he'd roar, "you'd be the world's biggest eejit if you told the government that you were single. Why the fuck would you do somethin' that stupid?"

Turnin' down free money, takin' a pass on a good grift — those were things you didn't do along the Back Channel. And the census scam was a good one, because the census workers didn't have any paper to verify or contradict what people were telling them.

Unrecorded births were common along the Back Channel. Most cabins didn't have a deed. Much work was done for cash or barter. The census workers knew this and long ago stopped asking for proof of what people were telling them. They just ticked boxes and moved on.

Family of twelve? Check.

Senior citizen with a bad leg and bed-ridden spouse? Check, check, check. You've hit the trifecta.

Everyone was in on it. A grift that could only work in a place like the Back Channel, because there wasn't much paperwork. A special place, where you could make up stories and there weren't no one around to call you on it.

She thought about that.

47

"I HEARD THE NEWS about Walter Crawley."

Griffin stood in the door to Yakabuski's office, her laptop under her arm. "He didn't leave a note?"

"Nothing so far. There's a safe in his study. We haven't been able to get into it yet. It's solid. It'll need some force to get it open. There might be something there."

Griffin nodded. Shuffled her feet. "Why would someone lock away a suicide note? Seems like the sort of thing you'd want people to find."

"I've never seen it."

"What I thought."

"There are some filing cabinets in the study that aren't locked. Desk is open, too. It's a partners' desk, must be twenty drawers in it. I'll have everything gathered up and sent to you. Might be something there."

"What about the work I've already done; the mortgage Crawley had with Tommy Coogan."

"Unfortunately, Walter Crawley is not around to explain that to us. And it is no crime to give someone a mortgage that nets no profit. Strange thing to do, but not a crime."

"Why don't we bring in Coogan, to explain it?"

"Because Tommy Coogan will show up with four lawyers, tell us he was doing a favour for a friend, laugh in our faces, and then leave. He'll be followed out the door by four laughing lawyers, each one trying to out-laugh the lawyer who just walked past us."

Yakabuski looked at Griffin and wondered if the foot shuffling was about to turn to stomping. She looked annoyed enough to have a temper tantrum. "There must be *something* we can do?" she said.

"There is. Go back to your computer and find the rest of the equation. We have half of it. We know what Tommy Coogan was doing for the water commissioner. Now, we need to know what the water commissioner was doing for Tommy Coogan."

"And why it's caused the deaths of eight people."

Griffin turned to leave. As she was heading out the door, Yakabuski said, "Walter Crawley killed himself rather than face the consequences of what he was doing with Tommy Coogan. His wife made the same call. Whatever we're looking for, Griff, I'd say it's caused ten deaths, not eight."

Born on the Back Channel. Murdered on the Back Channel.

Meaghan McKenna kept thinking about the problem. Her family had been one of the first to settle along the Back Channel, her great-great grandfather arriving in 1860, the first year of the land grants. Joseph McKenna came from Belfast and thought getting one of the first grants would guarantee he got good land. Would guarantee good fortune awaited his family in the New World.

He dug rock and cut stone trenches to drain water out of his grant, but by 1870 he knew cash crops would never grow in the soil. There were enough trees to build a log home, but that's all his land would give him — a place to shelter. If he needed income, if he wanted to *feed* his family, he would need to do something else.

Which is what all the settlers eventually did, the ones that stayed; they began foraging and scavenging and day-labouring along the Back Channel. Joseph McKenna worked in bush camps and on slag barges, learned how to trap and sold furs at the Port Henry market. In the winter he cut blocks from the Springfield River and sold ice.

Her father used to make jokes about that. How the first

settlers had it easy. "Sellin' ice," he'd say to her, "can you imagine that Meaghie? That's all you needed to do to make money back then, cut blocks in the river and haul it away."

Her dad made it sound like the good old days. Although she suspected that even if electric fridges had never been invented, if *electricity* had never been invented, her dad wouldn't be hauling ice off the Springfield River. Her dad didn't like work. That was the stone-cold truth about her dad. Hauling blocks of ice sounded like work.

Instead, her dad collected a government cheque and scavenged. His word: scavenged. Other people used different words. More than once, someone had come to their home and accused her father of being a thief, of stealing some missing object: a chainsaw, a fishing rod, a child's bicycle. Her father was big enough, and mean enough, that nothing ever came from those visits. No one followed up on threats made.

Although Meaghan paid a price, bullied at the Port Henry school by children who had lost their bikes. Until she learned to fight, and the bullying stopped. She also stopped going to school after grade five, and that helped more.

On days when she wanted to think fondly about her dad, she wondered if that had been his plan. Force her to become tough. Because she was Bobby McKenna's little girl and she would need to be tough. Maybe it worked like a song she'd heard once, where a boy became tough because his father had given him a girl's name. She couldn't remember the song . . . or the name.

But maybe that's what her dad had been doing, when he went scavenging on their neighbour's land. Toughening her up. Getting her ready to deal with the likes of the Murphys. And the Byrnes. And the Kellys.

She thought about that.

Griffin was back in Yakabuski's office, her laptop under her

BACK CHANNEL   245

arms. "You've got to see this."

She set the laptop on his desk.

"What am I looking at?" he asked.

"Deeds for most of the land along the Back Channel," she answered. "I found them in the land registry office in Toronto. They were registered in 1866. Haven't changed hands since."

"I thought it was Crown land along the Back Channel."

"Not according to these deeds. It's private land. Has been for more than one hundred fifty years. Open that file right there."

Griffin pointed at an icon on the screen. It was labelled Names — Back Channel. Yakabuski clicked on it and an Excel spread sheet opened.

"What am I looking at now?"

"The people who own the land. Hit that icon there and select 'view by name.'"

Yakabuski did as she asked, and the spreadsheet changed to a text document. A fifteen-line text document. Yakabuski gasped.

"Yeah, it does kind of take your breath away, doesn't it? But what does it mean?"

A few seconds later, Yakabuski asked, "Where on this computer can I find the minutes for that in-camera session of the Water Commission, the one where they agreed to raise the water level along the Back Channel? And Coogan's financials, call those up for me, too."

THOMAS COOGAN WAS ARRESTED that afternoon, taken in handcuffs from the corporate offices of Coogan Forestry and brought to the Water Street police detachment.

His lawyers showed up twenty minutes later. Yakabuski had been mistaken when he predicted there would be four. The lawyers came from one of Springfield's biggest firms, Stevenson, Lawrence, Cohen and LaPierre, and there were only two. Although two with the same last names as those in the law firm. The first two.

Coogan made no attempt to hide his anger when Yakabuski walked into the interview room.

"I'll have your job for this," he hissed. "You and that bitch cop you must be banging, you're both fuckin' dead. I'll have O'Toole eat you both for lunch. If he wants to keep his job, that's what he's going to fuckin' do for me."

"Tommy, you need to calm down," said one of the lawyers, patting Coogan on the arm. "We'll get this straightened out. I promise you."

The lawyers sat on either side of Coogan. Peter Stevenson was to his right, the lawyer who had just told him to stop making death threats in a police interview room. Sound legal advice that was probably costing Coogan eight-hundred dollars an hour.

To the left was Simon Lawrence, who did most of the talking. "I can't blame my client for being upset, Detective Yakabuski," he said. "Arresting him in his office? Was that necessary?"

"I consider Mr. Coogan a flight risk," Yakabuski said calmly.

"Don't be absurd. Mr. Coogan has lived in Springfield his entire life. His family has been here for generations. He is a pillar of the community."

"Your client will be arraigned later today on multiple charges of homicide," Yakabuski said. "Given his legal situation, Mr. Coogan may wish to be a pillar someplace else. I'm not taking that risk."

"Very cute, detective, but again, you can't be serious. *Multiple charges of homicide?*"

"You've left a paper trail, Mr. Coogan. Funny, don't you think? Paper is going to bring you down. How much money has your family made by selling paper? Any idea? Some people think that's ironic. I haven't decided."

Yakabuski opened the file folder in front of him and slid some papers across the table.

"That's the timber rights registry. Looks like you own the rights to most of the land along the Back Channel. You bought it two years ago. Why did you do that?"

"Because I'm in the timber business," Coogan answered in a sarcastic tone.

"No one else wants those rights. They haven't been owned by anyone since the 1800s. Why the sudden interest?"

Coogan didn't answer. Yakabuski took a photocopied document from the file folder and slid it across the table. "This is a mortgage that the recently deceased Sunny Crawley held with Springfield Mortgage and Loans. You're familiar with this mortgage, I believe."

For the first time, a flicker of curiosity flashed across Coogan's face. He leaned forward to look at the paper.

"We've traced that mortgage back to you, Mr. Coogan. You gave Sunny Crawley money to buy a summer home on Big Bear Lake. Mrs. Crawley, of course, was the wife of the also recently deceased Walter Crawley."

"What are you insinuating, detective?" asked Lawrence.

"I didn't bring your client here to make insinuations," Yakabuski said. "Here are the Crawley's bank statements for the past two years. There are no mortgage payments showing to Springfield Mortgage and Loans."

"And that is significant, because ... ? I'm still waiting to hear why Mr. Coogan was arrested this afternoon."

"Having fun, are we, Mr. Lawrence?"

"Detective, that's a highly inappropriate comment and I ... "

"Nothing wrong with enjoying your job," Yakabuski said. "Here's some more paper for you."

Yakabuski slid a sheaf of papers across the table. Coogan and his lawyers leaned forward. Eventually, Lawrence picked up the top sheet and asked, "What is this?"

"It's the minutes from an in-camera Water Commission board meeting last year. Stapled to that is the agenda for the public meeting of the board, to be held next month. It's item six you're interested in."

The lawyer picked up all the documents and started flipping through them. He read one page for a minute, flipped forward, then flipped back, continued reading.

"I'll save you some time, counsellor," said Yakabuski. "What you're looking at is the soon-to-be-announced decision by the water commission to expand the hydro-electric dam at Smoke Island."

The lawyer put down the papers. "And this has something to do with my client, because ... "

Yakabuski looked at Coogan. "You want to explain it to him, or do you want me to do that?"

Coogan didn't answer. Didn't move. Didn't blink.

"All right," said Yakabuski, "I'll do it. This has something to do with your client, Mr. Lawrence, because boosting the capacity at the dam means the water level on the Back Channel is going to be raised by two feet. A little bit more. Twenty-six inches to be exact. You can find the estimate in the minutes from the in-camera meeting. How much did you pay for your timber rights on the Back Channel two years ago, Mr. Coogan? Let me see, we have the number right here."

Yakabuski took his time flipping through the papers in front of him. Pacing was going to be important for the next few minutes. He wanted to make Coogan wait, then pull him up short, then make him wait, play him like that. If he did it right, and if he got lucky, Coogan might blurt out something that would be useful later in court.

"Ah, here it is. Well, look at that. One dollar an acre. That's as low as you can bid, isn't it, Mr. Coogan?"

He didn't answer.

"How much would you bid for those rights next year, with the river two feet higher?

Coogan remained silent.

"Can't say? Or are you just having trouble speaking? Well, you don't need to answer. I've asked around. If you can float timber down the Back Channel, which you could never do before, your timber rights become some of the most valuable on the Divide. Nearly 40,000 hectares of old growth forest, less than twenty miles from your mill on Smoke Island. That's paradise, isn't it, Mr. Coogan? All you needed to do was buy a house for Walter Crawley. It was a hell of a plan. When did it blow up on you?"

Lawrence was quick off the mark. Quicker than Yakabuski had expected.

"I'd be careful, detective. You may be moving beyond insinuation to defamation. You have a lot of dots, but those don't get connected in court because of some vague theory or notion. They get connected by facts. Which you don't have. Other than the mortgage, which is simply Mr. Coogan helping a friend. What do you have that connects him to the water commissioner? What do you have that connects him to your homicides?"

"Your client buys a house for the man who was instrumental in turning his worthless land into some of the most valuable in the region," Yakabuski said. "Land that was considered so bad, the timber rights hadn't been sold in more than a hundred-and-fifty years. You think that was coincidence?"

"The mortgage goes nowhere," said Lawrence. "The rest is a theory. There's not even enough here for an insider trading charge. For this, you bring Mr. Coogan from his office in handcuffs?"

"No . . . for this."

Yakabuski slid one last pile of paper across the table. There were fifteen sheets in the pile, and the first one was stamped York Land Registry.

"What are those?" asked Lawrence.

"Those are legal deeds for land along the Back Channel. A hundred acres for each deed. These are the names on the deeds. I wrote them out for you, Mr. Lawrence."

Yakabuski slid one more piece of paper across the table. Lawrence leaned over and gave his head a sad shake, before he had the presence of mind to stop.

The first six names on the list were people with the same family name as the six people murdered along the Back Channel: McKenna, Murphy, Ennis, Byrne, Kelly and Smith.

"It was a good plan," continued Yakabuski. "I'm surprised no one thought of it before. Raise the water level on the Back Channel and all those old-growth trees can be forested. All you needed to do was build a dam. Hell, you don't even need to do that. Dam's already there. You just needed some sluice gates closed. Water commissioner can do that.

"Such a simple plan. Not many moving parts. Not many people involved in the play. It must have been frustrating as hell, when you found out you didn't have timber rights along the shoreline, that it was private land and had been since it was registered in 1866. Wish I could have seen your face when the scheme blew up on you. When did you decide to kill the people who owned that land, Mr. Coogan? Was it right away, or did you have to talk yourself into it? I figure it was right away."

Yakabuski waited. It was the moment he had played for. The push-them-pull-them game was finished, and if it was his lucky day, Coogan would blurt something out before his lawyers had a chance to stop him.

"It wasn't me; it was so-and-so . . . "

It would be a lucky day, indeed, if something like that happened. Yakabuski was willing to settle for less. "How did you find out about . . . " — that would work. Even a look of anger, or defeat, would give him an incriminating detail to add to his testimony when the murder trial of Thomas Coogan began.

But it was not Yakabuski's lucky day.

Coogan said nothing. He looked to his lawyers, gave a slight nod and Stevenson opened his briefcase. He pulled out his own sheaf of papers and slid them across the table.

"Here is what Mr. Coogan has attested to in an affidavit. As you'll see, how Mr. Coogan found out about those deeds is rather important."

V

THE NEXT THING
THAT HAPPENS

LAST CLUE

Panama City, 1898

Electric light cast long shadows over the terrace of the café. The leaves in the nearby trees fluttered in the wind and the shadows seemed to dance across the tables. Electric light had come to this street only the year before, and the café was busy with people who had come to sit on the terrace and watch the dancing shadows.

Except for two men who sat as far from the light as possible, one young, not yet thirty it seemed to the man sitting with him, who was much older. The older one was dressed in shabby clothes, had shoes in need of cobbling, an animal-hide jacket that had seen better days.

The young man was dressed in denim pants and flannel shirt and did not look like he belonged in Panama. He took a long sip of his beer, then laughed and repeated what he had just said.

"You're Patrick Adams. Don't even try to deny it. You're caught."

The older man did not answer. He looked around the terrace, then through the open doors of the café, where there were more tables and a long wooden bar where people were standing, espresso cups and draft beer glasses in their hands.

"I'm not the man you seek," he said. "You should go home."

"Right — you're Philip Addison, retired land agent for the Panama Canal and Railway Company. I read once that fugitives like to use aliases containing the first letters of their real names. Always thought that was a foolish thing to do, but here you are — Philip Addison."

"He is a fugitive, this man you hunt?"

"Have you forgotten? You are wanted for murder, Patrick. You have a five-thousand-pound reward on your head. As soon as I finish this beer, I'm turning you over to the gendarmes."

"You are a bounty hunter?"

"Don't insult me. The reward is merely a bonus. This is revenge, Patrick. Sweet revenge."

"For what?"

"For swindling my family. My father got his land grant from you, paid his passage and steerage out of Belfast to you, but when the colony road was cancelled and we lost our land — where were you, Patrick?"

"You didn't lose your land."

"Ahh, you know something of this story? Starting to come back to you, is it?"

"I know, by the simple fact you are here, that you have been misled."

"Don't try to con me, Patrick. Maybe you could do that with my dad, but not with me. You had my dad bewitched. He sheltered you, said kind things about you to the day he died. Do you ever feel shame, Patrick, for the things you've done?"

The old man turned suddenly to face his companion. "Never ask that question unless you want the answer, son. And you don't. Trust me on that. You don't want to bear witness to my life."

The old man took a sip of beer and tried to contain his anger. The past should stay in the past, he thought. Where it belongs. Where you have worked to put it. After you've travelled five-thousand miles, had the weight of three decades of living put upon your back — a burden you will carry to the end — the past should have the grace and wit to leave a man alone.

It certainly should not be sitting across the table from you, making threats.

"Why do you think you lost your land?" he asked.

"The improvements were never registered. You disappeared, remember? You told my dad some cock'n bull story about getting them registered, but it never happened. When the colony was *abandoned, we became squatters."*

"You've looked for your deed?"

"Do you think I'm stupid?"

"Where have you looked?"

"In Springfield, where it'd be if it ever existed. You're caught, old man. I've spent years looking for you, and now I have you."

Not in York, thought the old man, and he was suddenly overcome with a great sadness. No one had found the deeds. They had been registered and forgotten.

He had been unable to stop the injustices done to the settlers he brought to the Back Channel.

His sadness grew, became a physical thing, a weight pressing upon his shoulders, a liquid pooling upon his eyes. The old man wondered if all things, given enough time, were doomed to fail. What empire had not fallen? What life had not ended? What — in the physical or spiritual world — was eternal?

These are old-man questions, he told himself with disgust. He was wasting time. He watched the shadows flitting across the tables and thought briefly about letting himself get arrested. He was an old man, after all, and there might not be time enough to hang him.

But he considered this possibility only briefly. He had once quested for adventure, sought the wonders of the world. He would not end his days as a captured supplicant, on his knees, defeated and mocked.

Nor would he feel guilt for what needed to be done now. The young man had been given good counsel. He had free will.

The old man shook the collar of his coat. "What did you say your name was?"

The young man told him.

"I remember your family. Your dad built one of the longest rock fences I ever saw."

"You remember the Back Channel now, do you?"

"Yes, I remember the Back Channel."

"You're Patrick Adams."

"What if I am? The path that brought you here was still the wrong path to have travelled. You needed to go home."

"That ain't happening."

"I know."

The old man put a hand inside his jacket and began rummaging in a pocket, as though searching for a billfold. "You think you can control what happens next," he said. "But you can't. None of us can. You only believe this because you're young and you think the world is fair and predictable — a place where people get what they deserve. The truth is, we know nothing. We predict nothing. The next thing that happens to us may be completely random, may connect with nothing that has gone before, and will not be repeated in the future. It is merely the next thing to happen."

The old man took his hand from inside his jacket and extended it across the table. A friendly looking gesture. As though the two men were about to shake hands.

"I'm sorry, son."

"I don't under . . . "

The young man stopped talking, a surprised look coming to his face. Then panic, when the bola tightened around his throat. The old man sprang to his feet and thrust his thumb into the back of the young man's neck, pushing down on the vagus nerve.

"It's an early night for you, my friend," the old man said, loudly enough for people at nearby tables to hear. "When you're old like me, you'll be able to hold your liquor."

When the young man lost consciousness, the old man patted him gently on the back and lowered his head to the table. While he was doing that, he unwound the bola and put it back in his jacket pocket. He rebuttoned the caribou jacket and left the cafe.

The old man walked in and out of pools of electric light, marvelling at their brightness. He figured he had a good ten minutes before things turned bad for him. Maybe less. It had always been difficult to judge such things.

49

THE NIGHT AIR HAD that crackle to it you get sometimes in late summer along the Northern Divide, when there's moisture in the air, but the seasons are about to change, a cold wind rolling in off the Divide when the sun goes down. You can hear a crackling. It is the air becoming a tangible thing, turning to snow, a snow that did not fall from the sky but formed on the ground, twirling eddies of white powder that move across the earth like a child's spinning top.

Yakabuski kept his eyes on the road in front of him as it dipped and turned through the bogs of the Back Channel. He looked for signs of ground snow. Or a flash freeze. It seemed like the sort of night when you could get either.

He'd wondered how Coogan had stumbled onto those land deeds. Nobody had done that in more than a hundred-and-fifty years. He'd also wondered why killing those people had been his response to the problem, instead of trickery, betrayal, theft — instead of using one of the preferred tools of the rich and powerful.

Why six savage murders?

Now, he knew. The smile on Coogan's face when he walked out of the interrogation room, his lawyers walking beside him like some cocky protection detail, their black briefcases swaying like cudgels — he couldn't get that image out of his head.

When Yakabuski had finished reading Coogan's affidavit, he'd pushed it aside and said nothing.

Eventually, Lawrence cleared his throat and said, "Within our office, we have discussed at great length the facts contained within this affidavit. We have examined whatever relevant case law we could find, and we are of the opinion that Mr. Coogan is not culpable, in any way, for the murders you're investigating."

"You've discussed it?" Yakabuski said.

"At length," the lawyer replied.

"And you have an opinion? Did I hear that right?"

"Yes."

"Well, I guess we're done here," Yakabuski said.

Lawrence flashed a stupid smile, as if thinking for a second it might be true. Yakabuski was done. Then he looked into the cop's eyes and saw his mistake.

"You have questions?"

"One or two. Why didn't your client come see us months ago, when bodies started popping up along the Back Channel?"

"He feared for his life from the person responsible. It's in the affidavit."

"Really? That's what he's going with?"

"He *still* fears for his life, Detective Yakabuski. I wouldn't make light of it. There was some talk in the office of asking for police pro—"

"Don't say it. Don't you dare. Your client knew why those people were being killed. He knew who was doing it. He's going to become rich because of it. He should have done something."

"So — *a crime of omission*, is that what you see here? What would the charge be, *exactly?*"

The two lawyers leaned forward, curious to hear the answer. When they did that, Yakabuski knew this also had been discussed in the board rooms of Stevenson, Lawrence, Cohen and LaPierre. What crime had their depraved, bastard client *actually committed?* With *his* hands. Under *his* orders. What was his *legal culpability?*

It would have been debated like a problem in a college seminar. He imagined the younger lawyers with their sleeves rolled up; the older ones springing for the pizza.

His stomach turned.

"I'm guessing the defence of ignorance didn't fly," said Yakabuski. "The benefit of the murders to Mr. Coogan was too obvious. He must have known. So, fearing for his life, the defence of duress — a guilty man so fearful of losing his life he lacked the free will to commit the crime — that's what you're going with?"

The lawyers didn't answer.

"I'm curious — was there a vote? Was there a show of hands down at your office when the defence of duress was discussed? I'm assuming Mr. Coogan didn't much care for an insanity defence."

The two lawyers held Yakabuski's stare a long time before their gazes skittered away. Lawrence began scanning the interrogation room: cinder-block walls painted a light mud colour. Oak table with so many cigarette burns it looked pebbled. Cement floor with stains you'd find in a mechanic's bay. No windows. Acoustic tiles on the ceiling so old they had begun to crack and there was plaster dust in the corners of the room.

He stared at everything in the room except Yakabuski. Same for Stevenson.

Coogan, however, never stopped looking at Yakabuski. He held his gaze with a smug smile on his face. Eventually he said, "I can assure you, Detective Yakabuski, that I feared for my life. I was quite *petrified*. I am prepared to sign another affidavit to that effect, if it helps you any. Although you know the person, so maybe it's unnecessary. Rather unstable, wouldn't you say?"

Stevenson patted Coogan's hand. "Tommy, you don't need to say anything. I think we're done here." He turned to Yakabuski. "You have Mr. Coogan's affidavit. He's answered your questions. Unless there is something else, we'll be leaving. *Is* there something else, detective?"

Yakabuski was tempted to say "not today," tempted to spit the words out in his best Clint Eastwood impression. But he was quickly embarrassed by the thought. Never threaten out of anger. If you need to threaten, be cold and quick about it, be as emotional as a man punching in for his day job.

His dad taught him that. Same way most dads along the Northern Divide taught their children that lesson. There was perhaps no quicker way to lose respect on the Divide than to threaten someone and not follow through on it. Not because you had proven yourself a coward (although there was that) but because you had used words in a careless and disrespectful way, as though they had no meaning.

The respect that working people have for language is astonishing. People who work for a living still believe words have meaning; still believe that when a bank tells them the house is theirs, then the house is theirs; believe that when the government said it was going to build a road to their town, there would be a road.

Clarity and truth are things working people value. For the rich and powerful, they are things to fear.

"Yes, we're done here," said Yakabuski.

Then he sat in silence. And watched one more robber baron walk away from one more crime.

The last few miles of the drive were dangerous. Even for someone driving a Rubicon, who knew how to drive the backroads of the Upper Divide. Yakabuski switched his headlights to fog, so he could better see the road. The crackling was louder now. Like the drone-hiss of insects.

That FBI profiler had been right, he thought. The killer was poor, and the motive for the killings had been money. The case might have been solved sooner if they had worked only that angle. Agnes McKenna's old boyfriends, Liam Burke and his meth labs, Walton and Donnie Murphy's hatred of the McKennas — it had all been a distraction.

He should have followed the money. The fact that there was no money to follow —that shouldn't have stopped him.

The dots that wouldn't connect, the riddle that couldn't be answered, it came down to money. He should have known.

The Rubicon passed the *Welcome to Port Henry* sign. Dropped into the valley. Then up and over the berm. Yakabuski was soon parked in front of a building not far from the old harbourmaster's house, the house that still had a faded *Past Hope* sign on its south-facing wall.

As he climbed the stairs, snowflakes began twirling around his feet. He looked up and saw a clear night sky. The crowns of the spruce and pine were starting to shake from the wind. Perfect conditions for ground snow.

He opened a door and entered a darkened room, waited until his eyes adjusted and then he could make out some boxes, a service counter, a portrait of an English Queen that must have been taken forty years ago. He walked across the room and through another door.

Where he found Stinton Halliday standing beside his kitchen table. Meghan McKenna was with him, sitting on a chair. Halliday had a sawed-off shotgun pointed at the girl's head.

50

FOR MANY SECONDS it was a static scene. No one moved. No one spoke. Even the inhalation of air from the three people in the living quarters of the Port Henry post office seemed to slow and then turn mute.

Eventually, Yakabuski said, "It's over, Mr. Halliday. Tommy Coogan has given you up. You need to put that gun down."

Meaghan was wearing her winter parka, the one with soot stains around the collar. The shotgun rested on her shoulder. Strands of blonde hair were tangled around the barrel.

"Whatta ya mean, Tommy Coogan has given me up?" asked Haliliday.

"Means he told us everything. He signed an affidavit. If you do anything to Meaghan, it's only going to get worse for you."

Halliday's eyes narrowed. "Don't see how he could've done that without gettin' hisself in trouble. That don't sound like Tommy Coogan."

"He found a way. He came into the police station with lawyers who helped him do it. How many lawyers you got, Mr. Halliday?"

The postmaster's hand tightened around the stock of the shotgun. Yakabuski could see his knuckles turning white. "You goin' to threaten me with lawyers?" he yelled. "I don't give two flyin' fucks about lawyers. I gotta gun on this girl. You got a *situation* here, detective. Don't you think that's what we should be talkin' 'bout?"

Yakabuski ignored the question. "How you doing, Meaghan?"

The girl dipped her head in a slight nod. Careful not to jostle the barrel of the gun. "Been better," she answered.

"How did you get here? Did he kidnap you?"

"No, I come to ask him some questions. I started thinkin' about some things, and I . . . "

"Hey, little girl — shut up!" yelled Halliday. "Don't go answerin' none of his questions. Anyone asks any questions 'round here, it's me." He turned back to Yakabuski. "Tommy's lawyers, what did they tell ya?"

"Thought you didn't care about lawyers."

"I don't . . . just wantta know what they told you. And why you're here."

"I'm here to arrest you, Mr. Halliday. For the murders of Walton Murphy, Agnes McKenna, Dorothy Ennis, Harold Byrne, Peter Kelly, Tobias Smith, Liam Burke and Peter Atkinson."

The postmaster's eyes glazed over as Yakabuski recited the names. As though he were bored. When he was finished, Yakabuski took his service revolver from the pocket of his windbreaker and pointed it at the postmaster's head.

"Hey! What the fuck you doin'?" Halliday yelled.

"Changing the situation," Yakabuski answered.

The silence in the room seemed infinite. A quiet that had wrapped itself around the physical world and become something tangible, something filled with the breadth and wonder and dread of all known things. As though everything in the post office had suddenly become essential and inescapable.

One cop.

One killer.

One girl.

Two guns.

It was all about to happen.

Yakabuski was the one to break the silence: "For a serial killer, you don't know that much about guns, do you Mr. Halliday?"

Halliday gave him an annoyed look. "What's that supposed to mean?"

"You got bird shot in that shotgun, don't you?"

The postmaster blinked. "What if I do?"

"If you shoot someone with bird shot, even if you're right close to them, the way you are with Meaghan, the person you shot has a better than fifty-fifty chance of surviving. Do you know what the odds are of someone surviving a 38-calibre bullet to the head?"

Halliday didn't answer.

"Don't feel bad; I don't know either. But I'm willing to bet they're not *good* odds. Care to find out?"

"You'd let me shoot this girl? What kind of a cop are you?"

"Yeah," said Meaghan, her voice sounding as puzzled as the postmaster's. "You'd let him *shoot this girl?*"

"I'm just letting Mr. Halliday know how it's going to play out for him. Before I ask him one more time to put down that shotgun."

"I ain't putting down this gun; I ain't letting you arrest me; I ain't going to get cheated one more time in this world."

"That's what this is all about, isn't it? Your family getting cheated back in the 1800s?"

"Everyone got cheated. Thought you already knew that."

"Mr. Halliday, I don't blame you for being angry about what happened to your family. What it was like for your ancestors, in those years before a road got built to Port Henry, I can't imagine it. I have sympathy for you, sir. A jury would have sympathy, too. Why don't you let the girl go, and we can talk about this."

"Let her go so you can put a bullet in my head? Think I'm a fool? She's the only leverage I got."

"What if you had a gun to my head? Would that be enough leverage for you?"

Halliday gave Yakabuski a suspicious look. "What are you talking about?"

"Let me replace Meaghan . . . on the count of three I point my handgun to the ceiling. You do the same with the shotgun.

When both guns are pointed at the roof, Meaghan gets out of that chair. I count to three again, and we lower the guns."

"You'll shoot me . . . no way."

"I can shoot you right now, Mr. Halliday. Only difference is going to be you'll have your gun pointed at me instead of her. It's a good deal I'm offering you."

"You're going to trick me. No way. You put that gun down or I'll shoot her. I swear to God . . . I'll shoot her!"

"Stop it! We can skip the count down. I'll go first."

Yakabuski raised his service revolver and pointed it toward the ceiling. Halliday stared at the gun a few seconds before saying, "I can take you right now."

"Maybe. A lot of things could go wrong, though. And you don't want to kill me right now. We need to talk."

"Why do I want to talk to you?"

"Because you need to know what Coogan has told me. You need to know how blown you are and whether there's anything left to salvage."

Halliday's jaw clenched and the shotgun barrel shook for the first time. Meaghan gasped and gripped the armrests of the chair. Yakabuski looked at the twin barrels of the shotgun and wondered if he had overplayed his hand.

And then the postmaster took the shotgun off the girl's shoulder and pointed it toward the ceiling. Meaghan slid slowly off the chair as Yakabuski started counting — "one, two, three" — and then both men lowered their guns, pointed them at the other man's head.

"So," said Halliday, "what lies did Tommy Coogan tell you?"

Meaghan scurried to a corner of the room and stood there, bent at the waist, her hands on her knees, taking in gulps of air.

"Stay there!" yelled Yakabuski. "You're out of this, Meaghan."

She nodded, her hands still on her knees. "Don't need to tell me twice," she said.

Yakabuski turned back to Halliday. "Coogan told us it was your idea, killing those people. He said you threatened to kill him, if he tried to stop you."

"He's a lyin' bastard."

"I believe you. But how did you learn about the scheme he had going with the water commissioner?"

"Weren't hard. I never seen the water commissioner up here before, then last year, it seemed like he was here every week. A lumber baron and a water commissioner getting all chummy. Only one thing that's *ever* meant. All I needed to do was figure out what scam they were running, and if I could throw a monkey wrench into it, maybe I could make some easy money."

A self-satisfied smile spread across Halliday's face.

Grifters can spot a good grift ten miles away, thought Yakabuski. What normal, law-abiding people never see, a grifter sees in technicolour. Tommy Coogan becoming friendly with Walter Crawley? Stinton Halliday saw that and knew there was something odd about it. Then he started looking for ways to profit from it.

"I understand why you were suspicious," said Yakabuski. "But how did you figure out what they were doing?"

"I'm the postmaster. I know everythin' that happens in this town. Remember tellin' me that, detective? You was tryin' to con me when you said it, but you weren't wrong."

Halliday told Yakabuski how he started monitoring the mail arriving for Coogan Forestry. Looking for some connection between the lumber company and the Water Commission. Mimicking the job Yakabuski had given Griffin a week earlier. But instead of Internet searches, Halliday was steaming open manilla envelopes late at night. Reading documents and resealing the envelopes with Crazy Glue.

His first month doing that, he found out about the timber rights Coogan had purchased.

"Rights that weren't worth a plugged nickel unless you could float logs down the Back Channel. And you can't do that unless the water is a whole lot higher."

He was starting to put the pieces together when the article about the old colony road was published in the *Sentinel*. Walton Murphy came into the post office with the newspaper and asked Halliday if he'd read the story.

"He wanted to know what I thought about the land agent story, whether it could be true, that the agent disappeared with documents that would have given people clear title to their land grants. And if it was true — could the documents be found somewhere?

"I found 'em two days later. At the land registry office in Toronto. You can see land registry documents online if you got a library card from the Toronto Public Library. They give you one if you list the Union Mission shelter as your address."

He cackled. It was a wonderful country.

He hadn't known yet how Crawley was going to help Tommy Coogan, but when he found the deeds, he figured he had enough information to put the squeeze on Coogan. He left a message at Coogan Forestry, saying there was a registered letter from the land registry office in Toronto, addressed to Tommy Coogan. He needed to come to the Port Henry post office and sign for it.

"I knew if he came in, he was guilty of something," said Halliday. "He was here the next day."

"Those deeds would have ruined their scheme," Yakabuski said.

Halliday snorted. "Would have been no scheme left. If it ain't Crown land along the Back Channel, the water commission can't raise the water level. Coogan didn't believe it when I showed him the deeds. He demanded to see the originals. I laughed at him."

"Why didn't Coogan just buy out the landowners?"

"I didn't give him that choice. I told him I'd take care of his

problem. All he had to do was make me a rich man. I didn't
have to sell him much on the idea, I can tell you that."

"Walton Murphy knew what you were doing?"

"That idiot? He never had a clue. I told him I'd find out about
the deeds, find out if that newspaper story was true, and then I
kept stallin' him. Told him not to talk about it to anyone. Keep
it our little secret."

That's why he cancelled his meeting with the professor,
thought Yakabuski. "Why did Murphy come to you in the
first place?"

"Hell, son, I'm the *postmaster*. I work for the *government*.
Who else in this town would a hayseed like Wally Murphy
ask for help?"

Meaghan was standing upright now, listening intently. "Why
was Murphy fighting with my momma?"

"Already told you — he was an idiot. He wanted to buy some
meth from your mother, but he didn't have any money, so he
told her he was going to be rich one day, soon as I found the
missin' deeds. Told your momma she was going to be rich, too,
and if she didn't believe him, she could ask me."

"Which is what she did," said Meaghan. "After that fight, she
went into the post office, made me and Robbie wait outside,
she was in there a good ten minutes or more."

"Seemed like more," said Halliday. "I told her I had no idea
what Wally was talking about, but I could see she didn't believe
me."

"So, you killed her," said Yakabuski.

"Had no choice."

"Didn't Murphy know what you were doing?" asked Yaka-
buxki. "When bodies started being found in the river, didn't
he suspect?"

"Wally was a greedy idiot. He just wanted to sell his land
grant. He didn't care 'bout much more than that. He never
saw the . . . *bigger picture*."

"Why didn't you kill him right away? Why wasn't he your first victim?"

Halliday hesitated with his answer. He looked over at the girl, then at Yakabuski. "He was a big son-of-a-bitch. Thought I'd save him to the end."

"And Liam Burke, how did you get the jump on a man like that?" Yakabuski asked.

Halliday snorted. "A man like that. Let me tell you somethin', detective. Men like Liam Burke don't respect men like me. I wear Canada Post clothes, give change for dollar-fifteen stamps, don't even own three coffee cups. Remember that, detective? The smirk on your face? I do. You thought you were better than me. Liam Burke thought that too, and that made him sloppy. He don't think that anymore. You won't either, in a minute."

He turned to the girl and smiled. "It was a pleasure killin' your uncle. One of the best days of my life."

He kept smiling at Meaghan, a depraved, self-satisfied smile. There was something grotesque about it. Something evil. Halliday was showing his true self now. The genial, clumsy postmaster had disappeared. As though he had been kidnapped.

Yakabuski realized that Halliday was a master actor, a man with many faces and many miens, but what Yakabuski was seeing right then was the real man, stripped of guile and caricature.

"You don't need to feel bad about your uncle," Halliday continued. "Don't need to feel bad 'bout your momma, neither. Nobody dies good up here, child. 'Cept you two. I'll be sure to make it quick."

Meaghan bit her lip. Put her hands back on her knees. It looked like she was going to be sick.

"Why was Burke on the tugboat?" Yakabuski asked.

"That's where I killed Wally. I told Wally we had business to discuss and needed some privacy; told him we should meet on his boat. He was such an idiot he believed that. Like it's hard to find private places 'round here. He had the boat anchored at

Buckhorn Bay. When I was done with him, I moved the boat into a creek in back of there."

"Why?"

Halliday looked confused. As though he'd suddenly been asked a question in Sanskrit. "Why did I move the boat? 'Cause I wanted it. He had a CIP tug. Those things last forever."

"But the boat was found abandoned. With Burke's body on board."

"I took Burke back to the boat. Didn't want his body turning up right away, but he made such a fuckin' mess, I didn't want the boat no more. I cut her adrift. Guess I'll have to buy a new one next spring."

Yakabuski looked at the postmaster in astonishment. "Mr. Halliday, Tommy Coogan has given you up. There's no getting out of this. There's no new boat waiting for you in the spring."

"I don't believe you. I got enough dirt on Tommy Coogan to put him down. No way that man talks."

"He already has. The smart thing to do now is to put your gun down, before this gets worse for you."

Halliday laughed at him. Yakabuski looked over at Meaghan, surprised to see she no longer looked nauseous. The girl was standing behind Halliday, looking right at Yakabuski and silently mouthing words he was having trouble making out.

Keep him . . . *talking?*

"Why don't we put our guns down?" said Yakabuski. "Let's talk this over like real men."

Are you a man? Yakabuski suspected that question would get Halliday talking.

"I'm man enough to be the last thing you ever see, you dumb bohunk," the postmaster said. "I'm going to turn my gun back on the girl and I swear to God, I'm going to shoot her. You told me everythin' I needed to know. If you want her to live any longer, you drop your gun."

"All right! All right! That's what I'm going to do," said Yakabuski, and he took his finger off the trigger of his service revolver. "I'm not going to drop it, in case it misfires, but I'm putting my gun down. You don't need to hurt Meaghan."

Yakabuski rotated his service revolver so that it sat sideways in the palm of his hand. He held it out for Halliday to see. The postmaster stared at the gun as Yakabuski began lowering it to the floor.

Lower. Lower. The postmaster followed the movement of the gun, Yakabuski bending down now, about to go into a squat and for a brief moment it seemed as though the air in the room changed, the colours changed; seemed as though the two men had been transported somewhere else, had become actors in a play, waiting for a curtain to rise, waiting for the hard call of action and fate.

They were still waiting like that when Meaghan took a sawed-off rifle from inside her parka and shot Halliday in the head.

EPILOGUE

That summer on the Northern Divide was one of the hottest and driest on record. By late August, there were many places along the Back Channel where the river was so low you could walk across it to Smoke Island and the needles on the white pine had turned yellow, many of them falling, as though they were hardwood trees, as though you were someplace South.

The Crown Attorney spent the end-days of summer and much of autumn going through the evidence Yakabuski gave her. The recently discovered land deeds. The timber rights for the Back Channel. The in-camera minutes from the Springfield Valley Water Commission. Affidavits from him and Meaghan McKenna, along with the autopsy reports for eight murdered people.

In late October she told Yakabuski there would be no arrests.

"Our killer is dead, Yak. Much as I may wish to prosecute Stinton Halliday, unless you have a way to bring him back from the grave, there's nothing for me to do here."

"You can't charge the person who knew about the killings and profited from them?"

"It's not a crime to profit from another person's misdeeds."

"Misdeeds?"

"You know what I'm saying, Yak. I have found no culpability for Tommy Coogan. Not for the murders, not for the purchasing of the timber rights, and not for any financial dealings he may have had with Walter Crawley. I'm sorry, but you have nothing but inuendo and speculation."

"Coogan buys the water commissioner a house and the water commissioner raises the water level on the Back Channel, which makes Coogan rich. That's speculation?"

"That a crime was committed? Yes, that's speculation."

Yakabuski sat there and thought about arguing but didn't bother. Clarice Thompson was taking a pass on this case, and once she did that, she was gone. He'd never seen her come back. That there was no crime in profiting from another person's crime was probably true.

It was, after all, the origin story for any place that was ever colonized.

He got up to leave, not wanting to hear anything else, not wanting to give the Crown Attorney, whom he liked most days, the opportunity to say something along the lines of, "Coogan can't help being lucky."

"I should get back to work."

"Sorry it turned out this way, Yak."

"No need to apologize. Just wish people got what they deserved in this world from time to time. I know you didn't come up with the rules."

"Maybe you're not seeing the whole picture, Yak. When they raise the water level on the Back Channel, the McKennas will be getting what they deserve, wouldn't you say?"

"I suppose."

"That girl and her family will never need to worry about money again. Look for the positives in this. It will help you."

"Good advice, counsellor. I'll try."

"I hope you do."

They shook hands and Yakabuski left. He was in his Jeep, driving back to the detachment when his phone rang. He looked at the number and saw the call was coming from Clarice.

"Yak, I'm glad I reached you. Forgot to ask you something before you left, so I can close the file on this rat fuck — excuse the language, but let's call it what it is, shall we."

"Sure."

"I noticed something in the file that didn't seem right. Won't change anything. We're done here. But I made a note to ask you about it."

"Go ahead."

"Why didn't you use your service revolver when you shot Halliday?"

Meaghan McKenna sat on her porch in a bent poplar chair that her grandmother had made many years before she was born. She stared out at the remains of her vegetable garden, the ground turned, the stakes put away for the winter. Beyond the garden was a dark, burbling creek, beyond that a dark pine forest, and in the far distance a tall stretch of land that would soon be blocking the sun.

"So, that's it?" Meaghan said.

"That's it," Yakabuski replied.

"She didn't ask no more questions about the gun?"

"No."

"Do you think she knows?"

"I'm not sure. I think she's trying to see the positive."

"What does that mean?"

"Means it's over."

Yakabuski leaned back in his chair. It was a peaceful spot, the McKenna front porch. He held his hand against the horizon and measured the sun at two fingers above the Divide. Which meant it would be dark when he drove home. The seasons were starting to change. In the evenings there was a chill in the air, and a thin crust of ice ringed the shoreline of the Springfield River most mornings.

If he could measure seasons the way he measured sunsets, he'd guess winter was also two fingers away. Maybe less.

"I want to thank you for everythin' you did," Meaghan said. "And Griff, too. Tell her I'm sorry 'bout kickin' her out. I was just mad there for a while."

"I'll tell her."

"I'd like to thank you, too, Rachel."

Rachel Dumont leaned forward in her chair and patted the girl's hand. "You don't need to thank anyone, sweetheart. What's happening to you now, it's what you deserve. What you've deserved for a long time."

"I suppose . . . but you've both been real good to me. And to Robbie and Aunt Lizzie. Don't know where we'd be without you."

Rachel kept patting Meaghan's hand. Yakabuski hadn't been sure about introducing them. Would that be blurring the line between personal life and work life? Something he once swore he'd never do.

But the more he thought about it, the more he realized they had much in common, Meaghan McKenna and Rachel Dumont. Born into families that would never be described as law-abiding, the McKennas not on the same level as the Dumonts, but the scorn, derision and suspicion each woman must have experienced when they were growing up — he doubted if it had been much different.

Meeting someone like Rachel Dumont, someone who had escaped her past, he decided that would be good for Meaghan. To know the world was filled with possibilities, that you weren't tethered to family history, or the place you were born.

"Rachel is right," he said. "There's no need to thank us."

"But there is. You puttin' me in touch with that lawyer, findin' a home for Aunt Lizzie, a doctor for Robbie, Rachel givin' me this here phone." Meaghan pulled a satellite phone from the pocket of her cardigan. "Tellin' me I could call her anytime I wanted. You've helped us a lot."

"We were glad to do it," said Yakabuski. "When are you planning on leaving?"

Meaghan looked at Rachel and they exchanged conspiratorial smiles.

"I'm not," she answered.

"I thought you were selling the farm and moving down to

Springfield."

"Meaghan's decided she doesn't want to do that, Frank," said Rachel. "Not right away, at least. This is her family home. She wants to stay."

"I'm going to sell the timber rights, not the land," Meaghan said. "Your lawyer friend came up with that deal. Even when they raise the water level, I'll be left with eighty acres of old-growth pine. Know how much that is worth?"

"I'm guessing a lot."

The girl laughed. "You're a good guesser."

"But why stay? With that sort of money, you can live anywhere."

"I don't want to live anywhere. I want to live here."

Yakabuski was getting ready to argue with her, getting ready to tell her a home could be anywhere she wanted it to be, didn't need to be a settler's cabin on the Back Channel of the Springfield River. People moved all the time and found new homes. Better homes. She could be one of those people.

But before he could fully frame his argument, he realized he would be wasting his time. She *wasn't* one of those people. Land meant different things to different people, and for Meaghan McKenna, for a lot of people along the Back Channel, it meant everything.

Maybe land is easier to love when no one else wants it. Maybe that was part of the attraction of the Back Channel. Maybe not. Yakabuski thought right then that he could spend the rest of his life trying to figure out what land meant to people, and still not have a clue.

"It might not be forever, Frank," said Rachel. "But this arrangement works for Meaghan. We've talked about it a lot. She's had enough changes in her life this year. Let the girl rest."

Yakabuski looked at Rachel and wished, right then, that they were back at his apartment, or her apartment, just the two of them. Rachel's heart was the best thing about her, he thought.

Although there was much to choose from.

Meaghan said, "I almost forgot. I have something for you."

"You didn't need to get us anything," said Yakabuski. "Hang onto your money, Meaghan. Don't spend it as soon as you get it."

"It'd be hard to spend it all," she said, and then she gasped and threw her hands over her mouth. "I can't believe I just said that. But I didn't buy you anything. I found you something."

"Found something?"

"Yeah — I think you're going to like it. Wait here."

The sun had begun to slide behind the Divide, the two fingers nearly gone, the crowns on the white pine turning dark blue, then dark purple. Yakabuski couldn't see the brook anymore. An eerie, premature twilight had come again to the Back Channel.

When Meaghan reappeared, she was holding a rusted coffee can. "Remember the postmaster saying if Tommy Coogan betrayed him, he was going to regret it?"

Yakabuski nodded.

"Well, when nothin' happened to Mr. Coogan, when he wasn't arrested or anythin', I started wonderin' what the postmaster had been talkin' 'bout. Was he makin' up stories, or did he really have some way of hurtin' Mr. Coogan."

It came to Yakabuski as quickly as an avalanche. With the same physical, blown-away impact. "He had a hidey hole."

"He did. I found it under the back porch of the post office."

She handed Yakabuski the tin can. Maxwell Original Roast. The lid hard to unscrew because of how badly the tin was rusted. Inside were three disposable cameras, four miniature cassette tapes, one cheap, cardboard-covered writing journal, and a tape recorder.

"I don't know what's on the cameras," she said, "but I listened to the tapes. You can play them on that recorder there. I read the journal, too. Until I got to the part about my momma, and then I couldn't read no more."

Yakabuski flipped through the pages of the journal. There were dates. It read like a diary. "He wrote about the killings?"

"Yeah, he did."

"What's on the tapes?"

"Him talkin' to Tommy Coogan."

"About what?"

"'Bout killin' people."

Yakabuski looked at the tape recorder in disbelief. "Killing people?"

"Yeah. They talked 'bout sports, too, and the weather, but mostly they talked 'bout killin' people. 'Bout how they were going to get rich after they'd killed some people."

"Meaghan, do you know what you've just done?"

"Course I know. Ya think I'm stupid or somethin'?"

Yakabuski was laughing as he screwed the lid back onto the tin can. "No, just the opposite. I better go. I have work to do."

Meaghan grinned. "When you see the bastard, make sure to say hi from me."

Yakabuski promised that he would.

ABOUT THE AUTHOR

© Julie Oliver

Ron Corbett is an award-winning journalist, broadcaster, and writer. He is the author of the Danny Barrett thrillers (published by Berkley, New York) as well as the Edgar and Arthur Ellis nominated Frank Yakabuski mystery series.

His non-fiction work includes Canadian best-seller *The Last Guide*, and the critically acclaimed *First Soldiers Down*.

Ron lives in Ottawa, Canada, where he works from a century-old home overlooking a fine river.

You can contact Ron at roncorbettbooks.com

You can contact Ron at www.roncorbettbooks.com

    BB

FRANK YAKABUSKI MYSTERIES

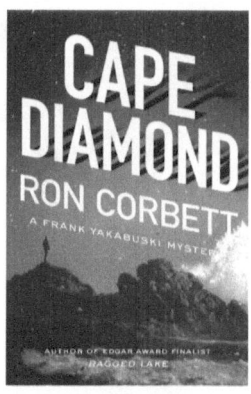

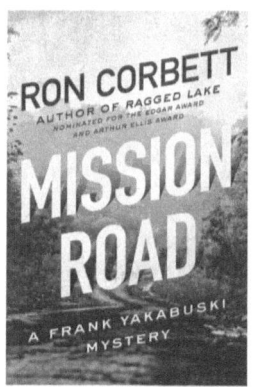

DANNY BARRETT THRILLERS

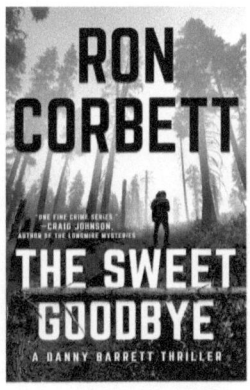

THE LAST GUIDE SERIES

www.ingramcontent.com/pod-product-compliance
Lightning Source LLC
Chambersburg PA
CBHW030648020726
47493CB00006B/1934